I0847588

Poinsettia Lane

Corina Bair

Cover art by Chelsea Kemp

First edition, November, 2024

ISBN: 979-8-9909467-0-5 (ebook)
ISBN: 979-8-9909467-1-2 (paperback)

Library of Congress Control Number: 2024920775

*This story is for everyone who doesn't know how to be themselves.
The soft hearts afraid of taking a risk.*

*May you break out of your shell
and show the world your true, beautiful self.*

Author Note

Hello lovely romance readers,

I have two important things to share with you before you read Poinsettia Lane.

First, this story takes place in a queer-normative world. There are multiple characters who are part of the LGBTQ+ community, but they do not experience discrimination, prejudice, fear of coming out, or any of the atrocities we experience in the real world by being part of this community. I understand that the characters' experiences are not representative of the world we live in, and I have done this intentionally. I hope you find relief in not only the lack of conflict and hate, but the unconditional love and acceptance this book brings.

Second, although this is a feel-good contemporary romance, please review the content warnings:
        - Accidental harm to animal (off page, but resulting injuries are seen on page)
        - Death of parents (off page, in the past)
        - Estranged family
        - Panic attacks (on page)
        - Open door sex scenes

Thank you, and happy reading!
Corina

CHAPTER ONE

Everly would give up her entire book collection for the ability to fast forward approximately twenty-four hours. She'd skip straight past the extravagant annual holiday party where her parents' old friends put on airs as they gather at her house. Much to her disappointment, time is an immovable construct, so the holiday party is unavoidable. She'll be forced to hear constant condolences and well wishes and "if only they were here to see this" while attempting to impress a bunch of people she doesn't like, or really even know.

Ladies and gents, the Moore Winter Holiday Gala, AKA the annual bane of Everly's existence and fuel to her crippling anxiety.

Everly's parents started the annual event well over 30 years ago, before either her or her sister were born, and when they passed, their friends expected Everly to continue to host it in their place. So she does.

Although she hates it, Everly tells herself that it's good for her to mingle and keep in touch with them. It keeps her parents closer, and it's respectful to their memories. Even if it does destroy her mental health for a couple of weeks every December.

Her night was spent tossing and turning, with visions of toppling Christmas trees, rotted hors d'oeuvres, and flat champagne. There was even one nightmare in which everyone was dressed only in their underwear. Realistically, Everly knows none of that will happen, but you try telling that to her other self, Anxious Everly. Anxious Everly is having a really hard time believing this will work out, and Anxious Everly gets very catastrophic when she hasn't had enough sleep.

Here we go again.

Everly takes a few moments to practice her breathing exercises, mainly so she doesn't feel like she's letting her therapist down, and then decides to do one last sweep through the lower level of the house to clear it of any debris or personal items. This task somehow ends up with her re-organizing the coat closet off the front foyer —entirely unnecessary—followed by folding the ends of the toilet paper in each of the restrooms like they do in her hotel.

"Maybe I need a pet," she mutters, stifling a yawn with her elbow, then startling when her phone buzzes across the floor next to her. "Frankie" flashes across the screen and Everly swipes to accept the video call from her best and only friend, only for them to cackle when they see Everly slumped on the cold bathroom floor in her robe and slippers, her hair up in a messy bun. Everly blinks in consternation at the situation she's found herself in as Frankie grins, sweeping their curly brown hair out of their eyes and squinting at her through the phone screen.

"What are we up to?" they ask.

"Heck if I know." Everly throws her hands in the air, lost.

Frankie nods, a sympathetic look on their face.

"Mhmm. Coffee first," Frankie says, circling their hand at Everly to encourage her to get up from the bathroom floor, then holding up their full mug in cheers when she does so.

Everly huffs as she shuffles into the kitchen, both grateful for her friend checking in on her and annoyed she let her anxiety get the best of her already. She's always envied Frankie's solid sense of self; they've known who they are and how they identify from a young age and have fully embraced it.

Everly starts the coffee, then returns her attention to her phone where Frankie is eyeing her expectantly.

"What?" Everly asks.

"I know you have a list," Frankie says. "Let's hear it."

Before she can pick it up, the doorbell rings.

~~~
~~~

* * *

"One, sec," Everly says, setting her phone and coffee on the console table in the foyer on her way to the front door.

Everly is so caught up in her own head about what she needs to do in the next couple hours that she doesn't check who is at the door before flicking the lock. As soon as she swings the heavy wooden door open, she immediately slams it shut again and whirls around, pressing her back to the door.

"Who is it?" Frankie yells from the video call.

"I don't know, some guy," Everly calls back. A really hot guy. All she caught was a glimpse of rich, golden-bronze skin, dark scruff, and strikingly light eyes, but it was enough to startle her right out of her senses. Why is there a hot guy on her porch? And why is she still wearing her robe, and slippers, and is her hair in a wet, disheveled bun?! God, she's a mess. Why does she always feel like such a mess?

From the other side of the door, a deep voice with an accent she can't quite place says, "This is 2574 Poinsettia Lane, right? I'm delivering the potted poinsettias and tree, from Magnolia? Magnolia Nursery."

Everly is pretty sure her eyes can't get any wider, and a nervous sweat is starting to bead on her brow. Did she just slam the door in the face of some poor delivery guy? Seriously, there must be something wrong with her. She tries to fix her hair as best she can, while also noting she doesn't have on a lick of makeup, then realizes it feels early still. Like, really early.

She quickly checks the time, noting that it's not even mid-morning yet. Did she not confirm the delivery time? She swears she had everything ready and planned down to the second. Turning around, Everly straightens her pink robe, pastes what she is sure is the fakest of fake smiles onto her face, and slowly twists the handle, opening the door.

"Hi, sorry about that, you startled me. Um, yes, the flowers and the tree, right this way and I'll show you where they need to go."

As she resists the urge to flee and shows Hot Delivery Guy through the empty foyer into the main entertaining room, he brings a whiff of fresh pine and earth inside with him. Nervous energy compels her to flutter her fingers around her hair and fidget with her robe. What must he think of her, answering the door in a short robe and damp hair? She should start putting a dollar aside for charity every time she embarrasses herself.

"So you want everything in here?" he asks, gesturing to the space around them.

"Oh, well most of it, yes. The tree definitely, but I'd like some of the poinsettias back out here in the foyer as well, and maybe even a couple outside on the steps? What do you think?" Why is she asking his opinion? This is her party, she doesn't need anyone else's approval on where the flowers go.

She mentally drops another dollar into the jar.

Smiling kindly, he replies "That will look really nice. I'll start unloading the truck. I'm Asim, by the way." He stretches the vowels and rolls his r's when he talks, and she gets hooked on how he says "the"—it sounds more like "zhe", which she decides is her new favorite pronunciation of any word, ever.

"Ah-simm," she tries out his name on her lips, pronouncing it slowly to ensure she has it right and flushing when his lips quirk at her in response. "Nice to meet you, I'm Everly."

Asim strides back outside and pulls up the back door of his delivery truck, while Everly spins around and sees her phone is still lit up with the video call. She grabs it, meeting Frankie's eyes that are just as wide as hers. Looking her up and down, Frankie presses their lips together in what may be an attempt not to laugh, but Everly chooses to take it as a look of commiseration at her unfortunate first impression with Hot Delivery Guy, Asim.

"Soooo," Frankie says, eyeing her. When Everly doesn't reply, they waggle their eyebrows and continue. "Based on the please-kiss-me look you've got going on, I'm gonna go ahead and assume he's hot and you're already smitten?"

"Oh my god, shut up! He'll be back in here any second." Everly whisper-scolds her friend. Unbelievable. "Why are you even still here? I'll call you back."

Everly doesn't wait for a reply and ends the call before Frankie can protest.

Just as she attempts to escape up the stairs to her bedroom, Asim comes back in with a massive tree trunk propped on his shoulder and the rest of the pine tree tied up and trailing behind him. Is this guy also a lumberjack? That tree is enormous, and she can't help but imagine the muscles he must have under his shirt, not to mention his thighs in those jeans look like tree trunks themselves. Who even wears jeans that fitted? Especially to do manual labor.

"Everly?" she hears, and it is clearly not the first time he's called her name. She looks up to see his head tilted toward her, the hint of a smile on his face.

"Yeah?" comes out of her mouth, breathy and soft, before her eyes go wide again. Great one, Everly. Bedroom voice. You're really making this first impression even better.

Thankfully, he doesn't call her out on it.

"You mentioned you want the tree in the other room. I'll get it set up first and then sweep all the needles out before I bring in the poinsettias so you don't have to clean around them. Where would you like it?"

"Oh." She turns and heads back into the front room with him. "If you could set it up at the far end over there, in the left corner away from the windows."

"Sure thing."

Just as she turns to make her second escape attempt, he calls out to her again.

"If you don't mind, why don't you walk me through the setup of this room while I get the tree situated. What are you imagining and what will go where? That will help me arrange the poinsettias to your liking." His voice is so enticing; somehow commanding and measured all at once. Her fingers itch to reach out and touch him. She wants to see if his sun-kissed skin is as warm as it looks, and if his arms are as unyielding under her touch as they appear to be when hauling around the pine tree.

"Right, yes that makes sense." Everly fists her hands in the hem of her robe. So much for changing into something more appropriate. She'll just have to make do and ensure her robe stays securely closed.

She describes the layout of the room; pointing out where the dessert table will be, then walking around the area that will encompass a number of standing tables by the windows, and lastly gesturing to the furniture up against the back wall which will form a more relaxed sitting area. He nods along with her and asks a couple questions, offering to move the furniture into position for her as well so he can place the flowers accordingly.

Everly thinks she would have to be out of her mind to decline another opportunity to see those muscular arms in action. Although she's not religious, she still turns her eyes skyward with a breath of thanks and a plea for willpower when he shrugs off his outer layer, revealing a tight gray t-shirt beneath that shows off his biceps in a manner that feels deliciously obscene. Everly now realizes why women in historical romances are always described as fanning themselves; she feels hot and flushed all over and could certainly use a brisk fanning.

She snaps her head around at his low chuckle, realizing she was pointedly looking up over her shoulder in an attempt to avoid ogling him, and he definitely noticed. Wide eyes meeting his, Everly clears her throat and walks over to the sitting area, intent on getting some space and sitting down for a moment, having completely forgotten they had just been talking about moving the furniture. Halfway down to sitting, he speaks again, and she freezes.

"While I'm sure you wouldn't add a significant weight to those love seats, they would undoubtedly be easier to move without you sitting on them." Seeing his sexy little smirk, she tips her chin up. He wants to tease? Fine, she can play this game too.

She chooses to complete her poorly timed journey, and primly sits herself down on the edge of the forest green velvet cushion.

"While I'm sure your monster arms would have no trouble moving either me or the chaise lounge, I have not yet decided how I want them to be placed."

There, she thinks, patting the flyaways along the sides of her face. That will show him who is in charge here. His eyes flick down to her long, bare legs where the robe has ridden up her thighs.

Everly does not expect the soul stopping smile that breaks out on his face in response to her admittedly snooty reply. She's never met someone so expressive. Those full lips give off an almost boyish grin, but the stubble surrounding them is all masculine. It heats her to her core and blanks out her mind.

"My monster arms, huh." His twinkling eyes scorch into her skin as Everly tries to maintain her composure. "We could test that theory, but I'm willing to bet they would have no trouble at all moving you wherever I desired you to be." His voice has lowered slightly, and he takes measured, confident steps toward her.

The breath sticks in her lungs and Everly does her best to hold her legs steady as she rises, pulling her robe back into place around her as she does so. He pauses a few inches in front of her, his eyes flicking back and forth between hers, and she can't quite decide what she wants to happen next. Is he going to kiss her? No, that would be absurd, he's working and she is a complete mess, they literally just met, and there's *no way* he is having the same thoughts as her right now. She reads too many romance novels, obviously. But what did he mean by that, if not what she thinks?

Asim raises both hands toward her, but he pauses halfway, affording Everly time to move on her own if she doesn't want to be touched. So much more gently than she expected, he places his hands on her upper arms and shifts her to the side. His thumbs brush back and forth over her robe before he lets go and steps back from her. She feels like a fish, snagged on his hook with her mouth gaping, unable to even look away.

"Alright then, where are we putting this lovely chaise?" he asks, emphasizing her previous word choice, though from the sparkle in his eye she doesn't think he's teasing her in a mean way.

Everly mentally pinches herself, then sucks in a breath as she strides back into the center of the room, eyeballing how she wants the sitting area to be set up and directing him on where to place the various pieces of furniture.

To her surprise, when Asim has the furniture fully arranged to her liking, he gestures for her to sit back down where she was before. Everly gives him a questioning glance before moving toward his outstretched hand.

"Have a seat," he tells her. "Make sure you like how everything else gets set up from this area, since you've already surveyed the others."

Shaking her head at the strangely considerate request and with a hidden smile on her face, Everly takes his hand and nearly melts at the warmth in the contact. Her surprised gaze flits up to his, and for a moment he looks just as stunned as her before she darts her eyes away again. Asim leads her over to the couch, where she attempts to gracefully sit back down.

Unfortunately, her version of "graceful" is not very, as she is immediately distracted by the powerful thigh in her very close peripheral vision, which in combination with his earthy scent engulfing her, results in only one butt cheek making it on the cushion and the rest of her nearly collapsing to the floor. Her saving grace is that massive hand encompassing hers, which prevents her from entirely losing her robe, all sense of modesty, and the little self respect she has left at this point.

"Oh my god, I am an absolute mess!" she says to herself, an embarrassed, breathy laugh accompanying the statement, not realizing this exclamation also came out loud enough for him to hear.

"I quite like it," is his soft reply. "If you think you're safely settled, I'll go grab the rest of the flowers," he says with a quick wink as he turns away and strides toward the front door.

Everly doesn't move a muscle while he's gone, too afraid to break this spell. When he finishes placing the bright red and burgundy flowers around the room, he steps back with a different sort of smile on his face. One that conveys a sense of satisfaction, maybe even pride.

"Beautiful," he says, eyes roaming over her and the poinsettias splayed around her in the sitting area. She's too afraid to ask if he's talking about her or the flowers, but her hopeful little romantic heart pitter patters all the same. Add to the swoop in her stomach the fact that her anxiety has started to creep back up on her, and she's torn between wanting him to leave so she can decompress, and hoping he has more to do so he stays a bit longer. Her uncertainty causes her to second guess everything, unsure how to act or what to say in this situation.

"Well, I think that's it. Do you want to take a last look around, let me know if you want anything else moved before I head out?" he asks.

So that decides it for her, then.

Everly pulls herself to standing, wishing he had offered her a hand again, if only so she can see if that fiery touch was a one time thing. It must have been a fluke, or she imagined it. Maybe his hands were just really hot from the hard work?

Taking a moment to look around, a smile creeps onto Everly's face. It really is a beautiful start to her decorating plans. Now she just needs to add the fresh pine branches laced with bright red holly berries, and string lights so everything glows. She checks the foyer, then follows him out to the front porch and down the steps to look back at it from the driveway as well.

Everly nods, "It really looks good. Thank you so much for delivering everything and helping me get it all arranged." she says, looking up at him with a genuine smile on her face. When was the last time she felt such a real smile, and one that came this easily?

"You're very welcome, Miss Moore," he replies, before giving her a polite nod and turning back to his truck. She takes a moment to admire him one last time as he opens the delivery truck door and steps up into the cab. As he pulls around the turn in the drive, Asim rolls the window down and props his forearm on it, and well, now she knows one more thing she likes about him.

"Take care," he says as he drives off, raising his hand once in a quick farewell.

CHAPTER TWO

Everly slumps against the front door after Asim leaves, hands over her mouth, vaguely baffled as a wave of confusion and relief washes over her. What in the world just happened? It feels like she's in some sort of hazy twilight zone, outside her body but somehow also feeling everything ten times more than she ever has before.

"Earth to Everly."

She jumps, her fingers knocking against her lips when Frankie claps their hands, startling Everly out of her weird, fugue state.

"You good?" Frankie says, and Everly shakes her head no, then nods a confirmative yes.

"Yeah, totally good," she says. "Wait, where did you come from?"

"I just got here, figured you could use some backup since it sounded like your morning was already thrown off. Also I kinda wanted to check out your Hot Delivery Guy, but it looks like I missed him," Frankie says.

Everly stares at them, a blank look on her face.

"Okayyyyy... I found your list," Frankie says, holding up the slip of paper. "I'll just get started on the string lights while you take a quick cold shower, yeah? Morning is nearly over at this point, the party people will be here before you know it."

Frankie's right. The morning has somehow sped away from her and she needs to catch up if she's going to get through this day in one piece. Everly nods her thanks and thumps up the stairs, as she had been trying to do the entire time Asim was here, but now feels much less imperative than it did before. She doesn't entirely understand what their interactions meant. She's confused about how the entire situation ended, because she's pretty sure he was interested in her, but then he left without asking for her number. She must have misread it.

A small voice still whispers that he was flirting with her too though, and that just maybe it did mean something.

Frankie leaves after getting some of the prep work done with promises to return in a few hours. Meanwhile, Everly's thoughts tumble around her head as she gets made up for the day, largely focused on Asim. Everly curls and pins her hair, smooths lotion down her legs, puts the final touches on her makeup. She finishes with jewelry and comfy shoes for now, pulling out sleek heels for later, and leaving her dress hanging on the back of the door. Everything is ready for a quick outfit change and touch up this evening before the guests arrive, so she checks her watch and compares it to her planning sheet for the day as she walks much more confidently back down the stairs. Now that Everly has her game face on, she can remind herself what is expected of her, and that she knows precisely how to follow through.

Everly straightens her list on the counter and refills her mug, inhaling the delicious scents of a heady medium roast.

Coffee is one of her favorite smells, even though she rarely drinks it. The rich, earthy scent reminds her of carefree mornings growing up with her parents.

They drank coffee only on weekends, so the smell always brings fond memories of relaxing in the kitchen together on Sunday mornings with jazz playing over the stereo. As she thinks about it, more memories pop into her head: her parents laughing with her mom clinging to her dad's arm; both of them dancing around the kitchen island, wrapped up in each other; quietly reading together in the soft sunlight after breakfast, her dad with a newspaper and her mom with a magazine or romance novel.

She doesn't have many memories of her sister, Addison, during these moments, and she frowns as she tries to figure out why. It feels foolish to assume her sister was enjoying the moment quietly as she was; her sister was rarely quiet. More likely, Addison was probably dancing along behind their parents, or still in bed after a night out with her latest boyfriend or girlfriend.

A shard of pain spears her heart. Everly misses those days. She misses her parents, of course, and she misses her estranged sister, but more than that she misses the sense of belonging. Of being part of a family and knowing she could turn to them any moment of any day. Of not questioning herself, or her place, or her value to those around her. Back before everyone she loved left her, when her mom would pull her shoulders straight and always give Everly a quick once over, checking her face, her outfit, how she planned to present herself to the world and nodding with approval. Her thoughts start to turn with slashes of hurt, confusion about who her mom wanted her to be and who she is now, questions about her sister and why they're so distant from each other.

Everly allows her mind to wander for half a second longer, but it brings up so many tangled emotions, she instinctively shies away. Guilt, shame, confusion, regret... all tightening her throat and compressing her chest until it's hard to breathe; it's too overwhelming to dive into, especially with everything else on her plate today. Before the tangle of sad loneliness and residual grief can well up, she shoves it all away, locking it in a mental drawer for later. Some future therapy session when she's feeling brave and has her life more put together.

Just on time, the party planner and event coordinator arrive to finish setting up the foyer and party area, and promptly direct other staff as they arrive too. This part is much easier for Everly, as she can simply stand back and supervise. Everly greets everyone politely, answering questions and nodding approval as needed.

All the while, she keeps thinking how different this is to when Asim was here setting up. She can't escape thoughts of him while surrounded by all of these gorgeous flowers. It's not solely how irresistible he looked, either.

He made her feel seen.

He made her feel beautiful.

And he listened.

He seemed to actually value her opinion rather than simply seeking her stamp of approval, a foreign concept for her. Everly can't remember a time when someone didn't want her approval on something, and prior to this morning, she wouldn't have even known there was a difference in valuing someone's opinion versus simply wanting their endorsement.

Everly's mind drifts to the day before, a subtle note of curious wonder flitting through her as mental threads connecting to each other pull her to replay her last therapy session.

"So, Everly," her therapist, Carrie, begins, her voice coming from the computer speakers clear and strong as they start a video session. "I know you have your parents' party tomorrow and that always brings up a lot for you. How have you been coping with it the last few days?"

Really just diving right into it then. Super.

"I've been okay. My anxiety is higher than normal, but I guess that's to be expected. It feels like a lot of pressure to make sure I do it right and that everything goes perfectly." Everly cringes and rubs her temple, looking away from the screen.

"What about the party do you think causes you so much distress?" Carrie inquires.

"It's like I have to be this perfect little socialite that they all expect me to be. But it's all fake. I'm pretending to fit in, pretending to laugh at their jokes, pretending to be happy to see them. Ugh, pretending I'm comfortable with that crowd is just so draining," she huffs. Everly doesn't see why it's so exhausting still after eight years of practice. She should be used to it by now.

Carrie drums her fingers on her desk before adjusting her glasses, then replies. "Do you remember what we talked about a few weeks ago, Everly, about your values and being your true self?"

Everly slowly nods, unsure of where this is going and whether she's going to like it.

"Well, I wonder if the reason you feel so emotionally drained interacting with these people every year is because you value honesty and integrity, and by pretending to be someone you are not, you're not living

up to your own values and who you want to be," Carrie pauses, tilting her head the other way. "What do you think about that idea?"

That sounds... like it makes a lot of sense. It's understandable that trying to be someone she isn't would be mentally taxing. Everly isn't sure what it all means though.

"So, what, am I supposed to just not laugh at their jokes? Tell them they're being snobby or something?"

Carrie smiles her little, knowing smile and Everly resists the urge to pout like a child. "I see what you're doing, and no, I'm not telling you to be rude or offensive. But I do think that bringing more authenticity into other areas of your life could help balance out the scales, so to speak. Where else do you think you could focus on being more yourself?"

Everly likes the sound of this much better. "Well I have been thinking about finding a hobby or maybe getting a pet. I just keep having this empty feeling inside and I don't know how else to fill it." She already knows what Carrie will say next.

"What else do you think you're missing? What else could fill that hole?"

Yep, called it. Everly twists her lips in thought. "I suppose I would like to be more social, maybe have more friends."

Carrie is already nodding. "I think that's a great start. Let's try to focus the next few weeks on socializing in an authentic way. This could really help with that feeling of emptiness and is a good way to build up your sense of self. Figure out who you really are and put that person out into the real world."

It doesn't get any easier after that. By the end of her therapy session, Everly's heart and soul feel picked apart and her brain exhausted. Despite that, she does feel a little more hopeful, and maybe even a tiny bit excited to start this journey toward authenticity.

Everly cocks her head and her eyes unfocus as her mind continues to follow this train of thought, connecting dots she hasn't noticed before.

Growing up, it was always about making the right impression, which then made others want her approval of them as well. Everly questions if she has ever really had any authentic relationships, apart from Frankie who doesn't care at all what people think of them. Then when her parents died, there were so many arrangements to be made and people needing her signature on one thing after another. Even her staff at the Sioria now, who she thought she had a good relationship with after working together for years, she realizes don't actually know her and only seek her out when they need her confirmation or support for something. She was only twenty-two and fresh out of college with her business degree when her parents died and left her the mansion and the Sioria Hotel in Stone Ridge, Arizona. Everly hasn't really tried to bridge the gap with her employees either, though. It's no wonder she ended up feeling like she's on her own so much of the time.

This is such a novel revelation that she can't stop her mind from circling it around and around her head, inspecting and critiquing and questioning it from different angles, and despite this, her anxiety can't seem to find any fault with it. Again, an unfamiliar experience for Everly, and one she thinks she might like. Is this what Carrie meant by being her authentic self? It's a bit scary, if she's being honest. Everly didn't really know how to do that at first, but she suspects her hours with Asim might have been a start. Could she be more of her real self around others too, like she was with Asim, and is more regularly with Frankie?

Think of them, and they will come.

CHAPTER THREE

Frankie swaggers through the front door to interrupt Everly's mind-blowing reflections, and immediately stops when they see her. Tilting their face and narrowing their eyes, Frankie plants both feet on the floor as though preparing for a throw down.

"Why do you look weird?" they ask.

"Gee, thanks," Everly gripes. "I'm just nervous! This is a big event."

"Nope. Not buying it. You do this every year and you get anxious every year and I know you. I know what your anxiety looks like, and this," Frankie waves their hand up and down to encompass Everly's entire body, "isn't it."

Frankie closes the remaining distance between them in three slow strides, giving her a narrow-eyed 'tell me or I'll pry it from your cold dead lips' look.

"And here I thought I cleaned up nice, all things considered," Everly mutters under her breath and rolls her eyes at her best friend, but knows she can't keep anything from them. Here goes this authenticity thing again. "I just... can't stop thinking about that guy."

Frankie interrupts with a dramatic gasp, saying "Hot Delivery Guy? Oh, I am so here for this," then yanks her arm, pulling her away from the bustle of the caterers and into a side hallway where they have some semblance of privacy.

"Alright, spill," they demand.

Everly puffs out her cheeks before letting the exhale trickle out.

"Yes, Hot Delivery Guy. He... well, I think we kind of hit it off?" It feels more real to say it out loud to someone else than it did just thinking it in her head. A little more absurd too.

Everly tries to remember the last time she went on a date or flirted with someone, and she's pretty sure it's been many months, if not a year or more.

Frankie's lips tighten and then they roll them between their teeth, trying to hold in a smile.

"Yeah, I mean, I don't know. There was definitely flirting, but you should have seen me. I was such a wreck, Frankie. I hadn't gotten ready at all yet, and I was this weird combination of nervous and excited at the same time. I think I rambled, like, a lot, but also I might be remembering it wrong and maybe I didn't say any of it out loud?"

Frankie gives in and lets out their contagious, booming laugh. Everly allows herself a self-deprecating chuckle alongside them.

"It's about time you got back out there, girl. I can't remember the last time you went on a date." Frankie's comments echo her own thoughts.

"I know, I know. I don't think it was really anything though, he didn't ask for my number and I only know his first name and that he delivers plants. There's nothing to follow up on, really."

Although they don't live in a big city, it isn't so small that she's likely to run into him by accident, especially considering that she's lived in Stone Ridge her whole life and has never seen him before. She'd remember someone like that if she did. Everly gives what she hopes is a nonchalant shrug in an effort to cover the spike of sadness at the thought of never seeing him again, and turns to go back to the other room.

"Hey," Frankie stops her with a hand on her arm. "If it's meant to be, it'll work out. You deserve some happiness in your life, so don't give up on him just yet. You never know."

Everly nods, but doesn't put much stock in their words.

"Alright, I'm gonna hang back here, man the kitchen staff and whatnot, but come find me if you need to, okay? I'll keep an eye out."

"Thanks, Frankie." Everly smiles at her friend, so very grateful to have someone like them in her life.

She heads back out to the driveway, ready to do one final walkthrough before anyone arrives. The event coordinator is off to the side talking into her headset, the party planner next to her. Honestly, Everly's not sure how their roles are different, but she hires these two every year. They work spectacularly together and it always turns out well, so she doesn't particularly care. If it takes some of the worry and pressure off her plate, she's happy to do it.

The pair walk up the stairs and step inside, making tiny adjustments here and there as needed. Everly is happy with the decor this year. Instead of over the top glittering and gold decorations as she's done in the past, this year features a more minimal style. The large pine tree is adorned with simple white lights and glows beautifully. There are fresh pine boughs with pinecones and burgundy holly berries on the window sills, with small white twinkle lights threaded throughout. The poinsettias are arranged in clusters and raised groupings around the tree and furniture, small fairy lights hidden amongst the foliage giving them an ethereal glow from beneath. The chandelier is on a dim setting so the entire room has a softer feel. The gentler, more natural decorations give Everly a sense of peace, which won't last once everyone arrives, but she's happy to enjoy it while she can.

Everly thanks the party planner and excuses her to go take a break before any guests arrive, then sits back down on the same chaise that Asim had placed her on earlier. Was that only a few hours ago? It feels like days, weeks ago at this point. As Everly looks around, she feels a sense of relief that it is nearly done, compounded with a lingering apprehension that the only thing left is to get through the party itself.

Sooner than she would hope, yet inevitably of course, the guests start to arrive. Her parents' friends from all over the country stroll through her front door, as well as the local city council members. Elegant evening gowns, sparkling jewelry, crisp suits and shiny shoes adorn the wealthy couples that arrive arm in arm. This is the part Everly despises the most. Pompous cheek kissing, delicate hugs where each person barely touches the shoulder of the other, fake smiles and, of course, the ever present "wish they were here" comments regarding her parents who have been buried for years.

Everly isn't prepared for one particular guest though, and heart stops in her chest when someone who looks eerily like her estranged sister, Addison, steps through the front door. Everly blinks, then spins away, scrunches her eyes closed, opens them and turns back.

The woman is still there, greeting an elderly couple she walked in behind, a beaming smile on her face.

"Addison?" Everly's voice is soft, but somehow her sister hears it and her eyes jump up, searching the crowd in the foyer until they lock onto Everly's.

Addison's mouth curves into a softer, more tentative smile, as she extricates herself from the couple and weaves her way over to Everly.

"Hey," she says, her voice equally soft.

"Hi," Everly says, dumbfounded, her brain completely offline.

"Hi," Addison says, her quiet smile turning into a mischievous grin. One Everly remembers all too well.

"It's really you," Everly voices her thought out loud, and Addison nods.

"It's really me."

"What..." Everly doesn't know what to say. Her mind is blank.

"Is there somewhere we can talk for a minute?" Addison says, and Everly walks in a daze past the kitchen, ignoring a gaping Frankie, and down the hallway to the laundry room, of all places.

"I guess this works," Addison says, quirking another tentative smile at Everly.

She's unable to return it.

"This is weird," Addison grimaces and her shoulders start to bunch up near her ears.

Everly lets out a surprised huff of a laugh. "Yeah, it really is."

"Should we start over?" Addison suggests.

"I think that would be good." Everly sticks out her hand. "Hi, I'm Everly, your long lost, very awkward sister."

Now it's Addison's turn to laugh. Shaking her head, she politely inquires, "Would a hug be okay? I'm more of a hugger than a shaker," before enfolding Everly in the comfiest, warmest hug she has felt in years. Everly's eyes prick with tears while she holds onto her sister for a significantly longer-than-average hug.

As they pull apart, Everly swipes at her eyes and tries not to notice her sister mirroring the movement.

"Everything looks amazing, Ev," Addison says, calling Everly by her childhood nickname. "The house, the gala..."

"Thanks," Everly draws the word out, feeling thrown off by her sister's apparent nonchalance. "So..."

"Um, yeah." Addison wrings her hands together and looks down at her feet. "I should have RSVPed, or at least given you a heads up, I'm sorry."

"Oh, that's okay." Everly's head is going to explode. This is the most uncomfortable moment of her entire life, and she has no idea how to fix it.

"Okay, um," Addison turns her eyes back up to Everly's. "I wanted to say, thanks for letting me be here."

"Sure, of course." Everly's mouth is working on auto-pilot at this point.

A heavy, awkward silence descends between them, only broken by the distant hum of the party. Everly's eyes drift to the door, though she doesn't want to be back at the party any more than she wants to remain here for another moment.

"We should probably get back out there," Addison says. "Can we catch up later?"

"Right, yeah," Everly says, her brain in a fog as she trails her sister back to the front of the house.

Addison hasn't attended one of these events since their parents died. Eight freaking years ago. Then she randomly shows up, without RSVPing, no notice or heads up, and waltzes right in the front door with a smile on her face?

This must be another nightmare.

Dream?

Whatever. Either way, there's no way this is reality. If she's not dreaming, Everly must be hallucinating.

She ducks into the kitchen rather than going back to the foyer and continuing to greet guests, needing a moment to sort herself out. Before she can so much as clasp her hands to her head, Frankie is there.

"What the hell?" Frankie whisper-shouts as soon as

she sees Everly. Their brows have disappeared under their floppy hair, and their eyes show white all the way around. They look how Everly feels.

"I..." Everly spins in a circle, her eyes darting around for answers, and Frankie grabs her shoulders to stop her. Everly shakes her head, though she doesn't know what she's saying no to.

"Are you okay?" Frankie asks.

Everly's head, of its own volition, continues to twist back and forth.

Frankie nods. "Okay, it'll be fine. We've got this."

They steer Everly to the sink and turn the water on cold, then stick her hands under it. Everly jerks in their grip, her eyes refocusing and coming back to meet Frankie's concerned gaze.

"Big breath," Frankie says, and Everly sucks air deep into her lungs.

"And out slowly," Frankie continues, "focus, Everly."

They search her gaze, eyes flitting back and forth between hers, and their eyes soften from concern into something a little less imperative.

"Okay?"

"Yeah," Everly says, "okay."

"Good. Now. You have guests to greet." Frankie hands over a towel to dry her hands. "We can have a breakdown or whatever you need to do later. Yeah?"

Everly nods, muttering a quick "later" to herself.

Frankie snags the towel back and then turns Everly toward the foyer, giving her a hearty pat on the back.

"You've got this."

Everly pushes her shoulders back with another slow breath, tips her chin up, and steps back into the party, doing her best to keep the swirling thoughts at bay.

Everyone looks genuinely surprised to see Addison, which results in more than a few sideways glances between the two of them when people think she isn't looking. Luckily, Addison is eager and ready for the attention; she doesn't look even half as uncomfortable as Everly feels.

Everly watches from the sidelines as Addison returns smiles and hugs, asking after people's businesses and families as though she hasn't missed any of the gossip from the last eight years. Everly is floored by this woman. Her sister has always been bubbly and outgoing, but in a more reckless and immature way. She supposes that's because she hasn't really known Addison since she moved out for college, and Everly shouldn't be surprised this is how she's turned out.

She fits in with this crowd perfectly.

Everly, on the other hand, has never fit in here. She doesn't like the person she pretends to be around all of her parents' old friends and acquaintances, but doesn't know how to be anyone else either since this is who she's been for years; it's who they expect her to be.

Frankie keeps telling her how wonderful the event is going, that everyone is happy and having a good time, to stop worrying, but everywhere she turns, she either sees Addison, or she sees flowers. Brilliant red poinsettias popping out at her no matter where she looks, reminding her of Asim and heating her cheeks.

Asim, who she wants to see again but doesn't know how to contact. Asim, with his kindness and charm, who somehow brought out a different side of her, one she thinks she likes. Asim, who gives her even more nervous butterflies in her tummy than she normally gets when she goes out in public, but for some reason she doesn't hate in this scenario. Asim and his biceps, barely contained in that t-shirt, that she wants to wrap her hands around to see if her fingers will touch or not.

Asim, who will not get out of her freaking head.

A few flustered hours and many glasses of champagne later, the party is finally winding down. The guests trickle out, repeating the same polite lines and gestures as when they arrived. Addison stands by the door with her, saying goodbyes and offering well wishes, which makes Everly feel slightly awkward, but despite that, Addison's presence is not unwelcome. Turns out Everly kind of likes having her sister there, and not only for her excellent buffering abilities.

After the last guest leaves, and while the hired staff begin their breakdown routines, Addison offers to help clean up. Everly isn't sure how much more socializing she can take, but this isn't an opportunity she can afford to pass up, so she agrees.

Frankie pops their head out from the kitchen and gestures with their arms and hands—what Everly assumes to be them asking if Everly wants them to stay or go. She nods her head for them to take off, giving a look that says she'll fill them in later. Frankie gives a thumbs up, then crosses their fingers with a raised eyebrow before ducking out through the garage with Addison none the wiser.

As Addison sweeps and Everly collects scattered bits of trash, they dance around the topics she is sure they both really want to talk about, but are too afraid to broach.

"How is California and the beach house?" Everly asks her sister, while her mind screams about how weird this is.

"It's great, I did some redecorating there as well. It doesn't look nearly as sophisticated and gorgeous as this place does though!"

"What does it look like? I'm sure you did a great job!"

The conversation is stilted, a bit too enthusiastic for this reunion, but they manage. Addison describes some of her favorite local beach spots, where she likes to eat, shows Everly a couple pictures of the beach house she's taken over the years and describes what has changed in the area since they last visited as a family. The conversation turns back to Stone Ride, drawing into the present again.

"The hotel looks so chic now, too," Addison says. "I hardly recognized the inside when I checked in earlier."

"Thanks, yeah it's been a lot of work updating it over the years. All the interior rooms were remodeled and I added the indoor/outdoor venue space." Everly bites her lip before continuing, not wanting to brag, but proud to share her accomplishments all the same. "The venue is consistently booked out nearly two years in advance."

Addison's eyes widen. "Wow, that's incredible, Ev."

A small ember of pride glows in Everly's chest, warm and tentative in its arrival.

"Do you want to unwind with one last drink before you head back to the Sioria?"

Addison's shoulders relax and she offers a smaller, more tired smile than the ones she graced everyone with during the party. Everly wonders if her sister was faking it the whole time too. Maybe she doesn't fit in with them as perfectly as she made it seem.

Addison takes a seat at the kitchen bar, and Everly leans back against the counter across the island from her.

"Thank you for hosting," Addison says.

Everly's eyebrows shoot up. She's unsure how to respond for a moment. She always hosts, because that's what everyone has always told her she should do.

"It's what mom and dad would have wanted," she replies.

"Would they?" Addison says, then shrugs. "Maybe."

Everly isn't sure what Addison means by that, but she doesn't have the mental fortitude to ask after the day she's had.

"Well, anyways, it's over and I have a year to rest before the next one." Everly is just saying her thoughts out loud at this point, which might not be the best for carrying a conversation, but again, she simply doesn't have the energy to care.

Addison looks like she's about to say something before stopping herself, snapping her mouth closed. She shrugs one shoulder this time, and looks back down at her drink.

"Did you have fun? It seems like it was a huge success, and that was quite the event to pull off on your own," Addison says, like it's an accomplishment Everly should feel proud of.

Everly doesn't feel proud, though. She doesn't feel any satisfaction or fulfillment at hosting such an extravagant event. If anything, she feels emptied out, drained but also relieved that it's done.

"I guess, yeah. I'm ready to sleep for days now that it's over."

She doesn't think her true thoughts on the matter need to be shared, except maybe with Carrie later.

Her sister drops the subject, turning the conversation to her stay for the next few days. She has some plans to meet up with old high school friends in the area, and mentions that it would be nice to see Everly again too. Everly's insides warm, a foreign sense filling some empty space inside her. She was hoping for the same, but didn't know if Addison would want to see any more of her.

CHAPTER FOUR

Twisting her office chair back and forth underneath her the next morning, Everly stares out the floor to ceiling windows at the desert view behind her desk, rather than the computer screen as she should be. She's relieved the weekend is over and the work week has started again; work is what she knows. Still, she can't help but reflect back on the day of the party and how it went. She's learned about redirection in therapy, and Carrie is adamant that redirecting her thoughts and preventing her tendency to ruminate on anxious topics will allow her to better handle her anxiety. It does seem to help when she can manage to actually do it, but unfortunately this morning does not look to be one of those days.

Interestingly though, her thoughts don't stick to the things they normally would, namely, the guests and her interactions with them. She has this annoying habit of going over every single thing she said, they said, how she reacted, and what her future omniscient self thinks she should have done or said that would have been exceedingly better. This is useless of course, as it only serves to make her feel worse. Today though, her thoughts are circling around two people in particular, and one of them wasn't a guest at said party.

Between her distress over the confounding situation with her long lost sister, and the depressing reality of not having a date with the hot delivery guy, she can't help but wonder what she is even going to do with her life. Does her sister want a relationship now, after all these years? Does Asim think about her constantly after their brief time together, like she does him? She decides to put pen to paper and make a list.

Lists, she firmly believes, fix everything.

Thoughts about Addison:
1. She seems friendly and has gone out of her way to interact with me.
2. She has good social skills and has clearly done well for herself.
3. What does she want?
4. Why is she here? Why now?
5. Options for next steps
   a. Don't do anything to upset the balance, let it play out as it will.
   b. Reach out to her and follow up on the tentative plans to get together again.
   c. Check in on her at the hotel / assess her in another environment, then decide.

Thoughts about Asim:
1. He is a delivery driver for the plant shop.
2. He is kind and charming.
3. He's the sexiest man I've ever seen.
4. I have no idea how to contact him, other than ordering more plants, which I don't need...
5. Find someone else?

With her brain more organized, even if she doesn't feel happier about the situation, she does have a clearer picture. Everly decides she can't do anything about Asim, so she will leave that up to fate or the universe (or maybe Frankie) to decide for her. As far as Addison goes, well, she's staying at the Sioria on the floor below Everly's office. It would take only a couple of minutes to walk down there and see how she reacts.

Everly decides to give it a day. She doesn't want to be too much too fast, and instead texts Addison a simple thank you for her help cleaning up after the party over the weekend, deciding to leave it at that for now. Spinning her chair around to her computer, she hopes she can actually focus on her work this time.

~~~

* * *

</div>
~~~

The next day, her first order of business is to follow up on her lists. Addison had sent a polite text back the day before, and Everly thinks an in-person visit is a good next step. As an early riser, Everly always gets to work before the morning shift starts, so she waits until a respectable hour to ensure she doesn't wake her sister up too early. As the clock hands tick forward, Everly loses patience and figures nine am sounds good enough; giving herself a firm nod to solidify this decision, she stands up, sets her shoulders back, and murmurs a quick "I can do this. I am capable." affirmation reminder.

Three minutes later, she's taking a deep breath and knocking on the hotel room door, shifting from foot to foot while questioning every decision she has ever made in her life. She hears a muffled "Ev?" through the door before the sound of the locks, and then the door swings open.

Addison does not look like nine am is a respectable hour. Her curly brown hair is a lion's mane around her face, and one cheek is lined and puffy from sleeping on it.

"Is everything okay? What are you doing here?" Addison asks, one hand rubbing the sleep from her eye.

"Oh, yeah everything's fine, great really. I just wanted to see how you were doing and ask if maybe you wanted to get coffee or something, but I can see you're not really up yet." Everly chuckles awkwardly, then clamps her mouth shut and bites her tongue before she really starts to ramble. They stand there in the doorway for a moment with the door cracked open and dead silence between them.

"Right. Coffee. I don't drink coffee, but if you want to come in for a bit there's complimentary tea. Which you know, obviously." Addison doesn't seem to be much better at this socializing thing than Everly is when they don't have the party connecting them.

"Sure, I can come in for a few minutes. I don't drink coffee either, actually," Everly confesses. "I just figured that's what people do so it made sense to ask."

Addison just nods, opening the door wider for Everly and waving one arm around as she walks back into the kitchen area of the suite. She has one of the nicer ones, with an open kitchen and breakfast nook, spacious sitting area, bedroom and connected bath. They do their best at small talk while the water heats to a boil, commenting on the weather this time of year, how it's just as Addison remembers it being, then take their tea to the balcony to enjoy said crisp morning weather.

Everly wants to ask so many questions, but isn't sure where to start, or if she even should. She confirms how long Addison is staying (until New Year's Day), if she has other plans (nothing set in stone), and Addison again asks about the hotel and comments on how stunning the updates and new designs are. After a moment of finger-tapping silence in which they both take too-hot sips of tea, Addison clears her throat, drawing Everly's attention again.

"Are you still friends with Frankie?" Addison asks.

"Oh, yeah, they're doing great. Running the coffee shop these days," Everly replies.

"Oh no way!" Addison's eyes light up and she looks fully awake for the first time this morning. "Did they buy it?"

Everly hums in confirmation, a proud smile curving her lips.

Addison sits back with a smile. "Good for them, that's really cool. I'll have to stop by before I leave."

"They'd like that. They were asking about you," Everly says, doing a double take when Addison's cheeks turn pink.

"Oh." Addison clears her throat but changes the subject before Everly manages to figure out why that topic turned awkward too. "How are the rest of the local businesses doing?"

"Great for the most part. Crooked Books is still up and running. I guess I don't really go anywhere else all that often."

"Is Mrs. Langdon any less grouchy these days?"

Everly laughs, and it finally breaks some of the tension between them. "Not even a little bit."

The conversation flows easier as they spend a little more time together, but it still feels weird, almost unnatural, to be so disconnected from someone she used to know better than herself.

The sisters schedule a time for Addison to come back to the house for dinner and drinks before she leaves, and they both end up with shy grins on their faces. Everly thanks her for the tea, debates offering a hug but decides it doesn't fit the moment, and offers a warm smile instead as she leaves. She walks back up to her office with a little more of a bounce in her step than she had on the way down a half hour prior.

~~~

Everly likes to think she's managing her anxious thoughts better today than she has been the rest of this week, despite the fact that she has no evidence to back up this belief. She's distracted randomly throughout the day for no reason at all, other than that she imagines she might run into him, her Hot Delivery Guy, who she would almost think was a figment of her imagination if she didn't have the plants at her house to prove the existence of someone, at least. So really, no, she's not actually getting a handle on things, but when she puts her mind to it, Everly is exceptionally good at pretending she does.

Later that afternoon, Everly skips out of work early to hang out with Frankie, who she hasn't seen since the party, although they do call or text multiple times a day whether they see each other or not.

Frankie owns the local coffeehouse a couple blocks down, also on the main street of their little downtown area. It's right next to their favorite bookstore, Crooked Books, run by Mrs. Langdon. She's this quirky old lady, who they are pretty sure has lived forever and is most likely a witch, with wild, curly red hair and a no nonsense attitude. Naturally, she has two cats that live in the bookstore, Luna and Harriet. They're about as sociable as she is. Mrs. Langdon doesn't allow for any "hooliganism" in her bookstore, which includes but is not limited to: carrying pens, markers, tape, drinks or liquids or food of any kind, sneezing, coughing, running, shouting or talking at any volume above a politely soft conversational level, along with anything else she might deem "ruckus" in the moment.

Truly it's a miracle her little store is still in business, as Everly and Frankie have seen her tossing many tourists and locals alike out her front door with words
~~~

along the lines of "unacceptable" and "intolerable" accompanying her signature scowl as she does it. They always wonder about those events, but don't ask, since she seems to have a soft spot for the two of them, and they don't want to push their luck. Everly and Frankie are sometimes allowed to bring their tea and coffee in—so long as it has a tight lid and they only drink it over the welcome mat, and leave it on the side table next to the front door when they aren't drinking it.

Sometimes the cats wander by them, without hissing or evil eyes, and one time Luna even let Everly pet her, which Frankie said was definitely a sign of their favor and probably why Mrs. Langdon tolerates their brand of "shenanigans". Everly thinks she just likes drama. Even still, they tread carefully, because being banned from the only bookstore in town would be an absolute tragedy.

Everly walks the couple blocks to Roasted Coffee House and enjoys how it has been a perfectly normal day so far, with no distracting men or stupid sexy arm muscles intruding where they don't belong. Frankie is actually working for once when she arrives, and she can see them wiping down tables through the window. The door tinkles softly as she opens it, and Frankie immediately comes over and flips the handmade door sign to "closed."

"Frankie," Everly draws out the end of their name in a frustrated whine. "Honestly, I have no idea how you make any money closing at random hours all the time! I did not come over here just to feel guilty about you closing down the shop because of me."

"I don't know why you assume it's about you," Frankie complains with a glower. "I have stuff going on too, you know."

"Oh my gosh, I didn't even think. Of course it's not about me, what's going on?"

They smirk back over their shoulder as they walk behind the counter to brew Everly a cup of her favorite Jasmine Green tea.

"I'm good actually. It was busy this morning but no one has been in for a minute, so I was going to close down early anyways to go wander around next door, see if Mrs. Langdon got any new smut." They laugh when Everly pretends to smack at their arm over the counter for making her think something was wrong.

"That's literally exactly what I need. Maybe she'll have a cute holiday novella, or a hockey romance." Everly is definitely on board with these new afternoon plans.

"Uh huh, feeling in the mood for a sexy strong guy after flirting with that delivery driver last weekend? I know how you feel about your hot hockey daddies, I'll keep an eye out for you."

When they turn around to wink at her, Frankie throws their head back and cackles at how red Everly's entire face and neck have turned. She cannot believe them. Why are they even friends? Yet for some reason, instead of stomping out the door like she considers doing, she leans back against the counter and waits for her friend to finish the tea.

They end up sitting around the coffeehouse and chatting for a bit instead of going next door right away. It's such a peaceful afternoon, Everly just wants to enjoy a bit of down time with her friend and relax without any stress hanging over her. They chat about the coffeehouse and some of Frankie's weird customers, and annoying customers, and the regulars they love. Frankie always has wild ideas of adventures and trips and projects they want to do, but really Frankie just loves to dream and hasn't ever set foot outside their small town. Everly can't deny it's fun to imagine though, and some of her favorite moments are spent with Frankie talking about the most ludicrous and unrealistic "dream vacations" that they will never go on. She even enjoys the comfortable silences they sit in together sometimes.

Everly breaks one such silence. "I saw Addison today."

"Oh yeah? How did that go?" Frankie sits up a bit and tips up their chin, eyebrows slightly pinched in concern.

Everly sighs and slumps back into the soft leather chair, cupping the dregs of her tea in both hands.

"I don't know how to talk to her. It's just so weird, you know? My long lost sister randomly being back and for no reason, what am I supposed to do? What am I supposed to say? I don't know why she came to the party or what she expects or what she even wants from me. It's kinda freaking me out."

Frankie nods and their lips pull down to one side thoughtfully. "Maybe she doesn't know either. It's a strange situation, that's for sure. What do you want to do?"

"What do I want to do?" Everly blinks a few times. What kind of a question is that? How is she supposed to know what she wants to do?

"Yeah, what do you want to do? Do you want to talk to her? Try to get closer, or do you want to keep your distance?" Everly can clearly see that Frankie is trying not to smile, and she can't help but feel like she walked into a trap somehow. Frankie tilts their head into their hand and waits.

"I guess... I do want to know her. We used to be really close, and I have so many questions. I don't know if I should ask them though." Everly considers this, realizing that maybe she does want a relationship with her sister. She can't think of a good reason not to, other than that it triggers her anxiety to think about it. Carrie would tell her to face her scary emotions, and in this situation, Everly supposes that means facing vulnerability and the possibility of opening up to someone who could hurt her.

"There you go." Frankie nods their head once, a solid confirmation. "It sounds to me like your heart knows what you want, you just gotta *listen*."

Everly squints her eyes. Listen? She thought she knew where this conversation was going, but now she's not so sure. Sometimes Frankie's logic can be a bit hard to follow.

A slow smile creeps across Frankie's face, causing Everly to lean away from them in slight alarm.

"Listen to your heart!" they belt out, as they jump up and grab Everly's hand, pulling her to her feet with them. "When it's talking to you, listen to your heart, there's nothing else you can do!"

Frankie spins Everly around on their way to the door, laughing and waving off her accusation that they're singing the wrong lyrics as they make their way next door for some perfect afternoon book shopping.

CHAPTER FIVE

A couple days later, Everly is pacing the same path over and over around the kitchen island. Addison is scheduled to arrive any minute, and Everly can't stop circling. Her thoughts, her pacing, her fingers twining around each other; her anxiety is peaking because waiting is the absolute worst. Just as she manages to stop her feet and take a breath, a knock interrupts her frantic mind.

Addison is here, finally. She's exactly on time, but Everly feels like she's been waiting for ages. She sucks in a quick breath, throws her shoulders back and pulls the door open wide. Addison looks as though she was giving herself a pep talk the whole way here, and it was only partially successful. Everly honestly doesn't blame her.

This is uncomfortable.

They walk back into the kitchen together after a quick greeting in the foyer. Their favorite childhood meal, lasagna, is wafting a comfortable garlic and melted cheese aroma through the air as it finishes up in the oven.

"Dinner will be ready in about ten, want anything to drink?" Everly says.

"Yeah that would be great." Her sister smiles with obvious relief. Alcohol always helps an awkward situation.

"I've got wine or we can make cocktails. Rum, vodka, I've got some fresh juice, tonic, and simple syrups. I think I have a couple of those frozen daiquiri mixes in the freezer too." Everly offers while pulling everything out for her sister to choose from.

"I'll have a cocktail, I'm not picky. Whatever you're having is great."

Everly sets out her ingredients and puts everything together to make her favorite signature cocktail, a Manhattan. She switches it up with bourbon or a dry vermouth here and there, but today she sticks to the traditional recipe.

"Oh wow, that's good!" Addison raises her eyebrows in surprise. "I might have to steal that recipe."

"Thanks, it's my go-to," Everly replies. "Boozy and delicious."

They clink glasses and manage to make adequate small talk without too much difficulty or awkwardness, and Everly internally congratulates herself for doing better than the morning she woke Addison up at the hotel. At least this time they're off to a better start.

When the timer goes off, she pulls the dish out of the oven.

"Lasagna?" Addison asks.

"I thought it might be nice, for old times sake," Everly answers, now questioning this idea. "Do you still like lasagna?"

"I do." Addison nods emphatically as if she needs to reiterate this point. "I love it, but I almost never have it anymore. And garlic bread too! Oh it smells so good."

Everly gets that warm fuzzy feeling inside watching her sister enjoy one of their favorite childhood dishes. It feels right to be eating this together, and Everly is relieved that at least she can do this well enough.

"We always loved this when we were younger," Everly says.

"I remember," Addison replies.

The silence lingers for a few moments, and Everly tries to decide how she should proceed. As she's questioning what she's supposed to do, she remembers Frankie's question.

What do you want to do?

"So..." Everly starts, then stops.

Addison looks up at Everly and raises her eyebrows, then nods slowly and gently sets her utensils down next to her plate, folding her hands into her lap.

"So," She replies.

"What... what even happened?" Everly starts and stops

again, unsure how or what to really ask her sister. "I mean, why did we stop talking? We used to be so close and then... after mom and dad died..." she trails off.

"I don't know. I can't even count the number of times I've asked myself that. I think about you all the time, Ev."

"You do?" Everly straightens up at this, blinking a couple times in surprise. She didn't expect that response, though she didn't know what else to expect either. On some level, she thought it was entirely her fault, that she had done something wrong or pushed her sister away. "I think about you too. I have so many questions but I don't even know where to start. I mean, why now?"

"I feel the same way. As for why now..." Addison trails off for a moment. "I guess it was a little impulsive, deciding to fly out here last minute, but I just broke up with my ex, like, a week ago. We'd been together a couple years and I didn't want to be alone for the holidays. Besides that, I don't know. I figured it was time. I just went for it, decided to come back for the gala and see if I can change things. I want to have my sister back and I know maybe it's too late, maybe you don't want me around, but—"

"No!" Everly says, voice louder than she intends. "I do want you around, I haven't known how to bridge whatever this gap is between us, but I really, really want to."

Addison's shoulders loosen and she slumps forward, putting her arms on the table and picking her fork back up, then absently twirling it around on her plate. Her cheeks puff out with a relieved breath, like the cutest little chipmunk Everly has ever seen.

"I'm really glad you came back, Addison. I'm sorry about the breakup and yeah, it probably hasn't been much of a better situation here. I know things have been weird and I'm awkward, but I want to fix things too."

"Oh thank goodness. I wasn't sure, I mean I thought maybe I was intruding? This is your home now, your town, your hotel, I didn't want you to think I was trying to come back in and mess up everything you've done or something."

That thought hadn't crossed Everly's mind once, and she shakes her head, upsetting the messy bun perched precariously on top of it, unable to even comprehend that her sister would think that.

"Addison, you've always been one of the most important people in my life. Even these last eight years when we haven't been talking, I never stopped caring about you. I've hated not talking, not knowing how you are or what you've been up to. I didn't know if I could reach out though or if that would be unwelcome. I thought I'd let you live your best life in San Diego and I figured you wanted to leave all of this small town nonsense behind you."

"Never. I never wanted that. Honestly, not talking to you has sucked. I hated it." Addison's eyes start to tear up. "I miss you so much, Ev. It hurts."

Everly isn't a crier, but hearing and seeing the emotion in her sister, she can't help it when her eyes start to fill too.

"It really has sucked," she replies with a mix between a sniffle and a smile. "So let's agree to not do that again. I don't know if I can do another eight years without you."

Addison nods, and tentatively gets up from her seat, holding out her arms. Everly jumps up and folds her sister into the fiercest hug she's ever given. A hug to make up for eight years of missed hugs. A hug that holds all of their shared tragedy, sadness, heartache, grief and loss. A hug to encompass their newfound hope in each other. A hug full of love and belonging. They hold onto each other for what feels like an eternity, and also will never be long enough. Addison reluctantly pulls away first, wiping her eyes as she does so.

"Well, I'm glad we got that cleared up. Turns out we are both idiots," she says with a watery laugh.

Everly chuckles with her, passing another piece of garlic bread and agreeing that yes, they are incredibly idiotic for staying away from each other for so long. They finish the rest of their meal with much easier chatter, and decide to take their drinks to the other room in front of the fireplace. Everly lights it up quickly enough; she likes the ease of a gas fireplace even if it doesn't give off the pleasant crackle of a wood one.

"What if you stayed a little longer?" Everly blurts out, and then looks down at her drink questioningly, as though it has the answers to where that question came from and why she let it out.

Addison awkwardly looks down at her drink too, twisting it in circles before replying. "I'll think about it, but... Well, I probably can't. I have to get back for work."

"Oh, right. Yeah, that makes sense that you'd go back after New Years." Everly understands, though she can't help but feel a little disappointed and rejected anyways.

"Maybe I can come back for another visit soon though?" Addison suggests.

"I'd like that," Everly says, smiling back at her. This push and pull, trying to stumble their way back toward each other is exhausting.

"Soooooo," her sister draws out the word, a hint of mischief twinkling in her eyes. Everly remembers that look; her sister was always getting into things and causing trouble when she was younger. Everly's hackles go up, wary about where this is going.

"Anyone important in your life these days?" Addison asks. "Boyfriend?"

It takes Everly a second to realize how hot her face has gotten.

"Oh my gosh, there is!" Addison is absolutely gleeful. "You *have* to tell me!"

"I mean, it's not..." Everly trails off, no idea what to say.

"I bet he's charming, to snag you. And hot." Addison draws out the h and snaps the t at the end of hot like it personally offended her. "So, where'd you meet him?"

Everly isn't entirely sure how to tell her sister that there's nothing going on, and it's just a random crush on someone she saw once. If possible, her blush gets even redder. She's fairly certain a tomato has nothing on her at this point.

"Okay, well, I mean we only met once," Everly says.

Addison twirls a hand for Everly to keep going while she takes a sip of her drink.

"He delivered the poinsettias and tree for the party," Everly blurts it out so fast all the words run together, then clamps her mouth shut.

Addison pauses with her lips still on the glass.

"And?" she says.

"And... that's it," Everly replies.

"What? That can't be it. Did you give him your number?"

"No, I was all flustered and he didn't ask for it, so I think that's just... it." Everly shrugs, trying to play it off like she isn't dying of disappointment.

"No way," Addison says. "If you like this guy, you have to see him again! He must work at the greenhouse, right? You could go see if he's there!"

"Oh my god." Everly cannot believe this girl. "You want me to go to his work? Like some sort of stalker?! That's insane, Ad." She uses her childhood nickname for her sister for the first time in nearly a decade, and it would have gutted her in the best way if not for the current distraction at hand.

"I mean not like, in a stalker-y way." Her sister rolls her eyes. "Just go pretend you need a plant or something."

If she's being honest, Everly hadn't even thought of that idea. She assumed he was a delivery driver, but what if he also works there? Or maybe she'll run into him between deliveries. How crazy is it that she's actually considering this?

"Just think about it. It's not every day you meet someone who makes you feel like that." Thankfully, her sister doesn't push too much and they move on to other topics. Addison fills her in more on her work and life in San Diego. They don't get into anything too deep, but that's okay for now.

At the end of the night, the women tentatively agree to another visit in a few weeks. Addison is going to check her work schedule to see if she can open up a long weekend and fly out again. They also agree to start texting and calling weekly until then, in an effort to get to know each other better and make up for years of missed opportunities. Everly is feeling happier than she has in years to be fostering this reconnection. She has her sister back, and that is everything.

~~~

New Year's Eve arrives, and Everly spends it with Frankie, as usual. She's had a few boyfriends in the past, but nothing serious or long term. Frankie's love life is similar, a few relationships on and off, but they don't have anyone they're seeing romantically right now
~~~

either. So here they are, clinking glasses with each other on New Years instead of kissing their one true loves.

"If you could kiss anyone at midnight, like anyone," Frankie asks with a bit of a slur from all the champagne they've had, "who would it be?"

Why does *his* face instantly pop into her head? Obviously, she should want to kiss some super hot, famous celebrity, someone like...

Why is her mind blanking on this? It's a simple question. Name a celebrity.

Any. Celebrity.

Frankie almost misses her internal freakout, but luckily misinterprets it.

"Why are your eyes so big? It wasn't a serious question. You don't have to answer it, but I'd definitely kiss Rachel from Friends. Not, like, Jennifer Aniston, but Rachel. And not her now, but like when she was..." Frankie trails off, then leans forward and slams their drink down on the table next to them, sloshing half of it out of the glass as their eyes get big too.

"Oh. My. God." Frankie imitates Janice, hands and all, also from Friends. "It's him! You'd kiss Hot Delivery Guy!"

Everly groans and covers her face with her hands, throwing her upper body back into the cushioned couch. Why can no one drop this?

"You have to see him again," Frankie insists. "If you're still hooked on this guy, you have to make it happen. I don't know how, but you're seeing him again. I'll order a freaking plant to be delivered to the coffeehouse and you can come wait for him to deliver it if I have to, I don't even care. We need to make this happen if you're still thinking about him!"

They are not going to drop this, Everly can tell. She debates telling them about her sister's idea, and decides if she's going to get anyone else's opinion, it'll be theirs.

"I was talking to Addison about this too actually, well, more like she was talking to me... anyway, she kind of had a crazy idea," Everly starts.

"YES. I love crazy ideas. Tell me." Frankie is ridiculous.

Everly loves them.

"Okay, well. She thinks I should just go to the

greenhouse and see if he's there."

"How did we not think of this already?!" Frankie almost looks pissed about it. "Of course you should go to the greenhouse. That's not crazy at all, that's just being logical and finding a way to get what you want. You do want him, right." It's not really a question, they both know she does.

"I mean, I wouldn't put it that way exactly," Everly tries to defend herself, but she can hardly get a sentence in around Frankie's excitement.

"No, I'm right. Addison is right. You want him, and the only lead we have is the greenhouse. I think you should do it."

"You don't think it's a bit creepy?" Everly really thinks their idea is dangerously close to stalking.

Frankie leans forward and grabs Everly's hand in theirs.

"Everly Anne Moore. You are not a stalker." Frankie says in their most serious voice. "You're desperate."

Everly can't hold in the surprised, snorting laugh that comes out of her mouth, and Frankie beams. They're proud, as usual, for being obnoxious. And also right.

"For real though," her friend says, squeezing her hand in emphasis, "didn't your therapist tell you to prioritize yourself? Aren't you supposed to be working on being your true self and taking risks or some such thing?"

They're right again. She is supposed to be doing that. With a sigh and a flutter of excited nerves in her chest, Everly gives in.

She's going to Magnolia Nursery.

CHAPTER SIX

It's possible, even probable, that Everly is procrastinating. She chooses to live in denial though, and blames it on Carrie, which she also recognizes is entirely delusional and for that reason she has no intention of telling her therapist anything about this thought process and decision making strategy.

She spends New Year's Day cleaning, attempting to relax, and mentally preparing, so when she wakes up the day after, she's ready. Everly made a list last night, obviously, and she woke up prepared to take names and kick butts. Or, make friends, rather.

First item on her list: practice.

Last session, Carrie said to focus on being herself. Everly isn't entirely sure what that means, so before she does it in a big way that truly matters with someone she wants to like her, she figures practicing around others would be a good first step. She's convinced herself that practice, consisting of spending time in places she isn't used to and talking to people she doesn't really know, will help. Starting at some of the local businesses.

She drives the short distance downtown instead of walking, then parks in the downtown lot rather than at the hotel, even though it's close. This way she has easier access to the other shops in the area and can run back to the car to drop things off if needed. Very practical.

So Everly sets off with a pep in her step. She chose her style and outfit carefully today; she doesn't want to put anyone off, so she went for a look that she thinks says "I'm approachable and easy going, but also sophisticated, and I have a sense of humor". Basically business casual, but that sounds way too boring in her head. She's rocking a comfy cream sweater, which she feels really makes her dark hair and eyes pop, tucked into a high waisted, herringbone-patterned skirt that hits just under mid-thigh. Her bright red stilettos add a pop of color, matching the red bag she has slung over her shoulder.

Fun, sophisticated, easy going and approachable. Nailed it.

Wandering into the local handmade shop, filled with all sorts of cute stuff from knitted hats for babies to gorgeous stained glass wind chimes, a little embroidered hoop catches her eye. It has a picture of a cheesy smiling lasagna getting stabbed with a knife and fork on it, that says "I'm feeling lasagnabout it" around the edges in bold lettering. Everly suspects it's a pun, but she has no clue what it's supposed to mean. It's cute though, so she picks it up as a little souvenir for Addison when she comes back to visit next time. Maybe she'll be able to decipher it.

Apart from the lady working the cash register who clearly has no interest in small talk this morning, there's no one else in the little shop, so Everly meanders her way down the block, popping in and out of each shop or business she comes across, but not having much luck on the socializing part of her goal.

She swears there are normally people outside laughing and chatting, sometimes even yelling down the street to one another. Of course when *she's* trying to be social though, everyone disappears.

Pursing her lips, Everly turns her feet toward the last stop of the morning, the candy shop. It's just opened for the day and smells divine. Sugary fuel is just what she needs to propel her into a more successful afternoon. Everly is wandering around inside, admiring the beautiful artistry of the truffles and candies under the counter, when she glances out the candy shop windows, almost like something pulled her eyes that direction. She sees someone walking into the local hardware store across the street, and a tingle shoots down her spine, a burst of adrenaline straight to her stuttering heart.

It's him.

Hot Delivery Guy just walked into the hardware store.

Asim is right across the street.

Everly immediately panics. Her heart beats a frantic rhythm as it tries to escape her chest, probably to go tearing across the street after him. Her thoughts spiral and she can't help but ask herself what she should do. Does she go in after him? Is that crazy? She was going to go to his work anyways, but if she can maneuver a happenstance run-in with him instead, that's much further away from the domain of a stalker. She could go in and pretend to shop around for... well, she's never been in a hardware store before. What does one buy there? Rope? That seems likely, but what would she do with rope?! Is she planning on tying him up or something? Actually... her brain tells her that doesn't sound so bad as far as ideas go. Even better, maybe he could tie her up...

Everly gives herself a violent, full body shake, scolding herself soundly in her head. Objectifying others is *not* what she is about. Yes, he's attractive, but come on Everly. Get your head out of the gutter, and *think*. There's got to be a reasonable way to make this happen.

After internally freaking out while staring with unseeing eyes at the assortment of candies under the counter, she belatedly realizes the sales person has been waiting for her to make a decision. Everly snaps to and requests a few of her favorite salted caramels, then decides to make a run for it ("coward!" Frankie's voice screams in the back of her head). Decision made, she pushes her way out the door while popping two of the sugary, salty squares into her mouth, and—

Asim steps out of the hardware store right across from her at the same moment. Their eyes connect, cementing her feet to the sidewalk. He's carrying a cloth bag, because of course he has reusable bags, but she can't see what's in it.

His face lights up and he glances both directions, checking the road before he starts walking toward her, which makes Everly realize she hasn't moved an inch, maybe not even blinked, and is just staring at him. She frantically chews, slurping up some drool before it can fall out of her mouth, and questions why on earth she thought eating two candies at once was a good idea. Or caramel itself. Caramel is never a good idea. Caramel is impossible to eat!

He makes it across the street and is only a few feet from her when his rich, clear voice makes her knees want to tremble.

"Well hello there," Asim says, still smiling at her as his deep voice seeps under her skin and sets her nerves on fire.

She tries to swallow too quickly, resulting in far too much sticky caramel not quite making it all the way down her throat, because her mouth has gone impossibly dry.

Everly is half choking, half mortified crying, and somehow also partly nervous laughing? Because honestly, what even is her life. Of course this would happen to her.

She manages to clear her throat after an eternity of torture and say hi back, though it comes out raspy, sounding like what she imagines a sun-baked lizard might sound like if it could talk. He reaches out to pat her back, just as kind as she remembered.

"Are you okay?" His eyes are a gorgeous green, filled with concern as they flit across her face.

She'd love to say yes, she's great, fantastic really, but now he's touching her and it's only making the situation worse because that causes all sorts of tingles and butterflies to erupt across her body, tightening the meager air left in her lungs. She feels too tense and closed in as she tries to fight against the panic taking over. Everly takes a clumsy step back from him so she has space to gather her thoughts.

Right as he asks, again, if she's alright, she offers him a candy from her bag, like some sort of creep who tries to entice kids with sweets. At least she doesn't drive a white van, she thinks to herself, and can't help but accept that this is going horribly wrong. She couldn't have planned it worse if she tried.

Luckily, Asim has much better social skills than she does. He politely accepts a caramel, tucking it into his pocket.

"Something sweet to remind me of you later," he says with a little smile, though the concern has only etched deeper around his eyes.

Everly isn't sure if him remembering this moment is a

good thing, as she really doesn't want him to remember that she can't even eat a candy or say hello properly, or what the sound of her choking sounds like.

"How have you been?" he asks in a valiant attempt to save the situation.

"Good. Great, yeah I've been good." Everly wants to slap a hand over her own mouth but manages to resist the urge.

Asim nods with a polite smile, "and how did the party go? I'm sure everyone enjoyed it."

He is sweet and kind, and wow did he have such long, thick eyelashes last time she saw him? They make his bright green eyes pop even more than they already do against his darker bronze skin. As he pushes the long sleeves of his henley up to his elbows, the muscles in his forearms flex with the movement of the bag shifting in his grasp, and holy mother how did she not notice the tattoos before?! Everly catches herself staring, imagining how far those tattoos go and what his muscles might look like underneath his shirt, before noticing his friendly smile has turned into a satisfied "I know what you're doing and I don't mind" type of smirk.

Everly experiences one of those deer in the headlights moments, and her immediate reaction, as usual, is to run. She starts to turn away, giving in to her instincts, but he catches her forearm. His hand is gentle but warm, and as she turns back, he briefly rubs his thumb back and forth over her sweater before letting go.

"It was really nice running into you, Everly." He says, gazing directly into her eyes. She could so easily get lost in those eyes. "I'd really like to see you again sometime."

Her brain stops.

Straight up ceases to function.

Her anxiety might have killed her brain all the way dead at this point, because somehow it's blank but also racing with too many thoughts to sort through. Her pulse skyrockets, and she forgets how to breathe, feeling like there's a mountain sitting on her chest. She offers an unintelligible, non-word mumble with a barely discernible "have to go meeting late" jumble of words, and nearly speed walks all the way back to the hotel, before remembering she parked in the downtown lot because, oh yeah, *socializing*. What an absolutely terrible idea.

She doesn't glance back once, her vision tunneled on the sidewalk in front of her while her pulse thunders in her ears.

Step, step, step.

Red shoe, red shoe, red shoe.

One foot in front of the other until she reaches the parking lot.

Everly is dreaming. She must be having a nightmare, because there is no way what she thinks just happened, is actually what happened. Surely, she didn't freeze up in front of Asim, ignore his polite request to see her again, and then quite literally run away. And yet, what other explanation is there?

Time jumps, and Everly finds herself sitting in her car, breathing way too fast and clutching a squashed bag of caramels to her chest with sweaty palms, feeling as though she just ran a marathon. She tips her head back against her seat and closes her eyes, trying to steady her breathing.

Sometimes it feels like she can't do anything right.

She smashes the bag of candy into the passenger seat before clenching her hands into fists and opening her mouth wide, letting out a long, silent scream. Her entire body is tense, eyes squeezed shut, neck taught and legs straining. It's over just as suddenly and she slumps back into her seat, entirely spent.

This day is a disaster.

~~~

Everly opens her door back up, not having moved the car an inch. She avoids the main sidewalks this time and instead sneaks through the back entrance of Roasted, coming in from behind the counter. She skirts around Frankie, in the midst of making something hot and foamy, and veers left into the back corner, keeping her head down. There's a little nook back here that can be perfectly arranged for hiding. Everly pulls a large potted plant to the side and tucks herself into the cushioned chair behind it, next to a small bookshelf. This is as much privacy as she can hope to get during the tail end of the lunch rush.
~~~

Frankie glances over, giving Everly a concerned frown. Everly just shakes her head and waves at them to carry on. She's not going anywhere anytime soon.

Everly wallows. She is truly astonished with herself and is having a hard time figuring out what exactly happened. Now that she's calmed down a bit and can think more clearly, she suspects she had a panic attack. She can hardly even remember getting back to her car, and it's nearly an hour later than she thought it was, indicating she lost quite a bit of time between running away from Asim and entering the coffeehouse. Everly pulls out her phone, types into the search bar and sure enough, she experienced most of the symptoms on the list.

Now that she knows what happened, Everly feels a little less idiotic, a little more concerned instead. She's been seeing Carrie for almost a year now, and overall her anxiety has gotten much better. She makes a note in her phone to talk about it during their session next week. This leads her to question how she can be herself without her anxiety getting in the way. As she's contemplating this dilemma, Frankie shuts down the coffeehouse again and pulls a chair up next to her.

"What's wrong?" They waste no time on pleasantries.

"I think I had a panic attack." Everly's voice cracks on the last word.

She can't help but be confused about what her emotions are trying to tell her. They feel all tangled up, and she's not sure how to sort them out.

"Are you okay? I didn't know you had panic attacks."

"I don't." Everly shakes her head slowly. "Or at least, I never have before. This was the first one."

"How about some tea? We'll do decaf, green tea doesn't have much caffeine anyways, but I know even a little can make it worse." Frankie is truly the best person she knows; they get up and grab a pot of hot water and riffle around the tea drawer for a particular tea bag, dropping it into a mug on their way back over. "Better to be safe."

Everly takes it gratefully, already feeling comforted having the warm mug in her hands and her friend at her side.

"Do you want to talk about what happened?" they ask.

"We can also just sit if you want. Or I can distract you, I'm pretty good at that."

"I don't know. I can't even get my thoughts straight right now."

"Distraction it is." Frankie launches into a story about their nemesis at the grocery store who keeps trying to steal their beans. This has been slowly escalating for a few months now, where the local grocery store owner has been hinting at and verbally tiptoeing around the mystery of where Frankie gets their infamously delicious coffee beans. Over recent weeks though, he's become more forward and demanding. At first, it's the same old story—he said, they said, he did, they did—but then Frankie leans forward and smacks their hand on the table.

"THEN," they say, "he had the audacity to threaten to report me to the city council!"

Now, Everly is fully invested. This may not seem like a big deal, but in their small town, the city council rules everything.

"He did not!" Everly gasps as her eyes widen.

"He absolutely did. Of course, I asked what on earth he would report me for, and he actually came up with something. He said, and I quote, "You're in violation of business hours." and he was so smug about it, too." Their lip curls up in distaste.

"Wait, you're in violation of business hours?"

Frankie leans back and rubs a hand across the back of their neck, glancing toward the wall of windows facing the street. "Well... you know how you're always getting on my case about closing down at all hours of the day?"

"Uh, yeah. Terrible business practice, but I don't see how that's a violation when you own the place."

"It is, actually." Frankie grimaces. "The city council passed it a couple years back: that any business on the main strip downtown has to maintain regular business hours "within reasonable expectations" whatever that means."

"And he's accusing you of not maintaining those regular business hours," Everly surmises, "because you're always closing shop in the middle of the day."

"You got it." Frankie sighs, and Everly turns her head toward the door where the word "open" is facing inwards, staring right at her, instead of facing out as it should be.

"You need to open back up. If he's threatening you... You can't keep closing like this Frankie." Everly implores them to listen, and Frankie nods in acquiescence. They stand and walk over to the door, flipping the sign before returning to their seat.

"If he does go to the council, you'll let me know? I don't have a lot of sway, but I do have some. They were all tight with my parents and since their passing, they always make a point to offer me whatever help I need. I can call in a favor. I'll help however I can," Everly says.

"Thanks. I don't want to ask that of you, but if it comes to it I will." They sit in silence together for a few moments, reflecting on the strangeness of their lives right now.

"Okay, I think I'm ready to talk about it," Everly whispers. Frankie nods and puts a gentle hand on her knee, waiting for Everly to continue. The soft touch helps to ground her, and she appreciates that Frankie knows and remembers this. "I ran into Asim, and I don't know, he started talking to me and I just panicked. I ran away and ended up back in my car and I think I was there for a while but I can't really remember."

"That sounds kind of scary. Do you feel uncomfortable around him?" Frankie asks, doing their best not to bristle.

"No, I actually really like being around him." Everly thinks about it for a moment. "I think it's because I wasn't expecting to see him. I was already feeling stressed being out, and then my plan to be social was failing so I was even more stressed, and then running into him so unexpectedly just really threw me off."

"That makes sense to me." Frankie reassures her, and they settle back into their seat.

"I'm not sure what to do now though. I made a complete fool of myself." Now that she reflects on it, she is feeling rather embarrassed about the whole situation. Her reaction was so out of the blue.

"What do you want to do?"

"Ugh," Everly glares at them. "This question again."

"Yes." Frankie counters her glare with a sassy smirk. "This question again."

Their left eyebrow goes up as they wait. Everly glowers at it. She's always been jealous that they can lift one eyebrow, it's such a useful expression. Hers just sort of contort awkwardly without any up or down movement when she tries.

Everly sighs and lets her head tip down toward her lap. "I hope he doesn't think it's his fault, or that there's something wrong with me. I guess I want to fix it. I don't like what happened, that's not me, and he asked to see me again. I want to see him again." She looks up at her friend with a self-deprecating smile on her face. "I just also don't want to look like a fool again."

Frankie looks like a proud parent sending their kid off to the first day of school. "You won't. Let's make a plan, we both know that will help."

Everly acknowledges that plans and a solid list fix everything, even though they betrayed her today, so the two of them begin. They go back to her idea of heading to the garden center under the guise of doing some plant shopping, since she still has no other way of contacting him. Frankie offers to go with her for moral support, but Everly determines this is something she can and should do on her own.

Everly and Frankie discuss what she will wear and say, backup ideas of what else she can say, what to do if he's not there, what to do if she sees him first and vice-versa, and anything else they can think of. At this point, she could not be more prepared if her life depended on it. It's the start of a new year after all, and she's committed to showing the world who she really is.

CHAPTER SEVEN

Parked in the lot outside Magnolia Nursery for seven minutes and counting, Everly is still sitting inside her car instead of getting out and walking into the main building as she is supposed to. Like a normal person.

But Everly's mind keeps jumping back and forth—she's not ready, she's ready, she's not ready. If she procrastinates too much longer, she'll be out of time and they'll have closed. It's times like this that she wishes she could just shake herself and stop overthinking everything. Maybe it's time to consider anti-anxiety medication again.

Everly starts to go over her hype speech again, when her phone chimes a text. Everly gave her sister a cute little bells ringtone so she doesn't miss it if Addison contacts her. It's been over a week now since she left to go back to California, but they've been doing their best to keep in touch.

Addison: Hey sis, it's been a couple days so
    wanted to check in and see how things have
    been going. What are you up to?

Well, that timing couldn't have been better. Maybe a small distraction is what she needs to calm her racing heart.

Everly: Oh you know, just sitting in my car
    outside the garden center trying to ward off
    a panic attack. The usual, how about you?

* * *

Addison: OMG!
Addison: You're finally doing it!
Addison: YES. Okay. You can do this, Ev. Talk
    me through the plan, what's the first step?

Everly: I suppose getting out of the car, or even
    turning it off and opening the door would be
    a good start.

Addison: Ha. Ha. Your snark isn't working on
    me.

Everly: Well I planned to go in and shop around,
    pretend like I needed a plant or whatever,
    and see if he actually works here or just does
    deliveries.

Addison: I like it. I'll be over here sending you all
    the brave, successful, you can do this vibes.
    Shoot me a "help" text if you need an
    emergency out!

Everly: Why would I need an emergency out?

Addison: I don't know. What if it turns out he
    has rotten breath or hates animals or
    something? No one's perfect.

Everly cracks a smile at that, because she can't imagine him having rotten breath or hating animals, but she appreciates what her sister is trying to do. She sends her a quick thanks and lets her know she'll send an update later. The distraction did help, and she feels a little more calm now than she has the last fourteen minutes since pulling up. Everly shoots into action before her anxiety hijacks her again.
    It's now or never.

* * *

~~~

The first thing she notices as she walks up the front path toward the building is the sound of tinkling water. There's a whole section of water fountains outside to the left of the path along the building, tucked in amid vibrant flowering vines, sculpted shrubbery, and potted trees, all waiting for their new homes. She loves how peaceful it sounds, and Everly huffs a soft laugh under her breath at how magical it feels when she spots a lazy yellow butterfly flapping around.

The door is already propped open, allowing fresh air into the main building. To her right is the checkout counter, along with some indoor displays and a staircase with a chain across it. Further to the left, the building opens up through a large, rolling garage door into a flourishing greenhouse. That looks like a bit much, so she decides to start at the displays here in the main shopping area.

Everly wanders, starting to relax a bit, even enjoying her time looking around at all the different plants, garden decorations, and cute pots. She runs her fingers over the leaves as she passes, feeling the different textures and shapes as she does so and marveling at the variety.

As she circles the next display, she feels a little spark on the back of her neck and Asim walks up to her, brushing his hands off on a small towel that he tucks into his back pocket.

"Everly," and there's that voice she can't get enough of, extending the first syllable of her name as though he's savoring it.

"Hi, Asim." Everly smiles up at him, unreasonably pleased that she got the words out without her voice betraying her, and she's also managing to keep the panic at bay.

"I'm so pleased you're here," he says, and she doesn't think anyone has ever said those words to her before. She likes the way he speaks. "Are you here for anything in particular?"

She wants to say she's here for him, but manages to refrain from embarrassing herself just yet.

"I'm just looking around. This place is beautiful."
~~~

"Thank you. I've put a lot of work into it," he replies.

Everly's jaw falls open, and his eyes crinkle in the corners. "You... own this place?" she has to clarify if that's what he meant, because that's a far cry from being a delivery driver.

"I do. Built it myself, and I live here too, right upstairs." He gestures to the staircase in the corner.

"Wow." Everly is impressed, to put it lightly. She knows how much work that takes. Inheriting and building upon something like she did is one thing, but building an entire business from the ground up is another entirely. "That's amazing."

"Thank you, it's a lot of work, but it's what I love to do." His eyes wander over the various plants, a small smile curving his lips, clearly proud of the space he's created. "Well, let me know if I can help you with anything."

He can't leave yet! She only just got here and found him.

"Yeah, actually..." Everly rushes to reply, then pauses, unsure what to say to keep him here. So much for those plans and backup plans. They've flown completely out of her head.

Asim raises his eyebrows in question, and she blurts out the first thing she can think of.

"I was thinking about doing some re-landscaping, and wanted to purchase some plants for the... terracing." She holds up the plant in her hands; one she picked up at random with a tag that reads "*monstera siltepecana*".

Asim gives her what might be an inquisitive look, glancing down at the plant, then back up at her face. He might also be trying not to smile, but he can't hide those twinkling eyes. She can tell he knows. Everly has absolutely no idea what she's doing, and he sees right through her. Instead of calling her out on it, he offers to help instead.

"Can I show you what I have in the native flora section? They'd be much better suited to the dry Arizona climate."

"Oh, sure, that'd be great."

He gently takes the potted plant from her hands, and while it takes both of hers to hold it, one of his nearly wraps around the whole thing. She thought there wasn't anything else about him that would turn her on, but she should have anticipated those hands. Strong hands, working hands, hands that he clearly knows how to use. Asim sets it back onto the display, next to a sign she hadn't noticed before that reads "tropical indoor plants." Right on cue, her cheeks heat up; so much for not embarrassing herself this time.

"Wait here." His voice is a gentle command that she's happy to follow.

Asim returns moments later pulling a cart behind him unlike any cart she has seen before. It's long and flat, without sides, and fat rubbery wheels, which makes perfect sense for a plant shop now that she sees it. Instead of going left into the greenhouse, he leads her through a double door in the back she hadn't noticed initially.

"Oh, it keeps going."

Immediately, her eyes widen and she tucks her lips into her teeth as she looks up at him. What a stupid thing to say. Why doesn't she ever think before she speaks?! If she was alone, she'd facepalm again at how lame that was.

"I never realized how big it was, or that there was more back here. It's very impressive." She explains, trying to save face.

"Yes, it keeps going." He quirks a sideways smile at her. "Would you like a tour?"

Everly's heart thumps in her chest.

"I'd love that."

Anything to spend more time with him, especially since it's actually going well this time.

Or, as well as can be expected when you're a bumbling ball of anxiety.

They leave the cart by the back door for now, and Asim walks her around the property, bypassing the "employees only" signs. He points out three more domed greenhouses in the back, as well as a large outdoor area with potted plants in place of a fourth one, explaining that each greenhouse is temperature regulated with fans and humidity control to create the right climate for each group of plants he has growing in them. He has some tropical and subtropical plants that he propagates and grows himself, like the one she was admiring inside, he says with a half smile and a little elbow nudge to her arm, causing Everly's cheeks to pink again, but she takes it in stride and smirks back at him with a one shoulder shrug. She's caught, and she doesn't care one bit because look where she is now.

Asim points out the other areas, plucking weeds out of pots and snapping off dead leaves as they go, and honestly, she's just happy to keep listening to his voice. She doesn't even care what he talks about, Everly just wants him to keep talking. Although, she reflects, she does find it fascinating how much he knows about plants and how much care he puts into them. She's more interested in it than she would have expected, but it's hard not to be when he speaks with such passion.

They wander back toward the public area and he snags the cart again as he leads the way to the native plants section for her landscaping.

"Many of the more popular plants used for landscaping are actually invasive to the area," he informs her, describing the detrimental impact it can have on the environment as a whole.

"Wow, I had no idea. Guess I came to the right place for help then." Everly grins up at him, biting her lip when his eyes sparkle in reply.

They slowly walk up and down the local flora aisles. She keeps sneaking glances at Asim, noticing his muscles flex and shift under his shirt as he picks up various plants to show her. Asim points out different varieties, commenting on the leaf colors, textures, shapes, sizes, how much or little water they need, what animals they attract or repel, and any other random fact that comes to him. He offers advice and suggestions based on the limited amount of information she's given him on the conditions of her terrace.

Everly feels so much more comfortable than she has the last two times they spoke, reaching out to touch the plants and ask questions about ones that catch her eye. Any she asks about or that he notices her looking closer at, he picks up and places onto the cart.

It's at this point that it starts to sink in what she's doing. Everly wasn't actually re-landscaping, but apparently now she is. She also has no idea how to do any landscaping or take care of plants in general, so now she needs to find a landscaper to figure out what to do with all these plants that are quickly filling her cart.

"You really know a lot about all this," Everly says, gesturing around as they weave through the aisles back toward the main building. He's pulling the cart along behind them and her eyes are drawn to him, glancing up and down his body as they go. Once or twice, she thinks she catches him doing the same to her.

"It's what I love." Asim's reply is simple, and it makes her both happy and sad. She doesn't have anything like that in her life, but she's glad that he does.

"Who is doing your landscaping?" he asks. They've just walked through the double doors to the indoor section, and luckily he isn't looking at her so she has a moment to decide how to answer him. She decides on the truth, or at least a partial truth.

"I haven't actually hired anyone yet," Everly says, looking down at her fidgeting hands. "I was only just starting to think about the project, but it looks like it's really happening now."

She isn't sure if she smiles or grimaces at the cart of plants, likely it's a weird combination of the two.

"I know a couple people who could do it for you." He stops for a moment, looking at her while he appears to be debating something. "Or... If you want, I could help with your project."

This is beyond what she dared to imagine or hope for. Of course she wants his help. Everly manages to wrangle in the crazy though, and thinks she does pretty well at remaining composed.

"That would be amazing!" She smiles up at him, and he instantly returns it, lighting up her insides. His smile is stunning. Asim was already attractive, but that look of pure joy transforms him into something else entirely.

He steps behind the counter to ring up her purchases and pulls out a business card from below the register. Asim writes down a number on the back, informing her it's his personal cell, and to call so they can arrange the details. Everly tucks it safely into her wallet as he snags a folded towel from under the counter as well, before grabbing the cart handle again and walking her out to her car.

As Everly opens up the back, Asim unfolds the towel

and gives it a quick flick, spreading it down in her trunk.

"So your car doesn't get dirty," he says in reply to the question she hasn't asked yet.

"Oh," she tilts her head at him, "thank you, I wouldn't have thought of that."

He gives her a quick little wink, or did she just imagine it, as he turns back to the cart. Next thing she knows, he's picking up two plants at a time and placing them into her trunk for her. Again, those muscles. Flexing and shifting underneath his shirt, it should be illegal for anyone to look that good. Everly could offer to help, but truthfully she would much rather watch, and Asim doesn't seem to mind. He glances over at her watching when he puts down his current armful, and she catches a glimpse of a smile as he turns back to grab the next ones.

Asim straightens once they're all in, dusting his hands again and wiping them off on the small hand towel he carries with him, which he tosses onto the empty cart when he's done. He closes up her trunk for her, then leans a hip against it.

"I'm really glad you stopped by," he says. This man is so direct, she's not sure what to do with it.

"Me too," she replies.

Good one, Everly.

Asim reaches out a hand and gently brushes along her elbow where it hangs by her side. She wants to lean into that touch. Before she can, he skims his fingers up the outside of her arm to her hair and tucks back a strand that has fallen out of place, then steps back, taking hold of the cart handle again. Everly is pretty sure he's just turned her into a statue; her whole body is tingling and she can't move an inch after that touch.

Asim tilts his head down, those unique green eyes piercing straight into her soul.

"Hopefully I'll see you again soon. Let me know if you end up wanting help with those plants."

At this point, she thinks she would do anything he tells her to. He gives her trunk a quick tap with his hand, and it snaps her out of her strange fever dream, allowing her to rummage in her bag for her keys.

As she's turning out of the lot, Everly takes a quick look back to see him leaning against the entryway watching her, massive arms folded across his chest. Everly waves, and he tips his head up, nodding goodbye. Her entire body heats, and she wouldn't be able to stop the giddy grin from taking over her face if her life depended on it.

~~~

Everly catches one last glimpse of Magnolia Nursery in her rearview mirror before her smile slowly fades and reality sets back in alongside her anxiety, and she begins to question everything. Did she imagine his flirting? Surely not, those smiles weren't fake, and she is sure he winked at least once, maybe even twice. No one winks unless they're flirting. But what if it's a nervous tic? Two winks seems like a lot, so it might make sense if it was a tic, or just a thing he does. Maybe the attraction is one sided and he simply doesn't want to be rude to her, or he could just be a flirt. He might flirt with everyone, and she's sure he would have no problem snagging anyone he wanted.

Outside the candy shop he asked to see her again, but he didn't say anything about a date or ask for her number. Is she too awkward? Everly knows she's physically attractive, but maybe after that last disaster he decided she's not worth it. He did write down his number for her, even though he said it's for the landscaping. Maybe that's just a side gig for him, and since he doesn't have a full landscaping business he gave her his personal number so she won't have to play phone tag with him via the garden center phone.

Her mind is spinning more and more the further away from him she drives, questioning the entire encounter, and she can't decide if that's because she's out from under his spell and seeing things more clearly, or because her anxious thoughts have taken over again—or more likely, a mix of both.

Everly tries her best to ignore it all when she gets home, unloading the plants with much more difficulty than Asim had loading them in, and lining them up outside on the driveway. Not sure what else to do, she retreats inside to make one of her favorite cocktails, deciding it's a good night for self care. Her jacuzzi tub
~~~

and hockey romance novel make for an excellent distraction.

CHAPTER EIGHT

Frankie doesn't close Roasted when Everly shows up the next morning. Obviously they can't wait to hear how the plant shopping/stalking went, and Everly desperately needs an outside perspective. She is way too in her head about it, and luckily for her, Frankie doesn't hold back.

Ever.

"Dude, you need to chill." They are clearly getting exasperated with Everly at this point. Turning away from the espresso machine, Frankie stomps toward Everly and slams their hands flat on the counter. Leaning forward, they look ready to smack Everly on the back of her head. "He gave you his number, he didn't have to do that."

The need to play devil's advocate doesn't abate, her blood heating for a multitude of tangled reasons. "But what if he was just being polite, or what if he wants a side gig landscaping. Maybe he's trying to go that direction—"

"No. I'm telling you right now. *No.*" Frankie slashes their hands through the air in emphasis from behind the counter, turning back around to finish the latte they were making for a customer who is eavesdropping with zero shame just a few feet away.

As they pass the customer their drink, Frankie comes around to her side of the counter and drops their hands onto Everly's shoulders, making her slump. "You want to know what I think?" they ask her.

"That is why I'm here." Everly doesn't intend to grumble a whine, but it definitely comes out that way.

Frankie angles the two of them toward the cozy back corner, the one Everly sometimes hides in.

"I think Asim realized you were having a hard time with him coming on to you."

Everly gets stuck on his name, and it takes her an extra second to catch up with the rest of their statement.

"Wait, no. I wasn't having a hard time with that. I was having a hard time with my anxiety getting in the way, it was just a bad day." Everly clarifies, although she also wonders if there's more to it than that, and if maybe Frankie's guess has some merit.

"Whatever it was, I think he saw it. I mean you pretty obviously freaked out, more than once." Frankie cocks their head, and Everly gives them this one, nodding in agreement. "I think he's backed off to give you space because you're clearly an emotional wreck at times—"

"Okay come on—" Everly interrupts, but Frankie cuts her off right back.

"—but that's okay because you're human. We're all a mess every now and then." Frankie concludes. "So... just think it out. Take some 'you' time, and decide if you want to put yourself out there."

Everly is trying really hard not to get defensive about this, because she does see that Frankie has a valid point. She also sees that Frankie is throwing the same message at her as before, challenging her to think about what she wants, rather than what she should do or what others would expect her to do, as she has typically done in the past. Not for the first time, she wonders if Frankie and Carrie are in cahoots.

"How about some of your favorite tea while you think it over." It's not a question. Frankie is telling her in their stern-but-loving way to sit there and think about her choices.

Frankie pats her leg before walking back over to the counter. As usual, Everly listens to them, despite feeling a little bit like she's just been put in time-out.

~~~

A few days later, Everly decides to give it a go. As she's thinking back over her conversation with Asim at Magnolia Nursery, she realizes he said he would help with the project, but he also offered to put her in contact with a landscaper he knows. She isn't sure now what he
~~~

meant by him helping, so this is her first order of business. She's going to call and ask what he meant—after writing out a script, of course.

She writes a few lines, then crosses them out and starts over. Tapping her pen against her paper, Everly thinks it over, going for more neuro-typical, less anxious mess.

What would Carrie say?

She tries again, sticking to bullet points, and finally comes up with a couple options that feel feasible.

Everly turns the business card over, the corner of her mouth twitching when she notices his handwriting is neater than she would have expected. She brings the card closer to her nose, eyes squinting as she looks at it more closely.

That is the cutest '8' she has ever seen. It's a little crooked, with a chubby lower loop. Everly drops the card onto the table and unlocks her phone. She taps in the number, double checks (and triple checks) that she typed it correctly, then hits the green call button. She immediately stands up from the bar stool in her kitchen and starts tracing her usual path around the island as his phone rings.

Just when she thinks he won't answer and starts to feel a dip of disappointment in her stomach, combined with a swell of relief for avoiding what is sure to be an awkward conversation, he picks up.

"Hello? This is Asim."

"Asim, hi" Everly replies, and she gets that same tingly feeling in her toes just hearing his voice again.

"Everly?" he asks.

"Oh, right! Yeah, it's Everly." And here she goes again, making a fool of herself. She's surprised he recognizes her voice over the phone, given how little she's actually spoken to him.

"I was hoping you'd call. How are the plants doing?" Asim asks, bypassing her awkwardness easily.

He was hoping she would call? Everly freezes, one foot hovering in the air mid-pace for a moment as she blinks rapidly and nearly forgets to answer his question.

"Um... huh." Everly glances around her kitchen, not really seeing it. How are the plants doing? She hasn't paid them much attention since heaving them out of the trunk of her car. "Maybe I should go check on them before answering that?" Her voice rises at the end, turning it into a question.

His laugh makes her heart skip a beat. It's full and deep, and warms her up from the inside out.

"I adore how honest you are. Yes, that would probably be a good idea. If you haven't watered them yet, you might want to do that too," he adds, and she can hear the smile in his voice.

"Noted, thank you." Everly gives a hesitant laugh in return. She's never had someone comment on her being honest before. She didn't realize that was a particularly strong character trait of hers, but maybe he's right. It certainly could be. If anything, she's more honest with him because of how open and honest he is with her.

"Could you do my landscaping?" she blurts, then slaps a hand to her mouth as her eyes widen in horror.

How is she already so far off script?! Everly doesn't want to pressure him into doing extra work if that's not what he intended, and that is certainly not how she planned to clarify what he meant when he said he would help.

In a rush, she continues, her hand now flapping madly in the air around her.

"I mean, obviously I'm not assuming, and if not that's totally okay. It's only that you offered to help but I wasn't sure if that meant you'd come here yourself or if it meant you'd help me find someone else. I shouldn't have put that on you." She's shaking her head quickly as if that will reverse time. "I can do it myself of course or probably my neighbor can help, he's always outside in his garden so I'm sure he knows—"

"Whoa, Everly, slow down." Asim's voice comes through loud and strong, and she realizes he's been trying to stop her for a while now. He continues more calmly when she cuts off her rambling. "Slow down, it's okay. I'm happy to help."

"Oh my gosh, thank you so much." She breathes deep in relief, her shoulders slumping before pulling up short again at his next words.

"On one condition," he states.

"And what's that?" The butterflies are back in Everly's stomach at the note of what might be mischief in his voice.

"If you'll let me teach you, if you'll let me show you how to plant everything and take care of them, then I'll come over and help you. I won't do it *for* you; we'll do it together." Asim's voice feels like a caress through the phone.

He wants to teach her? He wants to do it together? She's never been one for manual labor before, let alone literally digging in the dirt, but she's willing to do anything if he's involved. Getting down and dirty with him sounds like an afternoon to remember.

"That sounds great," Everly replies. "I'd love for you to teach me whatever you want."

There's a moment of quiet as the sentence hangs between them.

"Whatever I want?" he asks, and she can practically feel the smirk in his voice as he draws out the vowels.

Her skin flushes hot, and she's fairly certain he could hear the quick inhale she just took. She has no idea what to say, and she praises all the gods above and below when Asim smoothes it over again.

"Let's get started now then. I'm guessing you haven't planted the ones you bought the other day?" Asim moves on as if he didn't just set her mind reeling with possibilities.

"No, I haven't done anything. They're in the driveway." Everly somehow wrangles her thoughts back into the present moment and gives a fairly coherent reply.

"Okay, no problem. How about I come over this week to help with the design and we can start planting?" Asim asks.

Everly confirms a day and time, and they hang up with one last reminder for her to water the plants before then.

She drops her phone on the counter and stares at it, her mind and body feeling drained and energized at the same time; a fluttering mix of relief, anticipation, and nervous energy for what's to come.

Somehow Asim makes everything easier. When her anxiety doesn't get in the way, he's so comfortable and easy to talk with, to be around. Everly has never felt that way with anyone before; she's never met anyone quite like him. Someone who makes her feel like a better version of herself—one she wants to live up to—and who doesn't let her weirdness or awkwardness get in the way. She's never met someone who can so easily roll right past her eccentricities and seems to accept her as she is, obvious flaws and all, without any judgment. This is entirely new territory for her, and although it's intimidating, it's also a bit exciting.

~~~

"Hey Ad, perfect timing, I could use a break." Everly answers the video call and aims the camera toward her desk, showing Addison the plethora of paperwork stacked in organized piles all across it.

"Wow, what's going on?" Addison asks.

"Just reviewing end of year reports and comparing our prospective numbers for this year. How have you been?" Everly relaxes into her chair as her sister's bubbly voice rambles about how nice the weather has been, how they desperately need rain but she's enjoying the endless sunshine, about her trip to the beach with friends the other day, and her thoughts about some changes she's considering at work.

Everly is thankful that her sister is more talkative and social than she is, it makes it a lot easier to chat with her most of the time. Everly's learning that she just has to listen and give the appropriate responses, easy enough to do, until Addison turns it back to her.

"So you never told me, how did it go at the garden center the other day?" Addison asks, because of course she does. She's also learning that her sister is very thoughtful, and although her head is often in the clouds, she doesn't forget anything once she deems it important to someone she cares about.

"It... went," Everly says with a heavy sigh, rolling her eyes to the ceiling. "I mean it ended up good, but I'm just such a doofus sometimes. I don't know why I always end up embarrassing myself."

"You're just you. You might be a bit of a dork sometimes, but that's not a bad thing and you don't have to be embarrassed about it. It's cute, it makes you unique. It's one of the things I love about you."

"Thanks." Everly twists her lips to the side, she doesn't
~~~

know what else to say to that.

She isn't one for expressions of love or affection, not really having any practice with it for eight years, and although she appreciates hearing it from her sister, that doesn't make it any easier for her to figure out how to reply. Addison fills the awkward pause as usual, demanding Everly to tell her everything. Everly shares it all: the tropical plant mishap, the tour, her blunder with the whole landscaping debacle, the cart filling up, Asim passing her his number, how he so considerately loaded up her car, and finally, the follow up phone call. It actually feels good to get it all out, and she's eager to hear her sister's take on the situation.

"I am so jealous." Addison states.

"Wait, what?" Everly is completely thrown. "What in the world are you jealous of? Did you hear what I said?"

"Yes, I heard." A very annoyed huff comes from the other end, and Everly grins at the memories it brings up. With the bubbly, social side her sister had growing up, Addison was at times an angsty, opinionated handful when she was a teen.

"Okay, so what then?"

"You're so... you," Addison says again, then pauses and Everly assumes she's trying to get her thoughts in order. "I'm jealous of how forthright you are and I wish I could put myself out there like that. I feel like I'm always wearing a mask, but you're actually being yourself."

Everly has to laugh. If only Addison had the behind the scenes of how it actually went.

"Believe me, I'm also jealous of that version of me," Everly says. "I normally feel like I'm wearing a mask too. It took me ages to work up the courage to take it off, so to speak, and honestly, this whole being outgoing and being myself thing is pretty new. I'm not actually that confident, but I'm trying to be."

She wonders how much she should share with her sister, then catches herself, and takes a second to reflect on how much she wants to share. In no time at all, Everly realizes she wants to share everything.

"I've actually been seeing a therapist and it's really helpful. Lately we've been working on figuring out who I am on the inside, and bringing that person to the outside."

"I didn't realize you were going to therapy," Addison sounds surprised. "That's really cool. I've thought about giving it a try, but. I don't know. I guess it seems kind of intimidating." She nervously laughs out the last sentence, averting her eyes from the phone

Everly pauses, reflecting on how to move forward. She doesn't want to mess up what is turning into a very real moment for them.

"I'm happy to talk to you about my experience. Carrie, my therapist, is the best. She's also kind of the worst sometimes, but in a good way."

Addison laughs more genuinely at this, and Everly smiles along with her.

"For real though, no one is perfect, so I think everyone can benefit from therapy. It doesn't mean something is wrong with you. It just means you're willing to improve yourself."

Addison nods, "true."

She gets lost in her thoughts for a moment, eyes unfocused beyond the screen.

"I'd like to hear more, if you're open to talking about it." Addison's voice is tentative but Everly meets it with a smile.

"Of course. I'm happy to."

Everly reflects on her time in therapy and shares more of her experiences with Addison, answering some of her questions and talking more about what it has been like for her.

After their call ends, Everly sits back in her chair and swivels around to look out the windows over the landscape, admiring the meandering river as it sparkles with sunlight. She replays their conversation with a small smile on her lips. Their connection is growing, becoming almost tangible, and that alone is enough to make any day brighter.

CHAPTER NINE

Toward the end of the week, Everly deludes herself into believing she is mostly back to normal with fewer distracting thoughts, or at least she has gotten better at dismissing them when they do come up. Which happens literally every morning, when she comes down the stairs and sees the poinsettias in the foyer, and every night when she gets home from work and sees them on the porch steps. Truthfully, she's impressed she has managed to keep them alive this long. She's put more effort into it than she has anything in her life outside of work, and she's finally at a point where she can admit to herself that she wants to impress Asim.

Hopefully it means she isn't completely incompetent in the world of plants, maybe she has a chance of succeeding at this whole re-landscaping thing after all.

Everly tries her best to sit still while she waits, limiting her movements to tapping her toes rather than full on pacing; landscaping day one is here and she can't wait for Asim to arrive. The nervousness is a given, at this point she's used to the constant fidgeting and hint of nausea in her stomach, but the excitement thrumming through her veins is a welcome surprise.

She's also reciting her affirmation for the week on a loop in her head: "I can do more than I give myself credit for." Everly alternates this with quizzing herself while she waits, asking herself "what would Carrie say" in response to the intrusive thoughts as she sits in anticipation of his arrival, attempting to get her roiling emotions under control. She stares through the window above the kitchen sink, willing him to appear at the end of her driveway. Everly truly believes that waiting is the worst activity in the world.

What feels like days later, she hears him before she sees him, and Everly's jaw drops open when Asim turns into her driveway. He's riding a motorcycle, but it's not like any motorcycle she's seen before. For one thing, it's cream colored with brown leather seats and handles, and that alone is enough to catch the eye. As he revs closer up the driveway she admires the vintage look; sleek, curved lines and one big, round headlight front and center.

It's *pretty.*

Asim pulls around the circle and swiftly parks in front of the garage, dropping both feet to the ground and kicking down the stand with one booted foot.

Everly nearly sprints to the front door, flinging it open and tripping outside onto the porch before he's even turned his bike off. Standing this close, she can feel the rumble of it in her sternum, and it sends her pulse skyrocketing. Everly has little control over herself right now, eyes glued to the view in front of her as it feels like the world around her ebbs into slow motion.

She watches with rapt attention as Asim's hands rise to his helmet and pull it off. He rakes one hand through his thick, dark hair, pushing it back from his forehead as he swings off the bike and sets his helmet on the seat. He hasn't noticed Everly yet, and her body is rigid, stuck in place, feet cemented to the porch steps as she watches him.

Asim's eyes skim over the plants that are still lined up along the edge of the driveway before sweeping in her direction. As soon as those mesmerizing green eyes land on hers, Everly's insides melt even as her skin feels strung tight. The contrasting sensations are nearly overwhelming, but his smile sends all the anxious thoughts straight out of her head.

It sends every other thought out of her head too.

It's then that her eyes register what he's wearing. Asim strides toward her in a sexy-as-hell leather jacket, ripped and worn jeans, heavy work boots, and a t-shirt that she hopes is as tight as the glimpse she sees of it stretched across his chest hints at. He's pulled work gloves out from somewhere and sticks them in his pocket.

Everly, on the other hand, is not at all dressed for yard

work, despite scouring the back of her closet for appropriate options. She's wearing comfy black yoga pants that cling to her lower body with thick fuzzy socks pulled up over her ankles, a loose off the shoulder light green sweater giving just a hint of creamy skin, and her hair is down in wavy curls. Asim stops short of the steps, putting her slightly above him, then eyes the pair of poinsettias she has managed to keep alive on either side of her.

"Hello again," he says, lips curving into a smile as he looks up at her.

Everly clears her throat, trying to find her voice. Asim's presence is like a wave, taking over and sucking her under so she loses track of which direction she's supposed to be going.

"Hi Asim, thanks for coming." Everly is *so proud* of that response. I mean, look at her being all adult and mature and keeping it together when really all she wants to do is throw herself at him like a deranged puppy.

He flashes her a crooked smile like he knows what she's thinking. "I'm surprised these are still here." He angles his chin toward the poinsettias, and her chest blooms with pride.

He noticed.

"Honestly, me too." Everly chuckles at his questioning look, and gestures for him to follow her inside. "I've been trying my best to keep them alive. I don't know what else to do with them, so I guess I have a house full of red plants now."

Everly offers him a seat in the kitchen and a glass of water, intending to get right down to business even though she's not entirely sure where to start with this landscaping project. She assumes they need to make a plan and talk it out first.

It's pretty much her go-to process for anything and everything.

"You don't have to keep all of them," Asim says, and it takes Everly a second to realize he's still talking about the poinsettias.

"What else would I do with them?" she asks.

"Most people throw them out after the holidays," he tells her, though he doesn't look entirely happy to be saying it. Everly scrunches up her nose.

"I don't like the idea of throwing them away. They're still beautiful, and alive. It seems like such a waste."

"Maybe you could do something else with them. You could share them with friends or family," Asim speculates, but then notices how her body stiffens in response to that comment. Everly can't help it; any mention of her family has always brought heartache and loss in the past, and even though she's working on her relationship with Addison, there is no changing her parents' fate.

"What is it?" Asim asks, his accent heavy.

"It's nothing." Everly tries her best to relax and wave off his concern. "I assumed you knew, I swear everyone else in town does, but I'm not exactly close with my sister and, well, my parents passed away about eight years ago now."

"Everly," his face is carved with devastation, and he waits for her to look directly up at him. She does eventually, and although sad, his eyes are kind, with not a hint of pity. "I'm so sorry for your loss. I know you probably get that a lot, and I feel awful for bringing it up. I never would have suggested giving them to your family if I had known."

He reaches out and lays his hand so very gently on top of hers where she's picking at her nails. It's a nervous habit she can't seem to break.

"That's okay. You didn't know, and it was a reasonable suggestion." Everly pulls her hands from his and drops them into her lap, fisting the fabric of her sweater instead. She tries to make her voice nonchalant to match her words, but there's still a slight wobble to it. "Besides, even though I'm working on things with my sister, she doesn't live close anyways."

"Where does she live?" he asks.

"She's in San Diego. She's lived there since our parents died, actually." Everly doesn't know why she's telling him all of this, other than he's asking and is surprisingly easy to talk to.

"Is that why you aren't close? Because you live so far apart?" Asim's eyebrows crinkle in the middle, and the way he watches her so intently makes it clear he's invested in what she has to say.

"Maybe?" Everly isn't sure. "She was attending UCSD

when it happened. She inherited the beach house there, and I inherited this place here, and I don't know... I think we both must have gotten caught up in our own grief and trying to move on in our own ways. We just drifted apart and it lasted up until that holiday party actually. She's never come before, but she came this year." Everly pauses and takes a deep breath. "It's the first time I've seen or talked to her since the year they died," she confesses.

She can't look at him, but that doesn't stop her from hearing him suck in a breath at that confession, and Everly knows as soon as she looks up she'll see the judgment in his face. So she doesn't. Everly focuses on her fidgeting fingers in her lap, playing with a loose thread from her sweater.

Asim stands and walks slowly around the counter, only stopping when he's inches away from her. He swivels her stool gently so they're facing each other, giving her time to protest if she wants to. Asim places his hands on her upper arms, then slowly skims them down, picking her hands up from her lap and holding them in his to calm their movements again. Her fingers look delicate encased in his much larger grip, and she focuses for a second on the rough feel of his calluses against her skin. Everly still hasn't lifted her gaze, and after he transfers both of her hands into one of his, Asim nudges her chin up with his forefinger so she's looking up at him.

"Grief looks different for everyone," he says, slow and deep and with so much earnestness it takes her breath away. "It's okay to take whatever time and space you need, and when you're ready, if you want to, you can always reach out and see if she wants to reconnect."

Her eyes are glassy, and she's afraid to blink or they might spill over. She has no memories of anyone treating her with such gentle care and empathy before. After her parents died, it was all about planning and moving forward. Planning the funeral, transferring the properties, continuing their work on the hotel, and in general trying to get a solid foothold in this new world without them. There was never time for crying and softness and gentle condolences, not even with Frankie.

Or maybe she just never allowed herself that

emotional space.

Everly nods in response to his words, which unfortunately knocks loose a couple of those tears filling her eyes. Asim brushes them away, his calluses a soft scratch on her cheeks, then lifts her hands and kisses her fingertips before placing them back in her lap. His lips are soft and warm, and she wants to feel them again. He sits next to her instead of back across the counter, and he waits. Everly isn't sure what he's waiting for until she finds herself talking again a few moments later.

"I've been trying to reconnect with her. My sister. Addison." She clarifies. "She was here when you dropped everything off actually, she'd only been here for a little while before you showed up."

"Wow, gotta hand it to me," he says with a huff. "I don't think I could have had worse timing if I tried."

Everly musters a smile, though it's fleeting. "It was okay. It was a weird morning all around. We got together a couple more times while she was in town though and it got easier to see and talk to her, and we've been calling and texting since she left."

"That's great, Everly." Asim beams at her, straightening up a little in his seat.

"Yeah, it is pretty great isn't it." Everly's smile lasts longer this time. "We're doing pretty good I think, considering how much time we lost. What about you? Do you have family nearby?"

"Oh yes. My family is a lot." Asim's wide grin doesn't match the exasperated tone he uses to describe his family, and she can tell they're important to him. "And I mean that literally. I have four siblings. I'm the oldest at thirty six. After me is my sister, then two brothers, and another sister. We're all only a couple years apart and I have no idea how my parents managed all of us in one household."

"I can't even imagine." Everly knows her eyes are big, because she really can't imagine what that must have been like. She thought her one sister was a lot to handle growing up, but having four younger siblings must have been chaos most of the time.

"As I said, they're a lot. They're great though. We all grew up speaking Arabic, I'm grateful my parents didn't want us to lose that connection to our homeland, even though many people looked down on us for it. My parents still live in one of the suburbs north of Phoenix, which is where we grew up, but my siblings have mostly moved out of state. One of my sisters, Farah, the older one, lives in Phoenix too, so she's not too far, but that's it, and the rest of my extended family is back in Iraq." He says with a shrug, though she can hear in his voice that he misses them. There's still a light in his eyes, but it's dampened by talking about how far away everyone is.

"What part of Iraq?" she asks. "Have you been there?"

"I was born there actually, in northern Iraq, kind of near the border with Turkey. I haven't visited so much lately, but when we were growing up my parents made it a point to take us whenever they could. I know they miss their family that still lives there." Asim's eyes brighten again when he talks about his family, just like they did when talking about the plants he grows. Everly is shocked to find she isn't feeling any jealousy or hurt when he has something so wonderful that she doesn't, as she often has flares of envy when she sees families happily shopping or eating together downtown. She would love to hear more about his family, and maybe even meet them someday.

"Wow, that's a big move. When did you come to the US?"

"After my first sister was born, so I don't remember much of it. My grandparents passed and I guess my parents wanted to start somewhere new." Asim pauses for a moment, then continues with a softer note to his voice. "My bike is a replica of his, actually. My grandfather's. My parents say he had one just like it."

"Your motorcycle?" Everly clarifies, pointing toward the front of the house.

Asim nods, his eyes growing distant. "Yeah. I wish I could have met him, from what my parents say he sounds like an amazing man."

"I'm sure he was. It's really cool you have the same bike though."

Asim nods, a quiet smile on his face.

"So what made you move out here? I mean if your parents and sister are still in Phoenix, and your other siblings have moved away, why did you choose this random little town?"

Asim's eyes crinkle up when his smile turns to a crooked grin. "Okay, don't judge me." He says, holding his hands up to ward her off.

"I would never!" Everly laughs and playfully smacks his hands down.

"I wanted to be able to grow some of the native Iraqi plants," Asim says. He looks at her almost warily, like she might bite him if he says the wrong thing, and it surprises her that her opinion matters to him. "There's this pocket ecosystem that runs diagonally through Arizona, and it has a similar climate to parts of Iraq and southwest Asia. It makes it possible for me to grow some of the plants from there that I love."

Her heart thuds in her chest with an accompanying ache. This is one of the most beautiful things Everly has ever heard. Asim found a way to combine two of his passions, his culture and his plants, in a very real way that allows him to enjoy both on a daily basis. Everly wants that in her life too. She wants to enjoy those things with him, and she wants to discover and enjoy her own passions in the same way.

Everly forces a hard swallow of longing.

"That's beautiful, I'd love to see them sometime," she says, and his low chuckle starts a tingling in her belly, but she can tell from the soft lines of his face that he's pleased with her response.

"So." Asim rises and claps his hands together. "Should we see what we're working with out there?"

CHAPTER TEN

Everly leads Asim through the kitchen, around the back living/dining area and out the massive glass double doors to the red brick patio overlooking a wide, grassy yard. She doesn't have any shoes on yet, so she remains on the patio rug, curling her socked toes against the woven fibers, and points along the side of the house where the patio ends and the lawn begins. The yard is terraced there with a stone retaining wall intersecting the green grass, mortared stone stairs along one side leading down to the lower level.

"That's the area I had in mind. I think putting some plants along the terrace instead of grass would be really nice, but you're the plant person so if you have a better idea I'm all ears," Everly says.

"No, I agree," Asim says. "We can definitely make that work. I saw the plants out front on the driveway, do you have a wheelbarrow? I can haul them back here while you find some shoes." His lips press together and his eyes crinkle up again, sparkling with amusement as they flick down to her fuzzy-socked feet.

"Yeah, yeah. I like to be cozy, okay?"

Everly scrunches her nose, only a touch embarrassed that not only are they fuzzy, but they also have cute fox faces on the ends with the nose right over the middle of her toes. She thinks they're adorable. Obviously, it's not something she normally wears in front of others, but it's a little chilly out today so she wanted thicker socks for their yard work. Besides, she's supposed to be herself and not hide anymore, right? This is her daily contribution to that goal.

Everly points out the shed along the side of the house by the garage where Asim can hopefully find a wheelbarrow. She turns to go back inside, but looks back over her shoulder as she's walking through the doors, one hand braced against the doorframe next to her shoulder to see him striding confidently across the lawn. Everly thinks she could probably stare at him all day long and never get bored, then realizes how creepy that is and vows to rein in the weirdo vibes.

She manages to dig some old tennis shoes out of the back of her closet, throws her hair into a quick braid, and by the time she's outside on the patio again, Asim is already wheeling the last of the plants over. He's taken his leather jacket off and draped it over a patio chair, and yep, his long sleeved henley is exactly what she hoped it would be. Clearly worn, but not in a ragged way, it stretches across his chest and hugs his shoulders, thin enough that she gets a hint at the muscles of his chest and back as he lowers the wheelbarrow and unloads the plants. There is no hinting at those biceps though; those are on full display and Everly is not at all unhappy about it.

Asim steps around the side of the patio, brows slightly furrowed, nudging the toe of his boot into the grass and bouncing his eyes between the house, the ground, and the sky. He asks her about the lighting, her sprinkler system, and overall what aesthetic she's going for and what she wants to change. Everly basically wings it with her answers, as she doesn't actually know any of those things, and thinks she does pretty well all things considered. Asim chatters about what plants work well together, and discusses how they'll need to change her watering schedule for this area since the native plants won't need nearly as much water as the grass currently does. Everly nods along and they set everything out approximately where it will be planted.

"Is there anything else you have that can fill it in a bit more? I think I want a fuller look rather than so much open space," Everly says, one finger tapping her chin as she skims her eyes over their arrangement.

"Of course, how about this," Asim says, "I'll pull up the grass and we can see how far we get today. Once we have these in the ground with the proper space they'll need to fully mature, we can take a second look and pick up a few more things to fill in where you want? I have some ideas in mind, but a couple of the ones I'm thinking of are still in the back greenhouse as they aren't quite ready for sale yet. I wanted them to fill out a bit more first, but there may be a couple established enough to be planted in the next couple weeks."

"That sounds great!"

"Let's get to it." Asim picks up a shovel with far more enthusiasm than Everly thinks the situation warrants. She's assuming he found the shovel in the shed with the wheelbarrow, along with the other tools laid out on the patio, and truly he looks way too excited about the idea of digging.

"What should I do? How can I help?" Everly asks.

"I'll start tearing up the turf here, and maybe you can drag it off to the side so it's out of the way. We can decide what to do with it later." She helps Asim move the plants back to the patio for now, but keeps them organized in an approximation of the way they were situated on the terrace.

Then they get to work. It's impossible not to watch the way his arms flex and move with every strike of the shovel. As Asim cuts through the grass in neat squares and levers it up, his shirt starts to stick to the sweat forming along his back, and he pauses to push his sleeves up to his elbows. The tendons in his forearms are corded, making his tattoos look like they're moving while he works. His tattoo sleeve isn't the style of traditional Western artwork she had initially assumed it to be, but an intricate black and gray design of plants interspersed with some Arabic here and there. The writing is elegant, a beautiful script that intersects with the vines. She wants to ask him about it, but doesn't want to interrupt the methodical pace he has set, and now probably isn't the time for that anyways. Reminding herself not to be nosy, she refocuses on the task at hand.

Everly drags and stacks the slabs of grass the best she can as Asim digs them up, but the muscles in her arms are burning sooner than she'd like to admit and she's quickly short of breath. She had no idea grass was so heavy. She takes her sweater off after the fourth one, thanking her earlier self for thinking to put a tank top on underneath it, and puffs out a breath of air as she bends down for the next.

A short time later, Everly pauses to swipe a strand of hair from her sticky face with her forearm, then turns back to where Asim is tossing the next strip of grass in her direction. He slows to a stop while reaching back down for the shovel and his eyes scan her face, then down her arms, before connecting with hers.

Asim straightens up and strides over to her, pulling a small towel out of his back pocket and unfolding it.

"You have some dirt," he says as he raises the cloth to her cheekbone below her left eye. "Just here." The towel is soft and dry against her skin as he gently brushes it off; she wishes it was his hands rasping along her skin, not the cloth. His eyes are bright and his skin glistens in the sun.

"Oh," her reply is breathy, and that one word seems to be all she knows how to say at the moment. Standing so close to him, she picks up his earthy scent again and forces herself not to lean in and sniff him.

Asim quirks a smile, then playfully tugs the end of her braid, and suddenly she is burning for a whole different reason. That one action has moved the fire from her arm muscles straight down to her core, and her eyes flare when she instinctively holds in what she absolutely will not acknowledge was about to be a whimper.

He tucks the towel back into his pocket and turns around, bends down to pick up the shovel again—apparently oblivious to her body's reaction to him. Everly's eyes dart around, landing on the tools, his jacket, the patio table, searching for a reprieve.

"Do you want a refresh on your water? I think I'll grab some more ice for mine," she says.

"Sure, that would be great." Asim slams the shovel down into the grass again, and her eyes catch on his arms with the movement. She doesn't even notice she hasn't moved yet until he stops. Everly glances up at his face only to see the satisfied half-smile is back, and a flush takes over her cheeks at the look he casts her way.

"Right!" Everly doesn't mean to yell, but her body is out of control right now and she startles herself with how loudly she says it. Her eyes flare impossibly wider, and with a little jump, she turns and flees into the house, fairly certain she hears him chuckling behind her as she goes.

~~~

When she gets to the kitchen, Everly rests some ice on her neck in an attempt to cool her reaction to him, though she tells herself the hard work is the main contributor to her overheated body. She gives herself a little pep talk as she cools off. There is no reason to freak out; it's obvious they are both attracted to each other, and she can take this at her own pace. She's made a fool of herself plenty already, so Asim knows what he's getting into, and yet he's chosen to be here regardless. Wiping her brow with a damp paper towel, she leans against the counter and takes a few steadying breaths.

When she returns with fresh iced waters, he has most of the grass out of the top terrace already, and it's clear from the sweat on his brow he's been working hard. Everly suggests a break, so they both flop onto her patio furniture and he downs half the glass in one gulp.

"I honestly didn't think it would be this hard," Everly says, voice rueful as she looks at him from the corner of her eye.

Asim laughs and Everly smiles into her glass, having accomplished her goal of hearing it again. She crosses one leg over the other to stop them from bouncing and shaking the table between them.

"I'm used to hard work, so don't worry about it," he says. "I knew what I was getting myself into."

Everly sets her glass down and traces patterns in the condensation with the tip of her finger, collecting the cool water droplets along her skin before they drip down onto the table. She's not normally the best at talking to others, and this would typically feel awkward for her. Although it is a little uncomfortable at times, she attributes that to her normal level of anxiety that makes just about everything uncomfortable.

Overall, today has been... nice. Really nice. She doesn't feel pressured by him in any way. She doesn't feel like she has to fill the silences, or say certain things, or act a certain way, or even treat him in any particular way like she does with most other people. It's refreshing, and
~~~

Everly feels lighter just being around him.

Asim's phone rings, interrupting her musing, and he pulls it out of his pocket. Glancing at the screen before locking eyes with her, "It's my mom, do you mind?"

Everly shakes her head and he stands as he answers.

"Alo, Mama." Asim smiles at whatever his mom says, then takes a few steps away from Everly as he begins speaking in Arabic. He darts a sheepish look her way at one point, and Everly wonders what they're talking about. After speaking with her for a few minutes he shakes his head and hangs up, the corners of his mouth tilted up and a twinkle in his eye as he walks back over to her.

"All good?" Everly asks.

"Yes," Asim chuckles, "my mother is a busy body. Always wants to make sure I'm taking care of myself, and I made the mistake of telling her I was helping you out today."

"Why is that a mistake?" She tries not to feel hurt by his implication.

"Ah, I spoke poorly. It was a mistake telling her I was helping out a young lady with a big project, because now she won't let me hear the end of it and thinks grand-babies are on the horizon." Asim quirks a smile when Everly's face flushes. "You, on the other hand, are not at all a mistake."

Everly averts her eyes from his steady, sparkling gaze, unsure how to react to his words. He's so intense sometimes, but in a mellow way. Which doesn't make any sense, except that with him it somehow does. She clears her throat in the hopes it will clear her head as well.

"So, what's next?" Everly asks. "Now that the grass is out of the top terrace, is it time to plant?"

"I'm thinking it would be best to wait," Asim explains, "We'll need to replace the topsoil, and having some quality compost on hand to mix in when we plant everything would be beneficial too."

He scrubs a hand across his chin as his eyes take in the mess before them. Everly holds in a grimace, hoping it doesn't look as much of a disaster to him as it does to her.

"I'm thinking we spend a little more time tearing up

the grass on the lower terrace today, and then pick up there tomorrow. The shop isn't too busy yet as it's still a bit early for the spring rush, so my employees will be fine without me. I'll bring the truck over with a few bags of topsoil and compost tomorrow, that way I can take care of the sod too and you won't have to worry about it."

A bit flabbergasted that he's so invested in what wasn't even a real project in the first place, Everly agrees, even though she doesn't want him to leave so soon—despite already feeling exhausted and dreading the sore muscles she's sure to have tomorrow. She's quickly realizing she can't get enough of him.

~~~

A few hours later, she's freshly showered and sitting in her living room in front of the crackling fireplace with Frankie, and she is straight up gushing. Everly can't shut her mouth. She knows she's talking too much, and that it has been entirely about her afternoon with Asim, and yet she can't stop. Frankie was initially shocked, with wide eyes that barely blinked for minutes on end as Everly blathered on and on, and then they appeared to get used to it and realize this is their new reality. They settled in for the long haul and are now sitting with their legs stretched out, feet in Everly's lap while she absentmindedly massages them as she talks, ignoring Frankie's suggestive moaning when she kneads the arch.

Eventually her voice slows down, and Everly catches up with the current situation, realizing she's likely just talked for longer than she ever has in her entire life. Her face turns a little pink and she purses her lips, tucking her chin down into her chest and focusing on Frankie's feet.

"Well then," Frankie says when she finally stops speaking. They blink their eyes dramatically and pretend to wake up from a nap, raising their eyebrows and biting their lip to hold back a smile. "Hi. I guess you're good."

Everly throws her head back and laughs. She is good, and she doesn't remember the last time she felt this way.

"Sorry," she says. "I guess I'm... I don't even know. Happy?" And also kind of embarrassed about feeling happy? Or maybe just uncomfortable with the new
~~~

emotion.

"Yeah, I'd say you're pretty happy," Frankie confirms, one side of their lips tilting up. "I can't believe you just talked so much. Do you even remember half of what you said to me? Because I'll be honest, a lot of it didn't make sense."

Everly shrugs and rocks her head against the back of the couch. She wasn't really paying attention to what she said, but she can tell Frankie anything. All she knows is she has a lot of feelings and thoughts right now, and at the moment, all of them are good.

CHAPTER ELEVEN

Asim arrives the next day wearing a similar outfit of tight shirt and worn jeans, but to Everly's disappointment, no leather jacket. He's driving the same white delivery truck he used the first time they met, Magnolia Nursery painted in bold dark green on the side. He pulls around the circle of her driveway, then reverses so the back faces the lawn along the side of the house. After hopping down from the front, he walks around to the back and unlatches it, then nearly gives Everly a heart attack with the gun show he unknowingly puts on as he heaves the rolling door up. He pauses, arm stretched above him, and glances at the porch where she was waiting for him last time, but Everly is still inside watching from the kitchen window today. If she had pearls, she'd be clutching them. She didn't anticipate watching him like a sneak, she just didn't want to come off as too eager. Plus, she wanted to see what he would do if she wasn't outside waiting for him.

Asim doesn't disappoint. Instead of getting right to work as she half expects him to do, he strides across the driveway, skips a step up the porch, and is knocking at her front door before she can suck in a second breath.

Everly smiles with a swoop in her belly before she even has the door open, and as soon as it is, his eyes are perusing her up and down, getting stuck on her fuzzy socks again. Today they're sage green with big white daisies. She thought they were perfect for a day of gardening, and if the corner of his mouth tilting up is anything to go by, he seems to think so too.

"Cute socks," he says, glancing back up and turning

the full force of his smile on her.

"Thanks." She wiggles her toes so the daisies dance, then steps aside for him to enter. "I made lemonade, iced tea, and horchata. I don't know what you like, but I figured the least I could do was have some better cold drinks available than just water."

"I love water," Asim says, hand to his chest, pretending to be offended for a second. Then he squeezes her upper arm before dropping his hand to his side, leaving a scorch mark on her skin and a dreamy look on her face.

Smiling as he turns and walks next to her into the kitchen, he says, "but I love all of those too. I'll start with an Arnold Palmer, if you don't mind mixing some lemonade and iced tea for me."

Everly grins, loving that he's comfortable enough to ask for what he really wants and giddy to have him back in her house and at her fingertips. She's itching to touch him, but she isn't as naturally tactile as he appears to be. She was lost in thoughts of him last night after Frankie left, and she refuses to let that happen while he is right here in front of her.

"One Arnold Palmer," she says, handing him a glass and pouring some horchata over ice for herself. She's more prepared today in other ways too, now that she knows what to expect, with her hair already braided back from her face, dirty shoes ready by the backdoor, and wearing workout clothes. Everly also did some online shopping last night, and is unreasonably excited for her new gardening outfits to arrive in a few days. She can't wait to see what he thinks.

They walk through the house to the patio double doors, and Asim pulls something out of his back pocket. She expects it to be another rag that he always seems to have on hand for cleaning up, but she catches a flash of green.

"I brought you some gloves," he says, holding one glove open for her to slide her right hand in. "I noticed you didn't have any yesterday. These shouldn't be too hot; this brand is breathable but will also protect you. Just throw them in the wash with your clothes when needed and they'll be good as new." The fit is snug, but the material is thin and light enough that it doesn't bother her. As he helps her fit her left hand into the other one, she curls her fingers and then stretches them wide, wiggling her fingers inside the rubbery material.

"Thank you!" she says. "These are awesome, and they're my favorite color." They're a soft sage green, with cream colored grippy padding on the fingers and palm. She's also obsessed with the idea that he was thinking of her.

"You've worn that color a couple times now, so I figured it was a safe bet." He gives the socks poking out of her shoes a pointed look, and she bites her lip with a pleased half-giggle.

"True. I do wear a lot of light green." Everly likes how it compliments her creamy skin tone and dark hair, but these gloves have just taken the top spot of her favorite wardrobe items. Well, maybe second spot; her classic red heels are pretty much impossible to beat. She's a little flustered to learn he's observed her so closely, but then realizes she's watched him pretty closely too. Everly decides not to get in her head about it, and drops her hands down to her sides, rubbing the pads of her gloved fingers together. She might be able to manage her thoughts better today, as she already feels infinitely more comfortable around him, but the fidgeting is more difficult to stop.

"Where do we start today?" she asks.

Asim walks toward the wheelbarrow. "I'll need to do a couple trips with this—load the grass up in the truck and bring the topsoil and compost back here, we'll also need to finish pulling up the grass on the lower terrace."

That doesn't leave much for Everly to do, but she doesn't want to do nothing, so after he loads up the wheelbarrow, she heaves one of the slabs of grass into her arms and trudges along behind him. Asim doesn't notice until they make it around the side of the house to the truck.

"Everly!" He quickly grabs it from her, and she brushes her shirt off, doing her best not to look like she's already breathing hard. "We have a wheelbarrow for a reason, you know."

He shakes his head and his words are a bit snappy, but he's smiling at her, so she calls that a win and does her best not to let it ruffle her mood.

"I want to help," she replies, tipping her chin up. He apparently gets the message that she won't be dissuaded, so he tosses the grass into the truck and begins the process of switching out the wheelbarrow's contents without further admonishment. They're not talking, but it isn't uncomfortable like she expects it to be. It helps that after an exasperated sigh, he keeps throwing fond glances her way with that tilted smile on his lips.

Back on the terrace, Asim switches out the bags of compost for grass again, and suggests she start digging if she wants to help. She tilts her head as she looks up at him, eyebrows raised and side-eyeing the shovel on the ground.

Asim chuckles and picks it up, handing it to her. "It's not as hard as it looks," he says, "Make sure to use your back muscles, not just your arms, and I'll take over when I'm done with the last load." With that, he hefts the handles of the wheelbarrow like it weighs nothing and strolls across the lawn again, pushing it along in front of him as he goes.

Everly looks at the shovel in her hands, then shrugs and turns to the patch of dirt they laid bare yesterday. She remembers where a couple of the plants are supposed to go, so she picks one and decides to get started. Raising the shovel in both hands, she half heartedly drops it down into the dirt. Understandably, this doesn't do much. Everly wrinkles her nose and flings the minuscule bit she scooped up to the side, then pinches her lips together and puts more effort into it the second time.

She's surprised to see she's making some progress by the time Asim comes around the corner again, but unsurprised by the fact that she's panting like a dog and already dripping with sweat. Asim, on the other hand, looks like he hasn't even begun working yet.

"Hey, that's a good start," he comments on the dent she's made in the earth while dropping some bags of compost along the edge of the patio. He rips open the one nearest her, then holds his hand out for the shovel. "I'll trade you."

She gladly hands it over, then flops down on the edge of the stone wall and leans back on her hands, content to watch him work for a minute. Apparently, digging isn't as easy as he made it out to be, as he is soon sweating and breathing a little harder too, although he also has a decent sized hole to show for his efforts.

Asim pauses and walks over to the plants waiting on the patio. "This one was going to go there?" he asks, pointing to a fluffy grassy plant. It looks soft and breezy, like it's asking for her to run her fingers through it.

"I think so," she replies, side eyeing the wispy leaves.

With a shrug, she gives in to temptation and pulls a glove off, then slides her hand through the long leaves and seed fronds. They tickle against her palm.

Asim picks it up by the lip of the plastic pot as she pulls away.

"Deergrass," he says, "great for stabilizing the soil, and interestingly, ladybugs love to spend the winter hibernating in it. You'll probably see some birds snacking on the seeds when spring hits too."

Everly's eyes are fixed on him and she has to remind herself to blink. Asim has her rapt attention and doesn't even notice as he casually spouts off information while plucking a few dead leaves out of the grassy clump. He handles the Deergrass with intuitive care and tenderness, to the point that Everly thinks she might be a tad envious of a freaking plant.

Asim draws her attention back to the space between them as he shows her a trick to ensure the readied space is big enough. He sets the entire potted plant into the hole he prepared, then points out how it should be at least half again as wide as the pot it currently grows in. He scrapes some more dirt from the sides of the hole, then pulls the bundle of roots out of the plastic and sets it gently into the center. Asim encourages her to alternate filling in the hole around it with handfuls of compost and the dirt from the pile he made earlier. They fill it back in, mixing it all together and tamping it down with their hands as they go before moving on to the next one.

Working side by side, they get a couple more planted before Asim pauses. He stands and looks between the plants still sitting on the patio and the terracing in front of him.

"I think we might need to reorganize a bit," he says.

"What do you mean? I like the design we made

yesterday." Everly frowns, her eyebrows scrunching as she tries to see whatever flaw he's noticed.

"It's just that everything we picked out is all about the same height and size. I'm wondering if you might want a little more variety. Maybe something taller or more dramatic in the corner there." He points to the far corner of the patio where it meets the edge of the dirt section they've prepared. "It would give the space a little more depth and visual appeal, I think."

"Oh, yeah that sounds nice." Everly sweeps her gaze across the plants they selected, realizing he's right. They're all between one to two feet tall. "Maybe a tree in the corner there, and some sort of wider bush down below on the second level?"

"Now you're talking, you've got a good head for design." Asim smiles at her. "I have a few ideas for you. Why don't you swing by the greenhouse this week and we can pick out a couple things."

"I'd love that. Thank you so much for your help. Again," Everly says.

"You don't have to keep thanking me, I'm happy to be here, Ever." Asim calls her a nickname she's never heard before, but she loves it coming from him, especially with the way that accent makes it sound like a sultry purr. She likes everything that comes from his lips, honestly.

The blush creeping over her cheeks is mirrored in the soft tilt of his eyes as he smiles down at her, and Everly doesn't think she's mistaking the heat or hunger in his gaze when she catches him looking over at her throughout the day as they continue working. They get a couple more plants in the ground and Asim finishes tearing out the rest of the grass before calling it a day.

"Are you available Wednesday?" Asim asks, dusting off his hands on his jeans as he straightens and plants the tip of the shovel into the soil next to him. "If you want to come after close, I won't have to worry about other responsibilities when you're there and we can shop in peace."

"Yeah, sounds good. Wednesday is great." Everly, trying and failing to keep the grin from taking over her face, is inordinately pleased that he wants more alone time with her.

As she walks him to his truck, she does her best to

quell the fluttery feeling in her chest. Asim closes up the back, wipes off his hands and face, then walks back over to where she's standing off to the side.

"This may sound weird, but I had a lot of fun with you yesterday and today. I like sharing my joy of plants with others, so thank you," Asim says, piercing her with those green eyes and scattering sparks along her skin.

Everly huffs a laugh, hoping he can't tell how hot she is, and not just from the hard work they've done.

"I can't believe you just thanked me for putting you to work."

She makes light of it, but Everly gets the sense he doesn't do much for fun, and the hint of surprise in his voice indicates he isn't used to it. She likes to think she played a part in bringing more joy to his life, and she determines to make more of an effort to do so in the future as well.

Asim chuckles with her. "I like working hard, and it's worth it to spend time with you."

He tucks a lock of hair back into her french braid, then trails the backs of his knuckles gently down the side of her face, along her jaw and down the line of her throat. She's certain he can feel her pulse pounding out of her skin under his fingers. His face has gone soft, and he's smiling down at her. Everly's mind is screaming, begging for him to kiss her, touch her, do anything to follow up that sweet gesture that burned her to her core.

Asim almost gives her what she wants; leaning down, he brushes a gentle kiss over her cheekbone, and she feels his breath on her ear as he slowly straightens and drops his hand back to his side. All she can do is blink up at him for a moment. Her mind is blank, she's forgotten how to function.

"Breathe," he whispers, a sweet smile on his lips. She wants to feel those lips again, and she wants them on hers this time.

It takes her another precious few heartbeats to process what he just said, and then her body catches up with her lack of oxygen, agreeing with his instruction. Everly inhales a small gasp, sucking in air as a blush scorches her cheeks.

Asim's lips quirk into that boyish grin and he reaches out again to gently squeeze her arm. She's starting to find that gesture endearingly comforting. Asim turns back to his truck, hopping up into the seat and pulling the door closed. He rolls down the window as he starts it up and pops his head out, forearm propped on the edge of the open window. He thumps his fist twice on the outside of the door before saying "see you Wednesday, Miss Moore," and driving off.

CHAPTER TWELVE

The following days pass in a blur of distraction. Everly is all but useless at the hotel, so she doesn't even bother staying and trying to work. Luckily, she has a great team who are fully capable of covering for her now that she's going to take some time away from the office for pretty much the first time ever.

She is constantly daydreaming. Asim's knuckles gently brushing her hair out of her face, his palm on the side of her neck and fingers teasing through her hair, his stubble scraping across her jaw and his lips landing on hers. Her daydreams start as fleeting memories and quickly turn into steamy fantasy. Everly dreams of her name on his lips, and his muscles under her fingers. She imagines what he looks like with his shirt off, how she would wrap her legs around his waist, and what he might sound like if she touched him the way she wants to.

It's in the middle of one such reverie that she's very rudely interrupted by Frankie clapping their hands in front of her face.

"Get out of your head," Frankie grumbles as Everly nearly leaps out of her own skin. Thankfully, Frankie gave her a to-go cup with a lid for her tea instead of a ceramic mug, saving her from third degree burns.

Everly shoots Frankie her meanest glare. "Don't rain on my parade," she says, feeling petulant.

"The weather is doing that just fine all on its own." Frankie hates the rain. Most people in Arizona complain on the rare occasions it rains, but secretly they all love it. Rain is always welcome in Everly's book. Besides, rainy days are perfect for curling up in her favorite leather armchair at Roasted while reading and sipping a steaming mug of Jasmine green tea.

Frankie's not having any of it today though, and they haven't told Everly what has their pants in a twist. Maybe it's because Everly hasn't turned a page in over twenty minutes on account of the reminiscing and daydreaming, and Frankie doesn't like to be left out. They've been pestering Everly for "all the dirty details" about her weekend with Asim since their Sunday night video call, but Everly is hesitant, even after previously not being able to shut up about him, it feels like something is changing.

She feels different about Asim. Her time with him feels almost sacred, unreal, like it would be disrespectful to gossip about or minimize by trying to put into words the depth of what it has meant to her so far. There may also be a small fear in the back of her mind that if she talks about it, the beautiful bubble will burst and reality will come crashing in, taking him away from her. For now, Everly wants to keep it all to herself.

She settles back into her book, deliberately pushing her mind to focus on the words on the page, and not on what Asim will be wearing when she sees him tomorrow, or what casual touches he might grace her with, or if he will share more about his family or continue to spout random facts about plants. Everly is greedy for every little piece of him, and she needs to get a grip on reality before she completely loses it.

~~~

Everly is once again in the parking lot of Magnolia Nursery, and this time she has no problem jumping out of the car, the only one in the lot apart from the delivery truck. She wasn't sure what to wear for this trip, which is a rare experience in her world, so she went with another yoga pants and cute sweater combo. Everly practically skips up the path to the front door, noticing the sign is set to closed but the door itself is cracked open. She assumes Asim left it that way for her, so after stepping inside she closes and locks it behind her.

The large roller door leading into the attached greenhouse on the left is down, making the space feel
~~~

much smaller than it did last time she was here. Everly doesn't see Asim in this area, and no one responds when she calls out a questioning hello, but the back door is propped open too so she takes purposeful strides in that direction.

She swivels her head left and right after exiting the back as she picks her way through the aisles of plants. Calling out again, she continues to get no response, and doesn't see him anywhere. Everly is starting to wonder if maybe he was out front near the fountains and she accidentally locked him out. She opts to check the greenhouses while she's back here, remembering he mentioned he had some plants still growing and not yet ready that he wanted to show her.

The first greenhouse is closed up tight, the second is wide open with no Asim in sight, and just as she starts to walk toward the third, a large black dog comes trotting around the corner, tongue lolling out and floppy ears perked forward, surprising a startled laugh out of her.

"You must be Moose. Asim's mentioned you once or twice," Everly says to the dog, who pauses and wags his tail when he hears his name, then eyes her with his nose in the air. "Where's your dad?"

Moose's ears prick up and he turns toward the third greenhouse with a sign over the door that reads "hothouse." Moose bumps the door open with his snout and then bodies his way through, tail waving madly as he disappears into the building. Everly follows him inside, and her breath catches at the otherworldly beauty that greets her. There are lush, bright green plants organized in neat rows along benches and hanging from the rafters, some with leaves trailing all the way to the floor. The filtered evening sunlight creates a magical feeling in her chest as she blinks in wonder at how it refracts around water droplets and off of wet leaves, throwing tiny rainbows into the air all around her.

Everly has her chin tilted up, head twisting back and forth as she turns down the center aisle where she last saw Moose with his nose to the ground, and then nearly trips over her own feet as her jaw drops open. She snaps it closed before Asim can turn around and catch her reaction, but she can't seem to get her voice to work, or for her eyes to blink. She's pretty sure they've been scorched open by the sight in front of her, and blinking would be a cardinal sin because she wouldn't want to miss a millisecond of this experience.

Asim is in the hothouse, which is very aptly named, and he isn't wearing a shirt. All her mind is capable of processing is sweaty, glistening muscles. She was just imagining what he might look like without a shirt on earlier, and it did not come close to the reality in front of her now. His muscles are sculpted, but not rigidly defined. He's using a hose to water some of the plants, and his muscles flex and move as he raises and lowers his arm, rippling like a wave down his back as he maneuvers and angles it in different directions. Everly can't tear her eyes away. She wants to lick those defined lines down his back and across his arms, which is an absolutely ridiculous thought and so wildly out of character for her that she doesn't know what to do with it.

Everly carefully steps around and over empty pots and planting materials to make her way toward him when he raises the hose up higher to get to the plants in the far back row, and at this point she's close enough to see the veins on his forearm as he adjusts the angle of the spray. Everly can say without a doubt that she has never been jealous of a hose until this moment. First the deergrass, now a hose... She wants those hands on her, immediately.

Something alerts him to her presence, maybe he sensed he was being watched or Moose grabbed his attention. Asim glances over his shoulder, and his eyes widen when he sees Everly gaping at him. He quickly turns toward her, flipping a nozzle on the end of the hose to cut off the water spray, then clawing a hand through his hair in an attempt to sweep it back from his eyes. All it does is give him a messy bedhead look, which does not help her attempts at controlling the inferno that is her libido. Everly follows his gaze as it traces the line of her body down her skin tight leggings, and then slowly back up again. She can almost feel it, as though phantom fingers are skating along in the wake of his gaze, sending tingles up and down her spine and heating her from the inside out.

The moment his stunning green eyes meet hers is

explosive. She sees her own longing and intensity burning back at her, she has the sudden thought that she might be about to have a spontaneous orgasm. She heard that was a thing, but didn't think it was real, not until this very moment when it feels like it's about to be.

What must be an eternity later, Asim finally drops the hose and strides over to her. Everly starts to clear her throat, trying to find something to say, but he doesn't stop. He walks right into her space, palms the side of her throat with his thumb tipping up her chin and fingers tangling in her hair, and leans over her. Asim freezes with his mouth centimeters from hers, his eyes focused on her lips and his entire body tense. Her hands instinctively went to his chest as soon as he was within reach, and his heart pounds under her palm. Everly's fingers are trembling and her chest is heaving with stuttered breaths, but she doesn't think she's getting any oxygen. Her eyes keep flicking between his and his mouth, so close and yet so far from hers. Just when she thinks she might collapse, or scream, or die, he roughly grinds out through his teeth.

"I'd like to kiss you." Low and gravely, his voice strokes down her spine. Asim still hasn't moved, and the tension ratchets up between them. Somehow, his muscles harden even further under her hands, and she realizes he's waiting for her. He's waiting for a yes or no. For her permission or denial. Her brain is already shrieking "yes, yes, yes!" but her lips aren't following instructions.

"Please," she breathes out and it's barely a word, more of a whispered sigh, but he hears it, and he doesn't hesitate.

With a noise low in the back of his throat, his lips meet hers. It's not an aggressive kiss like she was expecting, though. His lips are gentle, although his hands are unyielding. He angles her head with the hand on her neck, and the other goes around her waist, holding her tightly to him. Everly doesn't even care that he's sweaty from working; she wants to be closer, and she wants more. She wants to be ravished. With a frustrated whine, she pulls at his shoulders, urging him on, and it sends him over whatever line he was holding himself back from.

Asim consumes her mouth with his, then moves down her neck, trailing licks and kisses and nips to her shoulder where her sweater has started to slip down. He lets out a discontented grumble when he meets fabric instead of skin and reverses course, making his way back up her neck again. Everly's body is shaking under his touch, shivering despite the heat. His lips are everything she dreamed they would be. She spears her fingers into his messy hair and yanks his lips back up to hers, taking her turn to thoroughly explore his mouth. She forgets to breathe and she never wants to take her mouth from his, but she feels like she might faint and isn't sure if it's from the heat of the hothouse or the heat of him.

She's debating how to get more oxygen without pulling her lips away when a cold, wet nose shoves its way between them. Laughing and stumbling a little, she pulls back from Asim and pats the dog's head.

Asim sucks in air, his chest heaving as much as hers.

"I guess he's the jealous type. Everly, I'd like you to officially meet Moose," Asim says, giving the dog a good neck-scratch, and Moose's tongue flops out happily as he pants up at them.

Taking the excuse for some space to catch her breath and her thoughts, Everly bends down to say hi to Moose and give him a few pats.

From the corner of her eye she watches him, Asim's chest still rising and falling with heavy breaths, and he reaches up, linking his hands behind his head and stretching as he breathes deeply. Everly can barely contain herself. Her skin itches under all her clothing, and that rather impressive display in her periphery is not helping the antsy feeling in her limbs. She re-focuses on Moose, giving him some extra pets and scratches, cooing softly to him so she doesn't give in to temptation and leap on Asim like she wants to.

They both look up from Moose at the same time, and Asim's eyes snag hers again. He truly has the most beautiful bright green eyes, with flecks of amber and gold streaking through them, a dark outer ring encompassing the green, and enviable thick, dark lashes.

Everly clears her throat, then blushes at how awkward that sounded. Asim raises his brows and grins at her, enjoying her flustered state while also giving her a chance to speak. She shakes her head and leans forward to re-tie her shoe, looking for any excuse to collect herself. She needs to snap out of it, and the voice in her head is telling her to get a grip already. Asim rubs the back of his neck, then grabs his shirt from a hook by the door, slipping it on over his head after quickly wiping away the lingering sweat with a dark green hand towel he had by the entrance.

"Should we get out of this heat?" Asim asks, pushing open the greenhouse door.

"Yeah, just give me a sex." It takes Everly a split second to realize what she said, and when she does she freezes in place, mortification sluicing an icy path down her spine. She's still half crouched, on her way to standing, and her mind is imploding. She's in denial; there's no way. She absolutely did not just say "sex" to him, instead of "sec". Surely, that was in her head.

Everly is too afraid to look. She slowly straightens her back and legs, standing to her full height, but keeps her eyes on her toes. Her face is on fire. Before she can figure out how to salvage this situation, his voice flows toward her from the door, the words slow and clear.

"No problem... a moment of peace... might be breast."

Everly's head snaps up, and her wide eyes lock onto his. His face looks utterly serious, but she can see the amusement in his eyes, the tight line of his jaw as he wrestles in a smile, and he slowly quirks one dark brow at her. She doesn't have time to think it through, her body just reacts.

Laughter bursts out of her, and suddenly she's hunched over again, with her arms wrapped around her middle as though that will somehow help contain her mirth. The giggles pour out of her mouth and her eyes start to water. She can't stop, and soon she's gasping, half in pain from the effect of her laughter on her abs and cheeks. Asim is laughing too, a deep, rumbling chuckle that only spurs her on.

Eventually they manage to get a hold of themselves, the laughter easing into hiccuping sighs, and Everly swipes her hands across her cheeks to dry her leaking tears, then across her forehead and the sweat that has beaded up from the hothouse. Walking out the door, she looks up at Asim, and he nearly stops her heart again.

He's always attractive, but she hasn't seen him like this before. The laughter has made him glow. He looks lighter, radiant, and he's looking at her like she's the only thing in this world worth looking at.

Everly averts her eyes and takes a deep, calming breath. She can do this, she can move forward like an adult.

"Sorry," she says, "I have no idea what that was. I'm such a dork sometimes." Her mouth twists to the side in a wry smile, and she shrugs one shoulder in an effort to minimize her discomfort in the aftermath of what can only be considered a complete loss of her mental faculties.

Asim steps in front of her and lightly touches her arm, snagging her attention so her eyes meet his again. His smile is warm and tender, and he uses both hands to brush the hair back from her face, gently holding her in place.

"It's a good thing I like your dorkiness then," he replies softly, and a smile slowly blooms across her face at the sincerity she sees on his. He takes her hand firmly in his much larger one and turns toward the outdoor plant section.

"Besides, that might have been the cutest thing I've ever seen." His voice is lighthearted and playful, so she's not entirely sure how serious he is. Regardless, Asim strides along the path as if they do this all the time. Like everything is normal, totally okay, and not at all out of the ordinary while tugging her along with him.

"Thank you," she says quietly, and Everly hopes he knows she means it for more than just the compliment.

Lacing his fingers with hers, Asim leads her to a number of plants he had in mind as possibilities for her garden. All of Everly's attention zeroes in on that contact. The heat of his palm, how the size of his hand encompasses hers, his thumb rubbing distracting circles on her skin. When he squeezes her hand and gestures to a row plants, Everly mentally nudges herself back into the present moment and picks the ones she likes best. She does her best to listen attentively to his advice and recommendations, rather than think about his lips or the calluses that line his palms. Asim is incredibly knowledgeable, but never acts as though he's superior or makes her feel stupid or silly for asking questions. If anything, he seems to radiate joy at her expressed interest.

A warmth has taken residence in her chest, and it thrums through her. Between Addison coming back into her life and the introduction of Asim, she honestly can't remember a time since her parents died that she has felt so light. This feels like hope. It also feels a bit terrifying.

As Asim guides her through row after row of plants, Everly tries to imagine the work that goes into this place and can only guess at how much it must have taken to build it from the ground up. She keeps trying to picture it as an empty piece of land, and she simply can't. It's like Magnolia Nursery was always meant to be here, as though it has always been and always will be right here where it belongs.

After she insists on paying for everything, Asim tells her not to worry about the plant delivery.

"I'll load them up in the truck and bring them with me this weekend," he says, which is when they've arranged to continue their landscaping work. He's got a couple extra employees on the weekends so it's easier for him to get away then.

Not having to worry about unloading the larger plants on her own is another weight taken off her shoulders by this man who has already dug his own little spot in her heart. She hopes for another kiss before she leaves, and is not disappointed. Asim leans down and gives her lips a soft brush with his, dragging his knuckles along her jaw as he leans back and leaving sparks in their wake.

"See you later, Ever." He smiles down at her, emotions flickering across his face, though she can't decipher what any of them might be. She's not sure she could untangle her own emotions right now either, so she lets it go instead of worrying—and that is a miracle in and of itself.

"Bye, Asim."

She aims a smile over her shoulder, stealing one last look at him as she gets into her car and pulls out of the lot, the smile stretching to take over her face as she drives away.

The weekend cannot come soon enough.

CHAPTER THIRTEEN

Time is flying by and somehow also crawling at a glacial pace. Everly doesn't know how it can go so fast and slow at the same time, but eventually the weekend arrives. She's been eagerly—and anxiously—anticipating seeing Asim again, which means the house is spotless because outside of work she's been stress cleaning for two days straight.

It's finally Saturday morning, she's been up for hours already, and she's peeking through the kitchen window, straining her ears for the first sounds of his truck rumbling down the road. Everly is excited not only to see him, but also for him to see her. She felt uncomfortable not knowing what to wear for their "gardening dates", as she's been privately calling their time together, so she remedied that with some online shopping. She would never admit to having gone overboard, but Frankie had no trouble accusing her of doing so when they video called the other night and Everly showed them what she bought. She's proud to say that she limited herself to only two pairs of rubber gardening ankle boots, even though there was a third she desperately wanted as well.

Everly wasn't exactly sure what would be best for clothing, so she got a few different outfit options to try, including the overalls she's chosen for today. They're a dark coffee brown with floral embroidery along the sides of her legs and on the front chest pocket, and she has the pant legs rolled up to just under her knees. She chose a light blue t-shirt to wear underneath as it matches some of the embroidered flowers, and of course, fuzzy socks. They're tradition at this point, and today they're hot pink dinosaurs with teeth chomping her toes. The sage green ankle boots she bought to match the gloves Asim gifted her are waiting by the doors to the patio, along with a new wide brimmed straw hat to protect her face and neck from the sun.

As soon as Everly manages to gain some semblance of control over her restlessness and settle down on a kitchen stool to wait, she hears what she hopes to be his truck turning into the driveway and immediately pops back up again, standing on her toes and leaning over the counter to look out the window. Sure enough, the Magnolia delivery truck is trundling up her driveway.

She can't wait, and she doesn't even try. Everly rushes to the front door and steps out onto the porch, standing at the top of the stairs again as Asim expertly maneuvers it into place where he can unload the plants directly onto the lawn, then opens the door. The moment Asim notices her, his face lights up. His eyes crinkle at the corner and a lopsided grin takes over his face as he pauses for a moment with his hand still on the truck door. Everly shifts her weight, giving him a fleeting wave and then clasping her hands behind her, twisting her shoulders back and forth in an effort to contain her restless energy as he slams the door shut and strides toward her, his long legs eating up the distance between them. She really hopes he doesn't think she's ridiculous or looks silly in her new gardening getup. His face splits into an even bigger grin as he gets closer and finally notices her socks, and she huffs out a pleased laugh at his reaction.

"How many of those ridiculous socks do you have?" he says in lieu of a greeting.

Everly's stomach drops, as does her smile. She resists the urge to step back and instead sticks her nose up into the air. No one will make her feel bad about her favorite socks, especially in her own home. "More than I care to admit," she says cooly, hoping she hasn't misjudged him.

"Good," he replies, "I like being surprised with a new pair each time. Keeps me on my toes." He gives her a little wink, and she realizes he wasn't judging her with his question. Ridiculous to her is a bad thing, but ridiculous to him must not be. Her shoulders relax and she exhales a relieved breath. Asim cocks his head at her, noticing her reaction.

"You thought I didn't like them."

Everly shrugs. "They're not exactly a fashionable choice." She looks down at her feet and wiggles her teethy-toes.

Asim tips his head the other way, like a bird trying to figure out its prey. "I don't know when I gave you the impression that I care about 'the fashionable choice,'" he says slowly, "but rest assured that you could wear a burlap sack and I'd feel the same way about you."

"Oh," Everly says, eloquent as always. "Okay then."

She resists the urge to roll her eyes, but she doesn't know how to respond to him when he says stuff like this. As usual though, Asim covers for her awkwardness.

"I do like the socks, with those tiny teeth about to nibble on your toes." He chuckles, and then his eyes skim from her feet back up the rest of her body. "And I really like your gardening outfit today."

Everly ushers him in, giving herself a chance to chill after that mini emotional rollercoaster, and they follow their customary routine of grabbing iced drinks and heading out back through the patio doors. Asim sees her shoes, with the gloves he gifted her resting on top of them, and although he's not facing her, she notices his pleased smile and the way his shoulders straighten slightly in response. She slips the boots on, plops the hat over her braided hair, and sticks the gloves in her pocket for now.

Turning to him, she grins and pulls the door open. "Let's go."

She's been ready for this for days.

They easily settle into their routine from last time with Asim digging the hole and Everly filling it in. Now that she knows better what to do, he leaves her to fill around each plant on her own while he gets started on the next one. They get a couple planted before Asim points out that he still needs to unload the other plants from the truck.

"I could use a break anyways," Everly says. "Why don't I grab us some refills from the kitchen?"

"Perfect."

When she gets to the kitchen with their glasses, she sees she left her phone on the counter and it shows a missed call from Addison, but she didn't leave a message. Everly's mind flies into overdrive, assuming something is wrong. Her sister might be in trouble, or hurt, or need her help, and although Everly recognizes this is her anxiety flaring up, logic doesn't come into play with her emotions very well.

She rushes to set the glasses on the counter and grabs her phone, returning the video call and pacing around the island while it connects.

"What's wrong?" she snaps as soon as her sister picks up.

"What? Nothing." Addison's eyebrows pinch together. "Why would something be wrong?"

"Oh, thank goodness," Everly says with a relieved exhale. "I saw the missed call but you didn't leave a message so I assumed the worst." She takes a deep breath to slow her heart-rate and flops onto one of the kitchen stools, resting her arm with the phone on the counter in front of her.

"What are you wearing?" Addison still looks confused, squinting her eyes as she leans into the camera, and Everly glances down at herself, having momentarily forgotten what she was doing right before freaking out.

"Uhh..."

"You're wearing a straw hat? And overalls?" Addison's entire face is scrunched up and she's looking at Everly like she's lost her mind. "Why..."

Her face suddenly clears and Everly hears her snap her fingers.

"Oh my god!" Addison's eyes go big and round, and Everly cringes at how loud she yells.

"Shhh!" Everly flicks her eyes up, glancing down the hallway that leads to the back of the house.

"Are you trying to impress Hot Delivery Guy?! Is he there right now?!" Addison yells in a stage whisper this time.

"No! I mean, I don't know, maybe." Flustered, Everly stops talking and glares at her sister. Addison opens her eyes wide and raises her eyebrows, waiting for Everly to explain.

"Fine, yes he's here right now. We were just getting started with the landscaping for the day." She relents and quickly recaps how things have been going. She doesn't know why Addison insists on calling him Hot

Delivery Guy still. It bothers her a little, as it feels disrespectful for some reason, like she's minimizing who he is, but now isn't the time to get into it. Everly pushes the annoyance away and re-focuses on the man in her backyard.

"You are so in trouble." Addison is grinning now. "You totally like him! I can see it all over your face."

Everly shakes her head, but she can't truthfully deny it. He's irresistible. She also doesn't feel like talking about this while Asim is right outside, especially when she isn't entirely comfortable with her sister yet.

"I should get back out there," she says, glancing at the doorway again. "What is it you called for though?"

"It's nothing. I just wanted to check in, but we can talk later. Go!" Addison says. "And have fun!" She wiggles her eyebrows and cackles just as Everly says bye and ends the call.

Everly stands there for a moment, tapping her finger on her phone as she wonders if she should have said "I love you" before hanging up. Most families say that to each other, right? She isn't sure, as she hasn't talked to anyone in her family for the last eight years to know, but she tries not to worry about it right now. She doesn't think she's ready to say that to her sister yet anyways, especially with so many new feelings getting all mixed up, and she really doesn't want to try to figure it out while Asim is here. Smiling to herself as she thinks about him helping her, she refills their drinks and heads back outside.

He already has all the new plants lined up with the others and is working on digging the next hole, but straightens and steps onto the patio when he sees her open the door.

"Hey," she says, "sorry that took a minute. My sister called."

"No problem," he replies with a polite smile, and reaches out to take his glass from her. "How is she?"

Everly doesn't answer for a second, her eyes getting stuck on his neck as he tips his head back and takes a mouthful of the lemonade.

She swallows to clear her throat before replying. "She's good, nothing new, we just haven't talked in a few days but I told her I'd call back later."

"I don't mind if you'd like to talk to her now." Asim sets the half empty glass down on the patio table as Everly shakes her head in response.

"Nah, she knew you were over and didn't want to interrupt. It's okay."

He nods, then turns with his hands on his hips to inspect their progress. Everly is relieved he doesn't push the topic of her sister any further.

"It's looking good so far, but I wanted to double check where you want some of these new ones," he says.

He walks over to a tree-like plant, which she recently learned (from Asim) is called Yellow Trumpetbush, and hefts it up, carrying it over to the far corner of the terrace where it meets the patio. He sets it down carefully, swiveling it a little until it's in the right spot, then takes a few steps back, tipping his head to look at its placement. Everly doesn't care about the tree-bush at all right now. She's back to watching him work, his face lined with thoughtful consideration, the way he moves with fluid purpose, the flex of his muscles and his shirt sticking to his sweaty skin. Her brain is beyond caring if it's impolite.

She snaps her head up when he twists around, looking at her inquisitively, and she assumes he must have asked her something.

"Sorry, what did you say?" Everly asks, aiming for an innocent look but knowing he sees right through her.

"I asked if you like it there, or if you want to see it somewhere else before I start digging?"

"Right, yeah that looks good." Everly barely glances at the small tree with pretty yellow flowers and nods, not really seeing it as she instead imagines him digging with his shirt off.

Asim casually slides it out of the way and begins slamming the shovel into the dirt again. Everly still feels stuck as she stands there watching him. After heaving a few shovels of dirt to the side, he notices she hasn't moved and pauses his work, propping the shovel next to him and leaning on it.

"While I certainly don't mind your eyes on me," he drawls, voice low and slow and far too suggestive for her already tenuous hold on her emotions, "I do have that one ready for you."

Asim aims his chin toward another of the grassy clumps that she now sees isn't planted, but is sitting bare-root in a hole ready to be filled in.

"Yep!" Everly startles and clumsily wrangles her gloves back on, kneeling down in the dirt and getting back to work. Asim's low chuckle comes from her left as he continues digging, and she can't help the corresponding smile that stretches across her face.

Everly doesn't mind the manual labor as much as she thought she would, even though she works up a sweat. She readjusts the leaves and flowers of each plant after Asim plops them in the hole, getting the angle and direction right until they look just so. She keeps glancing at Asim as they work. It's unreasonable for anyone to expect her to keep her eyes off him. Everly often catches him watching her too, and he smiles at her every time they make eye contact. It would be awkward with anyone else, but this is Asim, and together they just click.

They work for another hour or so, planting a couple medium sized plants with pretty purple flowers that read 'Larkspur' and some smaller daisy looking things, before Everly stands up with a huff, puffing air over her face in an attempt to whisk away the stray hairs that have fallen out of her braid. When that doesn't work, she tears her hat off and uses her sleeve to wipe the sweat from her forehead before slicking her hair back with her hands. Asim stops working too and glances up, giving her a quick once over, then he stands and dusts his hands off.

He pulls his usual hand towel out of his back pocket, giving himself a quick brush off, and then grabs one from the table that she hadn't noticed. He unfolds it as he walks over to her, then gently wipes her face. She blinks at him, unsure how to react. He tugs off her gloves one finger at a time and swipes the towel down her arms. It sends tiny tingles shooting over her skin, lifting goosebumps on her arms and neck where he passes the cloth over her flesh, and Everly shivers as his touch moves to the back of her neck.

She bites her lip to keep from whimpering, because even though he's only touching her with the cloth, it still feels incredible on her overheated skin. Everly hasn't dated in ages and she's not a one night stand person, so she hasn't had close contact with anyone in months, apart from the random hug with Frankie, which isn't the same. She's clearly touch-deprived, and Asim makes her feel more than she ever expected.

His eyes latch on her bottom lip where she's biting it, and she mirrors the action as her eyes skim down his face too. The long, straight angle of his nose, the dark stubble lining his cheeks, those full lips. Lips that have kissed her and set her skin on fire, and that she wants to kiss again.

Suddenly his thumb is on her mouth, gently tugging her lip from her teeth, then brushing over it in a feather-light caress. Her eyes fly back up to his, seeing they've darkened from their usual bright green. Her instinct is to bite her lip again, but he's preventing that, so she latches her hand onto his wrist instead, although it's unclear if she's preventing him from moving away, or stopping him from moving closer.

Asim startles slightly, looking down at her hand clutching his forearm, then blinks, taking a small step back from her. He turns his hand as it leaves her face, so her palm slides into his, and he clasps it lightly. Turning her hand over, Asim dips down and places a gentle kiss on her palm, and then the inside of her wrist, looking her straight in the eye and causing her to flush with heat as he does so, before gently returning her hand to her side.

He takes another small step back and smiles down at her. "We got a lot done today," he says.

Everly has to mentally shake herself to catch up with him when he turns the tables on her like this. She thought he was going to kiss her again, and she would have welcomed it.

"Yeah, we did." She steps to his side and surveys their work. "Still a lot to do though." Their to-plant pile is smaller, but they haven't finished the top terrace yet, and haven't even started planting the bottom one. Still, she's proud of the work they've accomplished so far.

"It's looking really nice. I think you'll be pleased when it's done," Asim says.

"Thank you again for your help." Everly smiles at him, feeling strangely shy in this moment. It's been a wild week, and she hasn't given herself much down time. Her nerves are starting to fray, and she's worried she will do or say something foolish again.

Although she would like him to stay, Everly recognizes that she needs some time on her own. A bubble bath is calling her name, and a long soak with a Hot Toddy sounds just about perfect for her aching muscles right now.

They agree to continue the next day, having gotten a good amount done so far. Everly walks around the side of the house with him to his truck, and although it's quiet between them, she notices again that it doesn't feel uncomfortable. It's a normal quiet, a calm silence, an understanding that it's okay to just be, and she enjoys it immensely.

CHAPTER FOURTEEN

Everly is desperate for Asim to kiss her again, even more so after their brief text conversation the night before. She messaged him last night, partly as an excuse to suggest he bring Moose with him today, but also to thank him for his kindness when she does something stupid. He had replied in typical Asim fashion.

Asim: Everly, you aren't stupid. Please don't
  think that. We all embarrass ourselves
  sometimes, but know that I don't think
  anything you've done is stupid or
  embarrassing. Quite the opposite, actually.
  I've immensely enjoyed spending time with
  you and am happy to help with your project.

Everly keeps reading that one line, "quite the opposite, actually" over and over again. Her brain circles around what it could mean. What is the opposite of stupid and embarrassing? Smart and put together? Everly can certainly acknowledge that she's intelligent, and typically is very put together, but that hasn't been the norm around him. She revolves around the thought that maybe he meant she's attractive; he did make a comment about her being cute once, and there's definitely chemistry between them so the idea doesn't seem outlandish. She is generally considered to be pretty by societal standards, but that doesn't mean her looks are to everyone's taste.

She continues to ponder his meaning as she eats a light breakfast of toast with melted goat cheese and honey, and mentally prepares for his arrival, doing her best not to let any intrusive or anxious thoughts twist what she knows to be true.

To her delight, Moose jumps out of the truck as soon as the door is open wide enough for him to squeeze through, and his nose dips to the ground as he zig-zags his way across the driveway, taking in all the scents of a new place. Everly internally denies the undignified squeal that pops out of her mouth, and rushes in her socked feet out to the porch. As soon as he hears the front door open, Moose's head swings in her direction, tail already wagging.

"Hi, sweet boy!" she says, not remotely ashamed of the baby voice she uses with him, because he is the best, most cutest, furry baby. Moose immediately trots over and noses into her, accepting her pets and praise while Asim ambles up behind him.

"And now I know the real reason you're interested in me," he says, giving Moose a pointed look. The words are rueful, but the tilted half-grin on his face tells her he isn't the slightest bit serious.

"Can you blame me?" she asks, grinning back at him from her crouched position next to Moose. "He's so cute. Aren't you? Yes, you're the cutest. I should get some treats for you, I think. Yes I should." The baby voice is out in full force and Asim shakes his head.

"Don't judge me." She playfully throws the words at him as she stands back up. "What does he need? Water, anything else?"

"Nah, he's good. He can just chill in the back with us, though I'll tie him to a long line so he doesn't get distracted and take off."

Everly nods and Asim clips an extra long leash to Moose's collar, leading him around the outside of the house while Everly goes back inside for her shoes. They meet on the patio out back, and she shares the ideas she came up with that morning, thankful Asim doesn't appear offended at her bringing her opinions to the table, even though it's his area of expertise. They agree on a task list for the day, then get to work outside with Moose keeping them company from a shady spot on the lawn.

He spends the morning roaming around, snuffling

through the grass and occasionally rolling in it, his legs thrashing wildly through the air and causing Everly to giggle at his antics, which subsequently catches Asim's attention and brings out that boyish grin she likes. At some point, Moose finds a stick to gnaw on, and she sighs at how adorable it is that his tail wags the whole time he's chewing on it and spitting out the little pieces that break up under his teeth.

When they break for lunch, Everly refills Moose's water bowl while Asim secures his leash to a new area of the yard for him to explore. They wash their hands and refill their drinks in the kitchen together before grabbing the deli sandwiches Asim brought and settling back out on the patio to eat.

"You didn't have to bring lunch, you know," she says. "I'm happy to feed both of us, since you're already doing me such a huge favor."

"I know," he replies, "but I'm also happy to feed both of us."

She rolls her eyes, knowing it won't do any good to argue and not really wanting to anyway. They chat as they finish their meals, mostly about Moose, and Everly soaks in Asim's rich tone and the way he adds extra vowels when he talks, the r's he rolls with his tongue and how his lips form the words as he speaks. Those lips... she wonders if she should make a move this time instead of waiting for him to do so.

Asim stands when they're done, strolling over to Moose to give him some love. She relishes the opportunity to get to know Asim better, and it's easy to tell Moose holds a special place in his heart.

She's happy Asim brought Moose today so she can see this side of him. The side that is playful and sweet, as he checks in on Moose periodically and makes sure he isn't tangled in his leash or out of water. Tossing a stick for him and playing a quick game of tug of war. Even the part that doesn't hesitate to stick his fingers under Moose's lip flap and pull out a goopy wad of dead grass that was stuck to his gum. It's gross and makes her nose scrunch, but it also makes her heart flutter—especially since Moose so easily lets it happen, his tail thumping the grass the whole time while his tongue lolls out the other side of his mouth. There's a sense of trust and companionship between them that Everly longs to be a part of.

A loud crinkling startles her and she shakes herself out of her daze. Asim tosses the crumpled up paper from his sandwich onto the table and leans back in his chair, legs stretched wide and his head tipped back into the sun. Her eyes trace the length of him as she sips her iced tea, gaze darting to the side when his head starts to tip back down.

His phone buzzes across the table between them and Everly sees the name "Farah" with a picture of a beautiful dark-haired woman light up the screen. Asim immediately smiles and swipes to answer, holding it out in front of him for a video call. Everly isn't sure what to make of it, but her questions are answered before she can even think them.

"My beautiful sister!" Asim beams into the camera and Everly's shoulders slump with relief. "To what do I owe this unexpected video chat?"

Everly hears a scoffing laugh from his sister and she hides her own smile, but then the woman questions where he is and before she knows it, the camera is panning in her direction. She flares her eyes and shakes her head no, but there's no avoiding it. Asim pulls her into the conversation with him.

"Farah, I'd like you to meet Everly. Everly, my sister Farah."

"Nice to meet you." Everly smiles at Asim's sister, and she grins back.

"So you're the one he won't shut up about."

Everly blinks at Farah, then turns to Asim, who has a scowl on his face. Everly bursts into a laugh at the peeved expression and Asim starts to pull the phone away, clearly trying to avoid the conversation.

"No, wait!" Everly grabs his wrist, keeping the camera where it is, and leans forward. "What has he been saying?"

Farah throws her head back and laughs. "Oh, my dear, the way he *pines* over you, asking me—"

"Okay, that's enough." Asim narrows his eyes at Farah and yanks his wrist from Everly's hold.

She bites her lip to keep in a laugh.

"We have a lot to get done today," Asim says to his

sister, "did you need something?"

"No, no, I won't keep you." Farah is still grinning.

"I'll call you later," Asim grumbles.

"Sure, sure, I see how it is. Bye, akhi!"

Farah winks as she ends the call and Asim swipes a hand down his face. Everly decides not to give him a hard time about it, instead asking what 'akhi' means.

"It means brother, or my brother," Asim explains, a note of fondness in his voice.

"Oh, that's sweet." Everly tries to keep the wistfulness out of hers, but she knows it comes through anyways. She misses having a close-knit family.

"Ready to get back to it?" he asks. She glances back at him as he stands and grabs the trash.

"Let's do it." Everly stands up too, stretching her arms over her head with a sigh. He snags his empty glass and takes it inside as well while she wiggles her fingers back into her gloves, and all too soon they are getting down and dirty again.

Sadly, not the type of down and dirty she's been quite literally dreaming of.

Every night.

It's unlikely tonight will be any different.

Everly feels hyper-aware of him today. Each time Asim glances at her, she gets goosebumps and her heart flutters in what would be a concerning manner in any other situation. She can't stop peeking at him too, and is caught more than once. He continues to smile at her every time, and he shot her another wink once when he caught her not even working, just blatantly staring. They talk easily with comfortable silences interspersed, and that's one thing Everly hasn't had a lot of experience with when it comes to other people. She has adequate social skills and does well in a professional setting, but when it comes to extended conversation, she's typically not the best.

It's different with him, though. They delve into more personal things today, topics outside of those right in front of them. Everly reflects on how she doesn't think she likes living alone anymore and has thought about getting a pet, which he validates, sharing what a huge difference having Moose in his life has been. Asim talks more about his business, how he started it and what it's like living above the main shopping area. They converse about the challenges and rewards of being business owners, and how isolating that lifestyle can be at times. Although their areas of work are vastly different, there are many aspects that are comparable, and Everly marvels at the feeling of understanding she gets from him.

She isn't used to being seen.

"So what was that party for? The holiday one, it seemed like a pretty big deal," Asim says, snapping Everly out of her latest daydream.

"Oh, that." Everly sighs, wondering how to explain and if she really wants to get into it. He looks up at her when she pauses, and his eyebrows draw together.

"It's not good?"

She waves a hand in the air, pushing away his concern.

"It's just a whole thing. The party, or *gala*," she draws out the vowels and rolls her eyes as she says gala, "as I'm supposed to call it. My parents used to host it every year, and it sort of fell to me after they died. I've been hosting for their friends ever since."

"For *their* friends? What about your friends?"

Everly shrugs, pulling her lips to the side and wrinkling her nose. She doesn't really have any friends apart from Frankie, but she doesn't want to tell him that.

"Why did that become your responsibility? It seems you don't enjoy it."

He's correct in that deduction. She has never enjoyed it, even when her parents were still alive and she didn't have to host.

"It's what is expected of me, I guess." Everly shrugs again, then accidentally hurls her handful of dirt at the hole a bit too aggressively and it splatters across her legs. She huffs and sits back on her feet, legs folded underneath her and hands on her hips as she glares at the ground.

"But it's not what you want." Asim is hitting one nail on the head after the other.

"No, it's not what I want." The words come out softly, with more emotion threaded through them than she intends.

Asim eyes her for a moment, his lips pursed.

"Maybe it doesn't have to be that way. If it's not who you are, you could change it. Do something different. I don't think it's fair of them to put so much pressure on you, and you have the right to say no." His voice is slow and steady, almost tentative, as if he doesn't want to scare her away.

"Now you sound like Carrie," Everly grumbles under her breath and picks up another trowel-full of dirt. Everyone acts like it's so easy to just do what she wants, but it's not. There are people relying on her, people who plan their entire holiday season around this party. She can't quit hosting it now, after so many years. Besides the fact that it's always been her family who hosts. It's tradition, and the elite love their traditions.

She flings the small pile of dirt at the plants roots, watching it crumble apart with the impact.

"Who is Carrie?" Asim is watching her with his eyebrows slightly bunched, having stopped digging and set his shovel next to him on the ground. He's working on holes for the smaller plants now, so he's using a hand trowel and is also on his knees a few feet away from her, though he looks like he wants to shuffle closer and is debating if she would welcome it or not.

Everly hadn't intended for him to hear her comment about Carrie, unsure if she wants to share that part of herself yet. She picks up another handful of soil, letting it slowly trickle through her fingers around the roots she's burying before answering.

"Carrie is... my therapist." She swirls her finger through the loose soil, creating a pattern of loops around the base of the plant. Everly isn't ashamed of going to therapy, but she knows many people hold a stigma or misunderstand it. She doesn't want to feel rejected or disappointed if that's his reaction, and she's glad he decided on giving her space rather than crowding her.

"You don't have to share if you don't want to. I didn't mean to pry into a personal topic." Asim is eyeing her carefully, his gaze flickering from her gloved fingers to her tense shoulders to her downcast eyes and back. Everly realizes as he gives her an out that she actually does want to share. She feels more comfortable with him than she thought was possible, and the fact that he didn't immediately scoff or judge her is a good sign.

"It's okay," she glances up at him to confirm he isn't looking at her in any negative way, then continues. "I've been meeting with her for a while now. She's really good, mainly she helps me with anxiety. You might've noticed." Everly twists her mouth to the side and grimaces as she thinks back on how her anxiety did its best to sabotage her the first couple times they met.

"Well, you definitely couldn't have missed it when I literally ran away that one time." She glances up again to see he's leaned forward, listening intently. He nods for her to continue, but doesn't say anything yet. "That's what happened. Outside the candy shop. I panicked and my anxiety took over and I ran away. I'm sorry." She twists her hands together, fighting the urge to jump up and run away again.

"It's alright." Asim's voice is softer than she has ever heard it. "I figured you were nervous or something came up, I didn't know you struggled with anxiety though. Thank you for trusting me enough to tell me, but please don't feel like you need to apologize for that."

Everly stares at him, stunned. He thanked her? Is that something people do when someone tells them they have a mental illness and go to therapy? Not in her experience, but then again, Asim isn't like anyone else she's met before so she shouldn't be surprised.

"That's... huh. Okay," Everly says, feeling her shoulders drop and her body relax back onto her heels. She's still trying to get her brain to start moving forward again. He offers her a gentle smile, then moves a little closer and asks what she meant earlier about him reminding her of Carrie. At the same time, he pulls that ever-present cloth from his pocket to clean the dirt from his hands.

"Oh, that." Everly huffs at herself. "She's been challenging me to be myself. Sounds silly, I know, but it turns out I don't really know who I am. So I've been trying to figure it out. I think..." Everly trails off, casting her eyes to the side and looking at the plants surrounding her instead of him.

"You think what?" Asim prompts her to continue when she hesitates.

"I think you've been helping me with that. With being more comfortable with myself, and being who I truly am." She's starting to blush and turns her face downward again in an effort to hide it, but then she notices his reaction.

Asim's thoughtful look transforms into a smile that takes over his face. His eyes crinkle up at the corners, and he slides next to her, taking her gloved hand in his.

"I have never been more highly complimented," he says, and gives her hand a squeeze, then brushes his thumb along the bare skin of her wrist above her glove, leaving goosebumps in its wake.

Everly is taken aback by him yet again. This man is unbelievable, and kind of strange, but in the best way. It takes her a breath to react in kind, and a smile spreads across her face too, deepening her blush. She pulls her hand from his and covers her cheeks with her fingers, not caring that she still has gardening gloves on. She needs the coolness of the rubbery material, and she doesn't want him to see her blushing yet again.

"Please, don't hide from me." His voice is tender yet firm. Asim wraps his fingers around her wrists and tugs her hands down, then gently brushes the dirt off her face. He traces his fingers lightly over her cheeks, painting the blush on them. "You're beautiful."

This, of course, only makes her redden further. Everly sucks in her lips, biting them between her teeth in an effort to hold in the protest forming in response to his compliment. She's beet red and likely covered in both dirt and sweat, probably as far from beautiful as she's ever been.

Asim lets his hands fall from her face, and is now tracing circles on her palm as he holds one of her hands open in his. Everly wishes she didn't have the gloves on so she could feel his skin against hers. His green eyes hold her captive, a willing victim.

"May I take you out on a date?" he asks.

"I would love that." Everly blinks in surprise when she doesn't hesitate in her reply. Her shoulders fully loosen, and her smile feels easy on her face. If this is what it's like to let your inner self shine, her therapist deserves a raise.

CHAPTER FIFTEEN

They haven't yet discussed the date further, but Asim said he had an idea and asked her to trust him to get it set up for them. She's only a little surprised by how easy it was to let go and trust him with it. Now that he knows about her anxiety, she doesn't have anything else to hide. Everly feels seen, validated and understood after their conversation today. The emotional connection between them is almost tangible. Imagine that; Carrie is right again.

They're little more than halfway done with the planting and it's starting to come together. The plants she and Asim picked out work well together, and Everly is pleasantly surprised by the colorful picture it's creating in her backyard. Asim left with Moose a few hours ago, and she's since showered and changed. Standing in the living room with floor to ceiling windows overlooking the backyard, she continues to admire their work, and her thoughts soon turn to their date.

Now Everly has to wrap her head around the reality of going out on a date. She hasn't dated in ages, and the idea of going out with someone, in public, is a little intimidating. If it was with anyone else, she knows she'd be freaking out right now. Everly can't stop marveling at her responses to Asim though, and the way her mind has started to quiet and calm when they're together. Anytime she's accepted a date in the last few years, her nerves would take over and she'd debate various back-out strategies until the last second. She's never really had a good experience with dating, truth be told—it's been less than stellar since the beginning.

* * *

When Everly was 16, finally feeling as though she fits into her body and flooded with hormones, she had her first real kiss with her first ever love.

She didn't even see it coming.

He kissed her with groping hands and too much tongue in his friend's stale basement at the tail end of a party, and when she didn't want to go further, he slid off the dingy couch in a cloud of dust motes and retreated to the bathroom. She spent the next few minutes trying to keep her eyes to herself as the few other couples were all messily making out and looking like they didn't have plans to stop. She inspected the worn, white ceiling and counted the speckles on each tile, she looked at the diluted green and brown stripes of the unraveling rug under her feet, she traced her fingers along the cracks in the dull couch cushion, and she tried her best not to bounce her knee or otherwise give in to the nervous apprehension lining her gut.

When he finally returned to her, he held out his hand and pulled her up with a smile she couldn't quite decipher. Relieved to have him back, Everly didn't question it. He walked her to his car, opened her door for her, then drove her home. She didn't entirely realize anything was off until he sat silently in the drivers seat in her driveway. He didn't speak, didn't get out, didn't move a single muscle, both hands white knuckling the steering wheel. He didn't even glance in her direction; instead, his eyes were hard and focused straight ahead through the windshield.

Heart in her throat and stomach full of lead, Everly murmured a soft "goodnight" as she opened the door and stepped out. She never heard from him again. He ignored her at school the next day, and every day after that. His friends snickered when she walked by. He had completely ghosted her, left the few messages she sent on read, and at times she almost wondered if she had made up the entire night in her head.

That was Everly's first experience with heartbreak.

Since then, it's been a string of short, disappointing relationships interspersed with long periods of being single. It got even worse after her parents died. The loneliness became so entrenched she didn't know if she'd ever escape it. Spending time with Asim feels different, though.

Everly wonders if he could be the exception. Maybe this time, it will stick. She's afraid to let herself hope, afraid to let herself truly feel, but the cracks in her armor are expanding and it's only a matter of time before her walls come crumbling down.

~~~

As usual, she can't stay away from Roasted for too long, and Everly's back there again today. She inhales the cozy scent of fresh-brewed coffee and sun-warmed wood, trailing her fingers along the back of a worn leather couch as she meanders her way to her favorite seat in the back. There are a few other patrons inside, and although she tends to avoid interacting with others as much as possible, she's feeling good today. Optimistic, even. She meets their smiles and her heart warms at their nods of greeting. Although she recognizes most, she doesn't know their names, which she acknowledges is unusual in a town this size, and she vows to fix it at some point.

Eventually.

When she's done fixing herself.

She's been spending so much of her free time with Asim, it feels like she hasn't seen Frankie in weeks. Realistically, it's only been a few days, but that's longer than they normally go without spending time together, and they're both feeling it.

Frankie wraps her up in a bear hug the moment they see her, and Everly clings to the familiar comfort of her friend. They smell like the coffee shop, warm and homey with a hint of bitterness from the fresh beans they grind each day. Pulling back, Frankie eyes her up and down, then grins one of those big, mischievous grins.

"Spill it, girl." Never one to dance around a topic, that's for sure.

Everly is already smiling back, and Frankie's eyes get bigger when they see the obvious joy on her face.

"Uh, yeah. I am here for whatever this is." Frankie swirls their hand around in front of Everly's face, demanding answers to all their unasked questions.
~~~

Everly relents, no longer wanting to keep her feelings a fragile secret, giving in to the excited happiness filling her voice as she tells them about her time with Asim. It must be infectious, because Frankie hasn't stopped smiling either. Everly gushes about the kiss, of course, and all the little touches, and how desperate she feels for more. Somehow, things are moving too fast and too slow at the same time. Her feelings have skyrocketed, and she's been avoiding fully acknowledging them. They're quickly bubbling up to the surface though, and she knows it's only a matter of time until she's forced to face the full brunt of her emotions.

"I have to meet him, for real," Frankie says. "I'm your only friend—"

"Hey!" Everly interrupts, but Frankie keeps going, barreling right over her.

"—and anyone who makes you this freaking happy deserves some free coffee or a high five or *something*." They almost sound exasperated, as though making Everly happy is difficult to achieve.

"What does being my only friend have anything to do with it?" Everly is trying not to pout, because while true, she doesn't see how it's relevant to the conversation. Her grumpy face is definitely about to make an appearance.

"Anyone who is important to you is important to me," Frankie says this like it should be obvious, with a silent *duh* at the end. "You've only got me in your corner right now, so it falls to me to vet and welcome anyone else who wants to join me over here on Team Everly."

Everly's eyes start to feel glassy and she blinks to clear them, pulling Frankie into a fierce hug again. What a rollercoaster of emotions she's going through today. It almost feels safer to just stick to her realm of anxiety.

"You're the best. I think you'll like him, he's so nice and chill and knowledgeable about everything. Plus, he has the *cutest* dog."

Frankie perks up at that. "Dog? Do you have a picture?"

"No, I should though. His name is Moose and he's this really sweet mutt, he looks like a black lab mix, and just such a lover. This one time, all I did was look at him and his tail started wagging. It was so cute, and he's obsessed with Asim, not that I blame him. Oh my gosh, and the way Asim plays with him and talks to him..." Everly restrains herself from rambling about Asim again. "I do have to keep stopping myself from freaking out though whenever I think about how perfect he is."

One minute she stresses because he seems too perfect, and the next she's feeling overjoyed at how perfect he is. Her brain can't decide which to land on, so for now it seems both are equally true.

Rolling their eyes, Frankie admonishes her. "You know that's the anxiety talking. No one is perfect, but that doesn't mean he isn't good for you. I mean that's why you're going on a date, right? To get to know each other better. See if it's a good fit."

"I wonder what he has planned," she murmurs to herself, imagining all the possibilities.

Maybe he'll take her to her favorite Vietnamese restaurant and they can share a plate of spring rolls while their knees touch under the table. Maybe a cute picnic along the river with the sun warming their faces, or a concert in the city. He'll have put together the perfect playlist for the drive there and back. Maybe he's planning a nighttime stroll under the stars, holding hands, kissing... She doesn't realize she sighs breathily at that thought until Frankie's cackle cracks through her musings and her eyes fly open.

"Oh my god." Frankie has their head thrown back and even goes so far as to slap their hand on their knee. "You have it bad. Where did you just go in your head?! Because from your face and the noises you just made, it must have been fantastic."

"I was thinking about what he might be planning," she says, and takes a sip of tea to help hide her face from her friend.

"With his dick?" Frankie asks.

Everly spews tea across the table, much to Frankie's delight.

"No! Geez Frankie, I can't believe you." Everly snatches a napkin from the next table over to mop up the mess, patting off her mouth and lips as well as the tabletop. Thankfully it was a small sip, and she hasn't gotten any on her dress. "You are the absolute worst sometimes, you know that?"

Her words and tone are grumbling, but she's smiling

anyways. They both know it's not true.

Frankie grins. "You might not have been then, but I bet you are now."

"I'm leaving." Everly playfully wrinkles her nose at her friend and crumples the napkin in her fist as she scoots her chair back, wooden legs scraping across the floor. Before she can even stand though, Frankie stops her with a hand on her arm.

"Okay, drama queen. I'm done, I'm done." They hold their hands up in surrender. "I'll stop, for real. I'm truly happy for you Everly, you deserve someone who appreciates you."

Everly leans back in her seat, tossing the napkin onto the table and accepting Frankie's words at face value. They might tease her relentlessly at times, but they also respect her boundaries and Frankie is honest to a fault. They turn the conversation to Frankie's business challenges, the ongoing drama with the grocery store guy, then to Everly's latest therapy project, that of being true to herself. Everly shares how much easier it is to be herself around Asim compared to anyone else, apart from them of course. She mentions how she shared with both Ad and Asim that she sees a therapist and they responded surprisingly well, in their unique ways.

"Points for them both in my book," Frankie responds, and Everly's heart swells.

"Oh! And Addison told me why she randomly came to the holiday party."

"Yeah? What'd she say?"

"She said she had spent the last couple holidays with her ex, but then she cheated on Addison so they broke up and she didn't want to spend the holidays there without her."

Frankie perks up, leaning forward in their seat. "She's queer?"

Everly shrugs. "We didn't really get into specifics or labels or anything, but I guess so, yeah."

"Huh." Frankie leans back again, eyes glimmering with... mischief? Interest?

Everly narrows her gaze at her friend. "What? What's that look?"

"Nothing." They attempt a casual shrug, but Everly isn't fooled. "Just interesting is all."

Everly won't get anything else out of them if the stubborn set of Frankie's jaw is anything to go by. She purses her lips and tucks her legs up under her on the padded cushion, returning to her own thoughts.

What would it be like to have more than one person in her corner, as Frankie phrased it? She sees the possibility of adding two more people, if things continue to go well with her sister and Asim. That would be more people truly caring about her than she's had since her parents died, and she's never really been herself on the outside, so that part of it would be entirely new. It almost feels like Carrie is sitting on her shoulder cheering her on, telling her to push herself and not give up.

CHAPTER SIXTEEN

Asim gave her a hint about their date when she asked earlier, telling her to dress nicely for being outside in the evening, and that only serves to increase Everly's excitement. She chooses to wear her favorite red heels— they make her calves look stunningly toned—and she pairs them with a classic Little Black Dress. Sleeveless with ruching along one side of her waist that accentuates her curves, it hits just below mid-thigh. The weather is warmer than usual today, so Everly isn't too worried about getting chilled once the sun goes down. Her hair is curled and pinned up on one side leaving her neck bared on the other, and she got her nails done earlier in the day with french tips.

Everly loves how fancy she feels.

She normally dresses up for work, but that's more of a professional business vibe. The only other time she's dressed up like this in recent years has been the annual holiday party, and she's never been able to enjoy it. This experience is completely different. She's had an afternoon of pampering, partly because it's fun, but also because her anxiety demanded some self care to calm her nerves before their date. Now Everly feels amazing, looks amazing, and is ready to have an incredible night.

Asim pulls up right on time, the delivery truck rumbling into her driveway, and Everly is floored when he hops down from the cab. He looks absolutely bite-able wearing impeccably fitted charcoal pants and a deep green button down that makes his eyes pop. With the sleeves rolled up to his elbows showing off corded forearms, Everly reminds herself not to drool, or stare, or beg him to skip the date and come inside where she can rip those fine clothes right off.

He takes long strides toward the porch, loosely carrying a bouquet of wildflowers wrapped in brown paper with a twine bow around them in one hand. Her heart melts, and her heels click across the floor as she rushes to open the front door for him.

As soon as she pulls it open, Asim sucks in a sharp breath, his eyes devouring her. His heated gaze travels from her dark hair pulled up and exposing one side of her neck, along the curve of her body to her hips, down her bare legs to show-stopping red shoes. His throat bobs as he swallows hard. Blinking twice, Asim quickly reattaches his eyes to hers, the stain of a blush darkening his cheeks.

Her heart flutters, then turns over with a heavy thud in her chest.

"Sorry." His voice is rough and gravely, and a muscle ticks in his jaw. "I normally have better manners than that but wow, Everly. You look... you're stunning."

She preens with his compliment and smiles at his embarrassment, thinking it's cute that for once she's thrown him off instead of the other way around. He thrusts the flowers out in front of him, clearing his throat.

"These are for you, obviously," he says, passing them to her and then rubbing the back of his neck with his hand. She thanks him, gesturing to him to follow her inside while she puts them in water. A soft groan sounds from behind her when she turns, followed by a low grumble; she's pretty sure he's scolding himself to "get a grip." Everly smirks, but doesn't call him out on it. She's rather pleased to have affected him so strongly.

Asim confirms he's ready to go once the flowers are in a vase, and then apologizes for the ride.

"I would have brought the bike, but considering I told you to dress up I figured that probably wasn't the best idea."

"That's okay, I don't mind the truck. You might have to help me get in though." Everly gives a nervous laugh as she eyes the step leading up to the truck's front cab. It wouldn't normally be a problem, but between her three inch heels and the length of her dress, she'd rather play it safe than sorry.

"Of course," Asim replies, holding out his hand and opening the door for her.

Everly places her hand in his, loving how it encompasses hers completely. His fingers and palm are rough with calluses, and she wonders what they would feel like on other parts of her body. Everly gives herself a little shake as he closes the door and rounds to the drivers side, recentering herself in the present moment. Now is not the time for daydreams.

Pulling into the parking lot for the local river boat that runs river cruises for the tourists, Everly smoothes her hands along her thighs. She's never been on it before, never really even considered it as she always assumed it was a tourist trap. Before she can ask, Asim tells her to stay put, then hops out on his side and rounds the front again, opening her door and holding out his hand to help her down. She smiles at him as she steps out, and he answers her unspoken question.

"We are taking a sunset dinner cruise. Have you been?"

"I haven't. I didn't even know they did that to be honest." Everly raises her eyebrows in curiosity as she looks around, noticing a few other couples who are also making their way across the parking lot.

Asim passes over two tickets to the staff waiting on the dock, then ushers her onto the boat. "Where would you like to sit?" he asks.

"I have no idea. Where do you think would be best?" Everly is happy to take his lead on this.

"How about up top? I imagine it will have the best view for the sunset." Asim places his hand on the small of her back, but isn't forceful or pushy as he does so. He simply rests it there, as if he doesn't want to lose her, or maybe he simply wants the physical connection. Everly likes it.

They're crossing the second of three levels on the massive river boat when they run into another couple she vaguely recognizes from around town. Asim greets them warmly, exchanging smiles and handshakes, and she thinks he even knows their names. Everly, on the other hand, does not.

She has never been comfortable in these types of

social situations; Everly hates random small talk and never knows what to say outside of expected encounters. She pastes a smile on her face as the couple chatters happily at Everly and Asim, asking him about his business and in return he asks about someone named Claire. They end up inviting Everly and Asim to join their table, but thankfully Asim handles it as smoothly as ever, politely declining their offer before excusing them to head up to the next deck. Everly takes a few deep breaths to calm the spike of adrenaline brought on by the unexpected socializing, and focuses on Asim's thumb rubbing slow circles on her lower back. It feels smooth through the fabric of her dress and is pleasantly soothing.

They find a table along the front side of the boat and order dinner and drinks as it starts to slowly meander down the river. Everly might hate small talk with others, but with Asim it isn't a problem. She finds herself happily chatting away, answering his questions and asking some of her own. He asks more about her therapy journey, and she shares her goal of taking risks to be more of her authentic self, and of course worrying less.

"It sounds silly, but I was so convinced it was an impossible task." Everly laughs at herself and Asim tilts his head in question. "This idea of overcoming my fear of... I don't know, myself? I guess? It feels like I've worn a mask and been a people pleaser for so long that it's scary to think about being who I really am on the inside."

"It makes sense, though," Asim replies. "We're all raised with certain expectations, of course they're quite different based on culture and gender and identity and whatnot, but still. I can relate to the idea of taking off a mask. I've gotten so used to wearing my professional persona all the time, that letting my guard down around you has been a bit intimidating, if I'm being honest."

"Wait, you found *me* intimidating?!" Everly's eyes pop wide and Asim chuckles in reply.

"Only because I wanted to make a good impression." He pauses, seeming to debate what to say next. "I admire your courage, Everly. In facing your emotions in that way. I know from personal experience it's often easier to ignore or avoid uncomfortable situations, but you've done the opposite."

"It's a new thing." Everly shrugs. "I'm usually an expert avoider."

"Is there anything I can do to help? With any of it, your self-expression, the anxiety you mentioned before?"

Everly's heart threatens to explode and she takes a slow breath to keep herself grounded in the moment.

"Asim..." She shakes her head. "You've done so much for me already, I don't think you even realize. Most people in my past would make fun or judge me when I do something weird or awkward or embarrassing, but you haven't been like that. And just... Like how you take control in uncomfortable situations and make it seem so smooth and effortless. I don't get it, I don't know how you do it, but it's made things so much better. It's made being around you so easy."

Everly averts her eyes, looking down at her napkin instead of him. That was a lot. It feels like she just flayed her heart open and laid it in front of him.

"Good. That's what I want," Asim says, reaching across the table and opening his palm for her hand. Everly looks at it for a moment before settling hers there, relishing the warmth he brings to her cool fingers.

Asim, it turns out, is familiar with anxiety. His brother struggles with it as well, and as their parents have never been very open about mental health, his brother turned to him as someone to talk to about it. There's a warm, floaty feeling in her chest as he talks about learning from his brother, one that expands into a fierce sense of pride. She's proud of herself for opening up again and she's proud of Asim for not only being supportive of his brother, but going further by making an effort to learn more about what his brother dealt with and how to help.

They've finished eating and are slowly sipping their drinks as the sun sets on the horizon, turning the arid landscape a molten gold. The setting sun strikes a path of glowing orange across the river, and the cloudless sky is transforming to pastel shades of purple and pink above them. Everly admires how it burnishes Asim's skin and highlights his eyes, bringing out the color and making them shine a brighter green than usual. He looks ethereal, as though his skin is glowing and his eyes carry magic.

Everly wants to get lost in him, but she's been on edge

about going on a date to begin with, plus a little nervous about one thing this whole evening. She's at the point where she's had just enough liquid courage to finally brave it and ask him. She looks over her glass at Asim, scanning his face in an attempt to gauge what his reaction might be. He lifts his eyebrows at her inquisitive stare, setting his drink down and leaning his forearms against the table between them. His full attention is intimidating and gratifying at the same time.

"I had an idea…" Everly begins, but then pauses as her nerves start to flare up again.

"I like ideas." Asim encourages her with a small nod and his lips hitch up on one side in a half smile. She takes a fortifying sip of her drink, then continues.

"Well, remember when we were talking about the poinsettias?" She's having trouble holding eye contact and her gaze keeps bouncing around the boat, down to her hands, the river, the landscape around them, only glancing at him for brief moments in between.

Asim looks momentarily taken aback, but nods, replying, "I do, yes."

"I thought, maybe I could donate them to others around town. Maybe the retirement apartments or nursing home, or some of the other local businesses, if they'd like." Everly stumbles over her words, and forces herself to take a breath before continuing.

Why is asking for help so hard?

Logically, she knows this isn't a huge deal, but emotionally she's terrified. Everly straightens her shoulders and glances up at the sky, then quickly back down, locking eyes with him.

"Will you help me?" she asks.

Asim cocks his head at her. "You'd like me to help you donate the poinsettias?"

"Yes, well, I mean I don't know how else I would, since they wouldn't fit in my car. Or well, they might or I could make a few trips, but you have the truck so I figured, oh but that's not the only reason!" Everly's eyes flare with panic when she realizes it sounds like she just wants to use him for the delivery truck. "I want to spend time with you too! I thought it could be fun to do together, like a date, well not a date really, but you know—"

Asim reaches across the table and swipes his thumb

along her lower lip, stopping her rambling in its tracks. "Hush darling, I'd love to help you."

Everly's lips part and she desperately fights herself not to kiss his finger, or lick it, or suck it into her mouth and swirl her tongue around it. He's effectively snapped her out of one thought spiral, and sent her straight into a different one. Thoughts of him, his touch, his lips, her lips...

Asim slowly pulls his hand away, eyes flicking to her lips as she licks them, tasting the remnants of the salt from his skin. Her eyes follow that finger until it disappears beneath the table, then they seek out his gaze again. She realizes they haven't spoken for long moments, and it almost feels like they're under a spell. Like they're the only two people on this boat, sailing down an enchanted river with the world a blurry, glowing gold around them.

The spell is broken when the waiter stops by their table, butting in and startling her back to reality, asking how they're doing and if they'd like dessert. Everly's emotions take another tumble, slamming back into the realm of anxiety, because what was *that*, and now she's expected to order dessert?! She didn't even know they offered dessert.

Her heart starts to thump in her chest as the waiter stares at her, reverberating through her body and tightening her lungs. She hears Asim request a few more minutes, and then the sound of his chair scraping across the deck as he stands.

He kneels down next to her, taking her shaking fingers into his hands and clasping them lightly between his as his eyes scan her face. Everly's eyes are downcast, focusing on their hands and her breathing as she frantically tries to suck in air. She is acutely aware of the fact they are on a boat, surrounded by people and water, and there is no escape. Everly has nowhere to run, nowhere to hide, nowhere to be alone. She's unsure why, in this moment of all moments, her anxiety has decided to flare, but it's here now and it won't be ignored.

Asim grasps her hands tighter in his, pulling her attention to him. He's just below her eye level, where he crouches in a half kneel, allowing her to look down at him while blocking out most everything else around them. She can see his lips moving, but only hears the blood rushing in her ears. All Everly can do at this moment is shake her head at him, unable to respond to whatever he's trying to tell her.

One of his hands glides up her arm, though she hardly feels it, and then his fingers trace along the side of her face. She barely notices that either, until his entire palm flattens against her lower jaw and neck as he cups her head in his hand. He massages the back of her neck with strong fingers, and she leans into it, increasing the pressure until it pushes the other sensations back. Her hearing starts to return, and her blurry eyes focus on his startlingly intense, green gaze.

"Everly? Can you hear me?" His voice isn't loud, but it is firm, concerned. She nods, but isn't able to speak.

"Breathe with me," he says, releasing her neck and placing one of her hands flat against his chest. Everly sees his shoulders rise with his inhale, feels his lungs expand under her palm, and she tries her best to follow along with him. Her breath stutters as she inhales, catching in her throat, but she manages to hold it for a second as he does before slowly forcing it back out.

"Again," he demands, and she doesn't have to think about it. Her body listens, responding to his authoritative tone and trusting him instinctively. They breathe together, in and out, over and over, and it gets easier with each breath. Asim's steady gaze is her lifeline, and he doesn't look away from her once.

When her blood has stopped pounding through her and her breathing has evened out, she's able to move on her own again and her thoughts come rushing back in. Mortified, Everly slumps down behind his massive body, using him as a shield as she searches the other tables on the top deck, hoping against hope that no one noticed her breakdown.

"Everly, look at me." Asim's gentle but unyielding voice commands her distraught gaze to return to his. "You're okay. No one noticed, we were quiet, and they've been enjoying their meals and the sunset. It's okay." Slow and calm, his low voice soothes her agitated nerves.

"Okay. It's okay," she whispers the words, clinging to his gaze and his hand.

"It's okay. You're okay," he reaffirms, nodding. He

takes another deep breath, pressing her hand more firmly to his chest, and she follows his lead again.

"Thank you," she says quietly, pulling her hands from his and clenching her napkin in her lap. "I don't know what happened, and I don't know what I would have done without your help. Jumped straight into the river, probably."

"You're welcome. If you want to talk about it, I'm happy to listen," he says. "Are you ready for me to get up? I can stay here, if you need." His eyes search hers, flicking back and forth, earnest and piercing.

Everly shakes her head, taking another deep breath on her own and looking back at him with a small smile. "I'm good now, you can get up."

Asim gently squeezes her arm in that comforting way of his, then stands and smoothly slides back into his seat. "Now, would you like some dessert? You don't have to, I'm happy either way, but if you'd like a suggestion I hear their chocolate mousse is fantastic."

Everly looks around, realizing what felt like hours was actually only minutes, and takes a moment to assess her body. She's feeling drained from the panic attack, and doesn't think a rich dessert would sit well with her at this point. "No, I don't think I'll have any. Please get some if you'd like though, I don't mind."

Asim simply smiles, and when the waiter comes back around, he declines dessert, requesting fresh water for them both and a hot green tea for Everly. She looks at him in surprise, wondering if it was a lucky guess or if he somehow knows she likes green tea.

"You mentioned it once," he says, "when talking about your friend. You said Frankie always makes you green tea, that it's your go-to comfort drink."

Everly's heart thumps in her chest for an entirely different reason now.

She doesn't know what she did to deserve this man showing up in her life, but she's becoming more grateful every day for the opportunity to get to know him.

CHAPTER SEVENTEEN

The sun fully set during Everly's panic attack, but the sky still holds beautiful shades of deep blues and greens. Asim moves his chair around the table closer to hers, and they watch the fading colors together. Everly turns in her seat, tilting her head back against his shoulder as he winds one arm around her, lightly tracing the skin along her outer arm with his fingertips. They're holding hands and pointing out stars as they appear in the darkening sky above them, and a wave of peace sweeps over her. Asim senses her quiet mood, or maybe he feels the same, and they spend some time in comfortable silence listening to the sound of the boat and other patrons chatting around them.

Asim murmurs here and there when something occurs to him, telling her more about his siblings and sharing a funny story about his brother nearly falling off a boat when they were younger. He clearly misses his family, but he's also spoken about how much he loves the community and his job here too. His voice is comforting, resonant and deep, lulling her into a place of calm and safety.

Everly wonders about his future; what his goals and ambitions are. Whether his ideals and dreams might align with hers, then if she's crazy and getting ahead of herself. She figures the worst has already happened tonight and they got through it, so she dives in.

"What are your life dreams?" she asks, eloquent as always.

"My life dreams? Hmm."

Asim tips his head sideways and rests his cheek

against the top of her head for a moment while he thinks. Everly relishes how natural it feels to be held by him like this.

"Well if we're talking career goals, I'd love to expand the business, be able to hire more locals and become a town staple. Bring joy to the community. I've actually had an idea I'd like to propose to the city council, I've been thinking about it for a couple years now and just never gotten around to it."

"What's your idea?" Everly tilts her head a little further, curving her neck to the side so she can look up at his face. He looks almost... bashful? She never would have guessed this massive, confident, easy-going man could look that way and she's even more intrigued now that she's seen it.

"I'd like to partner with the city to bring more decorative planters to the downtown area. Maybe contract with them to add some native, drought tolerant plants along the sidewalks and in pots downtown. I think it would be nice to replace a lot of the less sustainable landscaping there currently."

"That would be amazing." Everly sits forward and twists to face him. "Asim, that's a really fantastic idea! I can't believe you've had this in your pocket for years. How do we make it happen?"

Asim's eyes brighten as his eyebrows rise, his lips slowly curve up into a smile. "We?"

"Well," Everly backpedals, she didn't mean to insert herself into his life goals. "I mean, obviously it's your thing, but I know almost all of the council members through my parents. Kinda grew up around them, the people with sway, our families were all in the same circle. I could maybe help if you wanted, not that you can't do it on your own of course." She pinches her lips together, determined to stop the rambling herself before he intervenes again.

"I'd be honored if you'd help. I know plants, and I do well enough on the business end, but I don't know the first thing about bringing a proposal to a group of politicians." He smiles fondly and she returns it, shifting and settling back into the crook of his arm.

"You don't need to be nervous to share your opinions and thoughts with me, Ever." Asim's voice is a soft murmur above her, and she doesn't have a good response to that statement. She's quiet for a few moments while her brain spins.

"I'm..." Everly doesn't know how to say what she wants to say without sounding like an idiot. She glances at Asim, and his face is soft while he waits patiently for her to find the words she's looking for.

"I'm not that great with words," Everly rushes through it, cringing at how that very sentence demonstrates it perfectly.

"That's alright." Asim is unfazed, and she realizes that he truly means it. "Would it help if I asked questions? When you don't know the words?"

She blinks as her eyes unfocus, imagining what that would be like, before replying. "Yeah, I think, maybe it would."

"Alright then," he says. "Even if you don't have anything to say though, that's okay too. I don't mind the quiet." Asim strokes a hand down her arm and pulls her in closer, surrounding her in comfort and warmth.

Her throat is too tight to talk even if she knew what to say, so she bobs her head up and down before pushing herself a little deeper into his side. He gives her a return squeeze with the arm draped around her and she sighs, allowing herself to finally relax into his embrace.

The stars are out in full by the time the boat putters back up to the dock. Everyone files down the stairs and Everly happily slips her hand into the crook of Asim's arm as they cross the dock back to the parking lot. Asim helps her into the truck again before climbing in himself, and they drive down the twisting back roads to Everly's house. The interior smells like him and Everly breathes it in, trying to figure out the individual components that make his scent so unique. She picks out earthy notes, maybe the slightly smokey scent of amber with some sandalwood undertones. Whatever it is, she breathes it in like she needs it to survive.

Everly leans her forehead against the cool glass of the window, a content smile painting her lips as Asim rolls his window down and rests his forearm on it. Cacti and large desert brush sweep by the window as they drive, and Everly stares out past it all, reliving their evening together in her mind.

When Asim turns into her neighborhood and she sees the road sign for Poinsettia Lane ahead, she pulls her mind back to the present moment. Everly peeks at Asim from the corner of her eye, noticing his arm is tensed, muscles corded beneath his tattoos as he clenches his hand on top of the steering wheel. Before she can ask if everything's alright though, they turn into her driveway and he glances her way, eyes softening as he smiles at her.

He doesn't have to tell her to wait this time, and his hand is there to help her out of the truck again. He parked right in front of her porch steps, so the house lights cast a halo effect as she looks up into his eyes. Asim doesn't let go of her hand, instead pulling her closer before sliding one hand to her waist and cupping her face with the other, while her hands settle around his lower back. His thumb lightly strokes from the corner of her jaw to the tender spot beneath her ear, sending a shiver down her spine.

"May I kiss you?" Asim phrases it as a question, though his tone sounds more like a statement of fact, with his voice hushed and low, for her ears only. Everly nods her consent anyways, tipping her face up and leaning toward him. Asim's eyes flicker between hers for a moment, then he looks down at her mouth, lips slightly parted as he leans forward to meet her.

The first brush of his lips on hers feels like coming home. Soft and warm, she sighs into his mouth, melts into his hold. The second is more demanding, meeting her mouth firmly, tongue stroking the seam of her lips and requesting entry. Everly opens for him, and he lets out a low groan from the back of his throat the moment his tongue tastes hers. She lets him lead, and he is happy to do so, plundering her mouth with his tongue and exploring every inch of her.

They meet over and over again, lips and teeth and tongues colliding and dancing for position to be the one to taste the other. Asim's lips capture hers, refusing to let her go, and his fingers tighten where they grip her. His hand slides up her waist to splay across her ribs, just barely grazing the underside of her breast, and Everly's nipples instantly harden when his other hand tangles in her hair and pulls, tipping her head back for a deeper kiss. The slight sting in her scalp only increases her ravenous desire for him, sending tingles down her spine. In return, she threads one hand into his hair at the nape of his neck. The other is still fisted in the hem of his shirt.

Just as she starts to feel light-headed from the lack of oxygen, Asim pulls back, loosening his hold on her hair and leaning his forehead against hers, breathing heavily.

"If we don't stop now, I won't leave." Asim's voice is strained, like it took considerable effort to say those words to her, and his Arabic accent is heavier than normal. "I want you to invite me in. I want to tear you out of that torturously sexy dress and taste every inch of you. I want more, I want it all, Everly. But I'd also like to take things slow. Sex has ruined things for me in the past, and I would hate it if I let that happen with you, especially on a night that I suspect has already been a lot for you emotionally. I like getting to know you, and I don't want to push either of us into too much, too quickly."

Everly debates inviting him in despite his clear hesitation, but she doesn't know if she's ready for that either, even as her body is currently begging to climb him like a tree.

She slowly nods in agreement, rocking her forehead against his, and he briefly closes his eyes, then nods back. Asim peels his fingers from her ribs and slides his hand from her hair, gently cupping her face in both hands and dropping his lips down for another kiss, this one sweet and chaste. She slides her fingers from the back of his neck and lets them rest on the tense muscle of his shoulder. As he pulls back, he stops inches from her face, pinning her with those intense green eyes as they seem to search her soul.

Her favorite color, Everly realizes. In this light, his eyes are her absolute favorite color, or maybe her favorite shade of green has changed to match that of his eyes.

Easing back from each other, Asim's hands slide down her arms and he grasps hers lightly, giving her fingers a squeeze before letting go and turning to walk up the porch steps. He stops outside her door, shifting to look at her a step behind him and tucking in some of the stray hairs that came loose from his manhandling.

"This is the best evening I've had in years, maybe ever," he says, and Everly blushes, looking down in an attempt to hide the shy smile that blooms across her face. Asim bends down to meet her lowered gaze, and she pulls her keys out of her purse before meeting his eyes again.

"This is the best evening I've had in a long time too. Thank you for... everything," she says.

"Truly my pleasure." Asim still has a small, blissful smile on his face, and it warms Everly up inside. "I'll wait here until I hear you lock the door," he says, shoving his hands in his pockets.

Everly offers a quiet goodnight, turns and enters the house, locks the door behind her. She hesitates, then presses her ear to the door, hands splayed wide against it. Unsure what she's hoping for, she simply listens as he waits a beat before his steps slowly back away. Everly sighs, then slips out of her heels and walks through the foyer to the darkened kitchen, peering out the window to see him getting back in his truck before the brake lights flare and he drives off.

Happier than she can ever remember feeling, Everly gets ready for bed and slips between the sheets. She takes a deep breath and closes her eyes, hoping to dream of him and imagining what steamy scenarios her unconscious mind might come up with. Maybe they go swimming in the river, or skinny dipping. She imagines the bite of the cold water and the contrasting heat she'd feel from his skin, and goosebumps pop up along her arms. Everly wiggles around, feeling exhausted and yet somehow full of energy at the same time.

Her toes are sore from her shoes, her brain is tired from the mental gymnastics, and her cheeks hurt from smiling so much, but that doesn't diminish it in any way. It's been a truly wonderful night, panic attack and all.

CHAPTER EIGHTEEN

Asim texts her periodically over the next few days, checking in and sending Everly sweet little notes. They set up a time and date to donate the poinsettias during the upcoming week, and Everly compiles a list of places she would like to donate them to. In the meantime, she's overdue for some quality friend time with Frankie.

Snagging her phone off the bathroom counter, Everly hits the video call as she wanders into her walk-in closet and waits for them to pick up. She's back home from work at the hotel after an aggravating day involving two of their longest-standing repeat clients somehow double-booking the same luxury suite and it was an absolute nightmare to sort out. She debates whether to take a bubble bath now, or wait until she's done talking with her friend, but Frankie picks up before she can decide. Their sparkly, hazel brown eyes light up her screen, shelves lining the coffee house stockroom behind them.

"Hello, this is Frankie, who am I speaking with?"

Everly snorts a laugh.

"Yeah, yeah, hilarious." She deadpans, rolling her eyes into the camera.

Frankie laughs and props the phone up on a box as she unpacks and shelves supplies.

"So, tell me about your daaaate!" Frankie sings the last word and wiggles their eyebrows at her suggestively. "I heard through the grapevine that you two were, and I quote, "just so darn cute together" end quote."

"Wait, what?! You heard from who?!" Everly does not like the relentless gossip mill in this town, and she normally stays out of it.

"Oh, you know. Just Nancy, doing her thing. She said she ran into you both as you were finding a table. Told me all about it when she was ordering her coffee this morning. Said she offered for you to sit with them just to pull your leg and see what you'd do." They roll their eyes at this. "Old lady jokes, am I right?"

"So that's what her name was. Nancy." She narrows her eyes. "Such an old lady name too."

Frankie snorts. "Okay, okay. Enough about Nancy. How was it?"

"It. Was. Amazing." Everly flops dramatically onto her bed, hair splaying out around her. She hasn't stopped thinking about her date with Asim since the moment it ended. "Also humiliating, but mostly amazing." Everly tells Frankie everything, all the dirty details they've been wanting for weeks, finally feeling in a secure enough place emotionally to share it, and Frankie is eating it up like it's the latest reality tv show.

"Okay yeah, definitely a keeper," they say. "I can't believe you had a full on panic attack though, and on the boat? Why?"

"I have no idea. I mean, my emotions were up and down all day leading up to it, and I had been feeling nervous, so maybe it was a combination of everything? I don't know. I'm going to ask Carrie about it next session. I just hope it doesn't happen again," she says, sitting up and crossing her legs, sighing in resignation at the fact that it likely will, as that wasn't the first one in the last few weeks.

Frankie looks at her thoughtfully.

"It sounds like even if you do have another one, if Asim's around he can help you through it. From what you said, it doesn't seem like it even phased him, and based on that kiss... yeah. Girl, you're fine." They state this as though their word is law and there is no question about it.

Everly laughs, acknowledging Frankie's words are likely the truth. They spend some time catching up on both of their lives, and Everly putters around the house taking care of minor household chores she's been putting off. As they finally end the call over an hour later, Everly is smiling and humming to herself, putting the last of the clean dishes away in the kitchen.

She heads up the stairs to bed, deciding she doesn't need that bubble bath after all, and feels lighter than she has in years. Joyful to have a friend she can share everything with who won't judge her for her flaws, and eager to spend more time with Asim in the next couple days.

~~~

Asim backs the delivery truck up to the front porch steps, in the same spot he had it when he first dropped off the plants for the holiday party so many weeks ago. Everly is already waiting on the porch with the front door open, grin stretching her cheeks and hugging a cheerful red poinsettia in her arms, ready to be loaded.

As he jumps down and closes the truck door behind him, Asim sees her and grins back. Everly lifts one of her hands from the pot, clasping her forearm with the other, and gives him a small wave before wrapping it around the pot and holding it tightly to her front again.

"Ready to get right to work, I see."

"I'm excited!" Everly says, bouncing on her toes. She feels good about this decision, bringing a bit of joy and life to those in her community.

Asim skips up the steps and strides right over to her like he owns the place, sliding his hand to the nape of her neck as his lips take hers in a searing kiss above the poinsettia's flowers tickling her chin. Before Everly can so much as try to return it, he's pulling away and turning to open up the back of the truck. Everly rocks up onto her toes, a blissful feeling lighting up her chest.

They both start grabbing the potted poinsettias from inside and loading them into the truck. Once they get a few in, Asim suggests she hop in the back and start organizing them while he hauls the rest out to her.

Before she can finish saying "sure," his hands are around her waist and he's lifting her up into the bed of the truck. Everly gasps, the combination of his touch, his hands nearly encircling her waist, and the ease with which he lifts her sending her mind into a buzzing frenzy.

She shakes her head quickly, not letting herself get sucked into the distraction that is Asim right now. They
~~~

are on a schedule today and she won't be sidetracked from it. Everly shuffles into the truck's depths, scooting and sliding the potted plants around so they're secure and will be easy to unload when they get to their new homes.

Asim easily carries out four at a time with two in each hand, somehow gripping the lips of the pots together and dropping them into the truck for her to arrange. After only a few more trips, the house is cleared out and the truck is loaded.

"Well that was way easier and faster than if I had tried to do this all myself," Everly says, hands on her hips and her voice wry as she looks down at Asim from her vantage point in the back of the truck. Asim chuckles and waves her forward. She sits down at the edge with her legs dangling off, intending to reach for his hand, but he has other ideas. Once again, his hands circle her waist, and hers go to his shoulders as he lifts her down, setting her feet on the ground in front of him.

"That's way too easy for you." Everly's breath hitches in her lungs and she struggles to keep her eyes locked on his when what they really want to do is admire the tattooed biceps that are being lovingly hugged by his short shirt sleeves.

"Because of my monster arms?"

Asim's grin is playful as he crowds her space, reminding her of the way her mouth ran away without her permission the first time they met. Her eyes flare as he reaches up over her, and her mind blanks. Everly has no idea what's happening now, other than that she's surrounded by him. His broad chest is pressing into hers, her nose is at the base of his throat with his masculine, earthy scent invading her lungs, and his arms are raised on either side of her. She's ready to climb him like some sort of rabid spider monkey, when he abruptly pulls down the roller door to the back of the truck. Everly squeaks in alarm, nearly crashing her nose into his chin when she instinctively jumps away from the loud sound, inadvertently launching herself at him.

Asim throws the latch behind her before leaning back and meeting her gaze again. His eyes are twinkling with mischief and she narrows hers, pinning him with a glare as she wills her heart to slow. He knew exactly what he was doing and how it would affect her. Everly unclenches her fists from his shirt and lightly smacks a very hard pec in retaliation. She's pretty sure her palm stings more than his chest.

Asim's smile oozes male smugness. Everly whirls around, whipping him in the chest with her long, dark hair, and strides toward the passenger door of the truck. She hears his amused chuckle behind her, and acknowledges it with a secret smile of her own. She likes playful Asim.

A moment later, he climbs in next to her, his corded forearm flexing as he turns the key in the ignition.

"Where to first?"

"I was thinking that apartment complex for 55 and older, the one over on Elmwood?"

"I know the one." Asim nods and shifts the truck into gear, driving carefully down the driveway and turning out onto her street in the direction she indicated. Everly cracks her window open so she can feel the cool morning breeze on her cheeks as the neighbors' houses slide by outside the window.

"You don't think this is silly, do you?" Everly is having second thoughts, wondering if people won't want poinsettias in February.

"I think it's a really thoughtful idea, Ever. If I didn't think people would like it, I would have told you so." Asim has always been honest with her, and she has no reason to doubt him. Everly relaxes back into the seat.

They arrive a few minutes later and walk up to the resident services building. To her surprise, an older man, who she assumes must be the leasing office or building manager, walks right up to Asim with a warm smile on his wrinkled face and his hand stretched out. Asim meets him halfway, warmth lighting his face in return as they greet each other while Everly stalls behind him.

"Mr. Williams," Asim says, "great to see you again."

"You as well, young man," Mr. Williams says. "How are you? How's that old truck holding up?"

"Sturdy as ever, just as you promised." Asim grins, nodding his chin toward the truck behind him.

"Well, I'm just glad to see she's still chugging along. Happy she's in good hands, you know," he says, and Everly surmises the delivery truck must have been Mr.

Williams' at some point.

"What brings you two youngin's over here today, then?" Mr. Williams asks, and Asim turns slightly, snagging Everly's hand and tugging her in front of him, then placing both hands on her shoulders, squeezing gently in reassurance.

"This is Everly, she has some poinsettia plants she wants to share around town and this is one of the stops on her list."

Asim is beaming, she can hear it in his voice and she swears she can feel it lighting up the air around them. Is this what it feels like for someone to approve of her? She's afraid to let herself think that it might even be pride, because somehow that feels bigger and scarier than any other possibility.

Mr. Williams greets her with the same warmth he had for Asim, even though they don't yet know each other.

"Hi Mr. Williams, it's nice to meet you. Do you think any of the residents would be interested in a free plant?" Everly asks, biting her lip to stop herself from rambling about poinsettias.

"Oh that sounds just lovely, my dear." Mr. Williams readily agrees and she breathes a sigh of relief.

He helps them unload some of the potted plants and set them up outside the leasing office, then returns to his work inside, leaving the two of them alone in the lobby area. As they are working, a fair number of seniors walk by and Everly greets each one, offering them a plant with a smile on her face.

Some are interested, others offer a polite no thank you. There's one sweet older lady who eyes the plants, but she's using a walker and ultimately declines. Asim notices her looking at them though, and offers to carry one back to her apartment. Her face lights up, and she tells him what a sweet young man he is. Everly's smile grows wider watching him interact with her. He grabs a couple of the nicest looking ones and pulls them to the front for her to inspect, asking which one calls to her. She spends a moment looking them over, and even reaches down to touch the petals of one, which she quickly declares the winner.

Asim snags it, then holds out an arm, gesturing for her to proceed him toward the main hallway. She pats his arm before returning her hands to her walker, and they shuffle away together. Everly hears a happy "thank you, dear" as Asim gives her a sideways grin over his shoulder on his way out the door.

He returns only a few minutes later and they close up the truck, leaving a few in the lobby and deciding to take the next batch downtown to offer to the other local businesses. Everly saves a couple of her favorites for the hotel lobby, plus a funky looking one for Frankie at Roasted, and they distribute the rest. Almost everyone looks surprised to see Everly, which makes sense given her lack of sociability with others in the community despite having lived all thirty years of her life in this town. On the other hand, Everly is surprised to see how many people know Asim. He's greeted left and right, with people inquiring after Moose and the greenhouse and his family.

He says hello to Alex, who she learns is the genius in the back kitchen of the bakery, greets José who is pulling up weeds along the sidewalk and she assumes works for the parks and recreation department but doesn't get a chance to clarify, and stops for a chat with Luís, who is apparently a cashier Asim knows from the hardware store. Alex and Luís each take a poinsettia, but José declines, stating he has enough plants at home already. Everly had no idea Asim was so well known around town, and she side eyes him as they walk to the next shop.

"How do you know so many people?" she asks.

Asim shrugs, and his shirt tugs up underneath the pot of the plant resting above his hip, revealing a strip of smooth, golden brown skin. Everly wants to lick it. She yanks her eyes away before her thoughts continue down that path, focusing on the sidewalk in front of her as Asim replies. "When I first moved here, I missed that sense of community and family I had before. So I went out and introduced myself to some of the other business owners; tried to foster that sense of home I was missing."

"Did it work?"

"Sort of." Asim looks down at the poinsettia, his eyes tracing over the red veins, before glancing her way again. "I do feel a similar sense of community here, but there's still a hole. Something missing. That feeling of belonging, of family. Being unconditionally loved and accepted and known." He looks away, a red tint to his cheeks and his eyes latch on to the door ahead of them. He quickens his next couple strides and snags the handle, pulling it open and stepping aside for her to walk in ahead of him.

Everly wants to ask more, but clearly he isn't very comfortable talking about it right now. She lets it go and they focus on finding new homes for the last few plants.

Finally, they make it to Roasted Coffee House with the last one she picked for Frankie. Frankie's head swings around from behind the counter as they open the door and step inside, and when they see Everly, they drop the checkered hand-towel they were using and walk around the counter toward the two of them.

"Oh hey, I know you!" Frankie says, striding up to them and holding out their hand to Asim.

"You do?" Everly asks, looking between Frankie and Asim.

"Well, in passing. You stop in for coffee every now and then, right? Chaga, if I'm not mistaken," Frankie answers Everly and then turns to Asim for confirmation.

"You have a good memory." He smiles and shakes their hand. "Nice to officially meet you, I'm Asim."

"Frankie," they reply. "So what's up?" Frankie turns back to Everly and raises their eyebrows expectantly.

"I brought you a plant!" Everly holds it out in front of her with both hands, smiling as she thrusts it into Frankie's arms.

"Oh! Okay, cool." Frankie glances at Asim as they accept it, then looks back to Everly, their face carefully neutral. "Um, why?"

"I'm donating all the ones from the party. Asim is helping." Everly waves a hand in his direction, her words spilling over each other. "I saved this one for you though, thought you'd like it. It's kinda weird."

One side of Frankie's mouth tips up. "You thought I'd like the weirdo plant, huh?" They extend their arms, holding it in front of them as they twist and turn the pot to inspect it further. "It is a little misshapen, kinda short on one side and scraggly on the other."

Everly shifts her weight from one foot to the other, Asim's hand coasts lightly along her back.

"Yeah, it'll do," Frankie declares, her eyes meeting Everly's again as they grin at her. "Here we go."

Frankie slips around Everly to get to the front window where there's a wide ledge holding knick knacks and a couple other plants. Moving around a few of the items, they make space and shove the potted poinsettia into the mix, re-shuffling a few of the smaller things and then stepping back to assess their work.

"Looks good," Asim says.

"Looks *perfect*." Frankie beams at them and bounces over.

"Thanks for thinking of me," they say, enveloping Everly in one of their signature over-the-top engulfing hugs. She squeezes her friend back, her heart happy and a grin taking over her face.

"So, you two want to stick around? Tea and Chaga," they point to each of them respectively as they name their preferred drinks, "on the house."

Everly glances up at Asim, a question in her eyes. She'd love to stay and for them to get to know each other a little more, but she isn't sure what his plans look like for the rest of the day.

"Sounds good, I'd love to," Asim says, and Everly bites her bottom lip in an attempt to hold in what feels like a very silly, very giddy smile.

They spend some time hanging out, the three of them talking about their day and getting acquainted with each other. Frankie asks where else they've stopped by with flowers, which is when Everly realizes that both Frankie and Asim are huge town gossips. Frankie learned long ago that Everly couldn't care less, and they gave up trying to talk to her about any of the goings-on in town, but to her consternation, Asim knows nearly as much about everyone's business as Frankie.

They swap stories, Frankie leaning forward with their elbows on their knees while Asim animatedly speaks with his hands, and Everly relaxes back into the soft leather seat, sipping her tea and eyeing them with amusement.

Sooner than she'd like, Frankie has to get back to work, so Everly and Asim stand up to leave, thanking them for the drinks and exchanging hugs. Asim holds the door open for her, then slips his hand around hers as they walk back to the parking lot. Everly swings their hands a little, her heart dancing when he glances down and winks at her, a cozy half smile tilting his lips.

With the truck now empty, Everly has a new sense of accomplishment, with a hefty dose of contentment curling around her heart as well. It fills her chest to bursting, but not in a scary way like the anxiety does. She feels proud of what they've done, and more fulfilled than she has in years. Part of her is tempted to minimize this experience, to say it wasn't that much and isn't really a big deal. The other part of her, the part that has been breaking out of its shell, the part that hears Carrie's voice on her shoulder, tells her to embrace it and that it was a purposeful step forward. That it's okay to feel good, to be proud, and to acknowledge that today has been meaningful for her.

Everly holds her shoulders back and tips her face into the sun, closing her eyes with a smile and letting the wind whip through her hair on the drive back to her house.

CHAPTER NINETEEN

The landscaping is nearly done, and Everly anticipates it'll be finished with another day or two of work. Asim is on the lower level digging out the final large hole for the hummingbird bush, and she's up top filling in the last of the smaller ones. Once they have these done, there are only a few of the small to medium sized plants left to finish up on the lower terrace. She's wearing another new outfit today; loose cutoff jean shorts that show off her legs, and a light yellow cotton work shirt, loose and fluttery around her curves. As usual, Everly has her hair braided back underneath her sun hat, and she's wearing her gardening gloves and boots.

Asim looks as delicious as always in his fitted work jeans and a t-shirt that might as well be painted on, the tattoos curling down his forearm taunting her. It's truly a sin that she isn't able to spend all her time admiring him, but alas, someone has to finish this up and he's already said he will only do it if she helps. So Everly grumbles under her breath, turning her focus back to the dirt in front of her rather than the dirt on his delectable backside.

"What was that?" Asim sits back on his knees, and Everly loses her view anyways.

"Nothing!" Luckily, Everly's face is already flushed from working in the sun. Asim's been flirting with her relentlessly today, and it hasn't escaped her notice that he seems to delight in making her blush.

"Mhm." Asim narrows his eyes at her, then turns back to filling dirt in around the hummingbird bush. "I think we can finish up with the planting today."

Everly is more than ready to be done sweating, but a twinge pinches her stomach at his words. It's so easy to be around him, and working together is strangely soothing to her soul; she's slightly terrified of what happens after, if they'll still have this connection or spend time together.

She's been trying to avoid the slew of anxious thoughts that have been threatening her the last few days. They primarily revolve around this topic, of what will happen once they finish this project. Will she still see him every week? Will their dynamic change? Will he enjoy spending time with her if they aren't doing something he clearly loves? Her breath turns shallow as her thoughts start to race, questioning what—if anything—they have between them while a cramp in her chest makes it even harder to breathe.

"And once everything is planted, then what?" she asks, hoping the tremor in her voice doesn't betray how confused and fragile she feels inside while her mind continues to race.

"You'll need some sort of ground cover. Mulch or rock, something like that to fill in between and help maintain the moisture under the soil." Asim pauses, eyes sweeping over the lower terrace around him. "So we'll get that sorted out."

Everly barely hears him, hardly recognizes that he's speaking and she certainly doesn't process his words. She's entirely focused on her breathing, trying to get it back under control and stopping her thoughts from swirling to darker and darker places. Forcing herself to surface, to come back to the present moment, she glances up just as his voice starts to register as actual words that she understands.

"Then that's it, we're done," he says.

Everly freezes; her entire body locks up. *Then what? That's it. We're done.* The words ricochet around her head and she feels the blood drain from her face as he confirms every horrible thought she's been avoiding, the ones she was just trying to pull herself away from.

We're done.

We're done.

Asim stands and dusts his hands off, having finished with the hummingbird bush, and looks over at her. His eyes flare wide and he leaps onto the top terrace next to her, placing a hand on her forehead.

"Everly, are you okay? You're pale as death, do you need water? Something to eat?" Asim asks.

She doesn't respond.

She can't respond. Everything has shut down, because her worst fear has come to light. It's as she thought, once the landscaping is finished, he has no reason to be with her anymore. *We're done.*

"Let's get you inside." Everly feels Asim's strong arms band around her from a distance, like she's not fully connected to her body anymore, and next thing she knows, he's carrying her across the patio and inside the house. Her hat falls off along the way, but she doesn't even try to grab it; she feels immobilized, helpless, as if she's sinking to the bottom of an icy lake, lethargic and disconnected from reality.

Asim props her on a chair in the dining room before rushing to the kitchen, returning a moment later with a glass of ice water and a cool cloth that he dabs gently on her forehead.

"Drink this," he says, kneeling in front of her chair and holding it up to her lips. "Steady now. How do you feel?"

Everly doesn't know what to say, but those words won't leave her head. *We're done.* She shakes her head, trying to dispel them, trying to get them out, but it doesn't work. She feels her lips moving around them, and she whispers, "we're done" as she stares at the glass in front of her without really seeing it.

"We're done?" Asim pulls back, confusion written across his face as his eyes dart between hers. "We will be soon..."

He cocks his head when she flinches at his words, letting his sentence trail off, eyeing her as her breath stutters and her eyes turn glassy before she twists away from him, curling her arms protectively around herself.

Eternity passes in the silence between them and Everly nearly loses herself again before he breaks it.

"Oh no, my sweet Ever, I didn't mean you and I. Is that what you thought? No, I meant the project. We're almost done with the project. Your anxiety thought I meant us, didn't it?" He pulls her off the chair onto the cool stone floor, cradling her in his arms and murmuring to her.

"No my darling, I am most certainly not done with you. You and I, we have so much left to our story." His arms are wrapped around her and the icy feeling starts to thaw as his words penetrate the fog in her mind.

"We are *not* done," he emphasizes, clearly trying to get it through her head.

Not done.

Everly blinks, moving her lips to the new words. "Not done," she whispers again.

"Not even close," he says. "I'm not even close to done with you, my darling Ever."

His arms are still around her, and she's picking up more of his words, letting them sink into her brain. His lips graze the top of her head, and she notices the feeling of one of his thighs against her back, the other underneath her legs as she sits sideways against him.

Not done. Not even close.

My darling Ever.

Everly sucks in a deep, shaky breath, and wrenches her eyes up to his. "You meant the project," she says and he nods, holding her eyes steady with his.

"Of course, you meant the project. I'm so sorry, oh my god I'm such a—"

"Don't you dare finish that sentence," Asim interjects. "If you say anything mean about the beautiful woman I'm dating, I'll have some seriously unhappy words for you." He glares down at her, but a smile twitches the corners of his mouth.

"Dating?" Everly looks up at him, and then squeaks when he squeezes her tightly.

"Did I not take you out on a date?"

"I... yeah." Everly is still catching up with everything after the world slowed around her and then snapped forward again into light-speed.

"So, if we're dating, does that mean we're going on another?" She peeks up at him through her eyelashes, his arms still banded around her.

"I certainly would like to, what do you think?" he asks.

Everly nods her head, tucking it in against his chest underneath his chin. "Yes, I'd like that too." Her voice is soft, and all at once, the surplus of frantic energy and tension drains from her body. She slumps against him, exhausted.

They sit in comfortable silence for a few more minutes, Asim's hands following a soothing path as he rubs up and down her arm before he gives her another gentle squeeze and stands up, picking her up with him and placing her on her feet.

"How about a break. Let's have a snack, and then see how you are feeling?" he asks, and Everly's stomach grumbles, answering for her.

She snorts a grimace at herself and takes his hand, pulling him into the kitchen with her. Everly keeps sneaking glances at him, afraid every time of what she will find in his face when he looks at her, not wanting to see evidence that his words were a lie. Pity, revulsion, disappointment, rejection. Her anxiety tells her they're all there on his face, clear as day, they must be. She finds none of them though, and she wouldn't believe it if she hadn't experienced this type of open acceptance from him before as well.

They put together a simple plate with some cheese, fruit, and veggies, sitting side by side at the kitchen counter. Asim doesn't stop touching her, and she relishes each one. His arm brushing hers as they reach forward, his knee bumping hers as he twists on the stool, his hand grazing hers in passing to and from the plate. It builds a slow heat, and she knows he's doing it on purpose.

Feeling rejuvenated, Everly proposes they head back out and try to finish up the planting today. It's still early afternoon, so they have plenty of daylight left, and she won't let one little misunderstanding ruin their day.

~~~

Everly swipes her gloves together, standing and taking a step back from the terrace. They've finished filling in the last clump of deergrass and Everly is sticky with sweat from her forehead down to her toes. She takes her straw hat off and fans her face with it as she walks back up to the patio and plops down into a shaded chair.

Asim chuckles at her theatrics, pulling the bottom of his shirt up to wipe off his forehead, and Everly shamelessly lets her eyes wander down the ladder of abs to that delightful 'V' near his hips. Asim catches her, of
~~~

course, and he stalks in her direction, sending her heart into a gallop before it takes a nose dive when he veers at the last second toward the remainder of his ice water instead, then thumps down into the chair next to hers.

"Good work out there," he tells her. Everly peels the gloves from her fingers and drops them on the table.

"You too. Thanks again, I never would have done all this without your help."

Asim eyes her for a moment and she raises her eyebrows.

"How are you feeling?" he asks.

"Oh," Everly tucks a stray hair into her braid as she forces herself not to look away from him. "Good, much better. Thank you."

"Good," he says, and turns his attention back to the plants. "Now we just need to water them." His eyes gleam as he says it, glancing her way. She's not sure what that's about, but her gut says he's up to something.

Asim heaves a breath and then stands back up. "I noticed a spigot on the side of the house, but no hose. You have one in the shed, maybe?" he asks.

"Sure," Everly says. She has no idea. Hose or no hose, she's taking a few more minutes in the shade.

Asim huffs a laugh and strides across the lawn to the shed, then disappears inside. Everly perks up when he comes back out with a green hose coiled and draped over his shoulder, massive biceps flexing as he hauls it across the lawn to the house. She doesn't have any of the fancy watering attachments that give it a nice even spray like what he has at the greenhouse, but that doesn't seem to bother him.

He attaches one end to the spigot and turns the water on, then cinches the hose closed as he uncoils and drags it closer to the terrace. Everly stands and steps to the edge of the patio, ostensibly to help, but really just to get a better view. He uses his thumb to disperse the spray and lets it rain down over the plants on the lower level. Giving them a good soak, he turns his attention to the top terrace, nearer to Everly's location.

His eyes flick to her, and his mouth pinches. Before she can react, he adjusts the angle of his thumb and water shoots straight toward her. Everly shrieks, throwing her hands up and leaping back from the cold spray.

She holds her arms out and shakes them off, trying to wrap her mind around the fact that he just sprayed her with a hose. Like a child. She blinks down at herself, feeling a bit like a wet rat, then hears his bellowing laughter.

Everly looks up from swiping the water off her arms, eyes slashing toward him, narrowed in a playful glare. He has his head thrown back and the hose is loose at his side, water sloshing onto the grass next to him. She doesn't waste a second of his distraction.

Dashing down the two terrace levels faster than she has ever moved in her life, Everly snatches the hose from his hand and turns it on him before he can react. She's not nearly as precise with dispersing or aiming the spray as he is, so she sets her sights on quantity rather than quality.

Everly drenches him and jumps out of his reach before he has a chance to react. Water blasts him directly in the chest, and his full-bodied laughter turns into a growl. Asim pins her with a look so full of heated anticipation it makes her core clench, and then he leaps toward her. She matches his movement, dancing backward and cackling when his arm swings out and just misses snagging her waist. He would have had her if her wet shirt wasn't stuck to her like a second skin. She turns the hose on him again, soaking his hair, the rest of his shirt, and one entire pant leg. Asim laughs and swipes water out of his eyes, combing his hand through his hair and then letting out a roar, coming at her a second time.

With a yelp of alarm, Everly attempts to skip backward out of his reach again, but this time she slips in the wet grass and stumbles, her feet skidding out from beneath her as her body twists in the air. Releasing the hose, water goes flying in every direction as she flails her arms in an attempt to latch onto anything that could stop her fall. She scrunches her eyes shut, bracing herself for impact, but before she lands, she feels an arm band around her waist.

Instead of hitting the ground, she simply stops, hair hanging down around her face and breath wheezing out of her lungs. Everly opens her eyes slowly, sees a massive hand splayed out on the grass just inches beneath her face. The moment stretches, time warping around her. She haltingly turns her head, eyes tracing up the bulging arm to a shoulder, which is when her head can't turn any further and her hair blocks her from seeing more.

"You didn't really think I'd let you fall, did you?" Asim's voice rumbles in her ear. She gasps a breath, filling her starved lungs after the air was punched out of them from his arm clamping around her. That's when she notices his chest is pressed to her back, and he's holding her horizontal against him. His breath gusts through her hair and Everly shivers, tingles cutting down her spine. Asim rolls so he's lying under her, his back in the grass with her looking down at his face instead of his hand.

He's wearing that boyish grin she loves, eyes twinkling with laugh lines creasing around them. His arm is now around her waist, holding her chest tight to his, his heart hammering against hers. Asim's smile slowly fades as his eyes roam her face and neck.

"You okay?" he asks, his hand coming up to smooth the hair back from her cheek.

"I'm good." Everly smiles at him, then looks down at her shirt between them. Her eyes widen when she sees that her light yellow shirt is now transparent, the comfy bra she's wearing underneath clearly visible. It's nothing super sexy (because yard work), but it's also much less than a typical sports bra since those always feel too confining to her. Her nipples are practically stabbing him through her wet clothes.

Asim's eyes follow hers and flare with desire. His hands drop to her hips and he rolls them again, putting her on her back underneath him. His weight on her feels incredible and Everly reaches up, running her hands along his arms and across his shoulders to link her fingers together behind his neck. Everly's breathing is heavy, her breasts grazing his chest with every inhale. She hasn't been this close to him in the daylight like this before, and her eyes are taking advantage, perusing every inch of his face so close to hers.

Her tongue sweeps across her bottom lip and Asim's eyes darken. She gives in to temptation, and pulls. He is an immovable object though, and she pulls herself up to him instead of what she intended, which was to yank his head down to hers. As soon as their lips touch, Everly doesn't care, and Asim gets sucked into her just as fiercely as she does him. His arms band underneath her as he props himself on his elbows, holding her off the grass with one hand splayed out between her shoulder blades and the other diving into her hair, angling her head and deepening the kiss.

When she hears herself moan into his mouth, the sound startles her back into the present moment and Everly remembers where they are. Lying on the grass, in her backyard. Although she would love to stay in this moment with him forever, she's pointedly aware of the fact that she has neighbors and does not want to be caught romping about in the yard, while soaking wet no less.

Noticing her change in demeanor, Asim pulls back and looks down at her, a slight crease in his eyebrows. Her eyes dart around, ensuring there are no nosy neighbors staring at them, and Asim catches on quickly. He stands, holding his hand out for her and lifting her to her feet. Everly attempts to brush herself off, as does Asim, but now that they've both been thoroughly watered the dirt just smears to mud across their skin and clothes.

"Well," Everly huffs. This was a fun idea in her head, and the cool water certainly feels good on her sweaty skin, but she hadn't accounted for what happens after the fact. She's also shocked that she didn't once think about how she's literally muddying up her pristine appearance, and even now that she realizes it, she doesn't particularly care.

"I suppose showers are in order," she says, glancing in his direction.

"I do need to water the upper plants, so they get settled in," Asim says. "Why don't you go shower while I finish up out here."

Everly doesn't mind that arrangement at all, though part of her does wish he would join her. She starts to turn away when he snares her wrist and tugs her back into his chest for a quick peck on the lips, then the tip of her nose, before spinning her around again toward the house.

Smiling, Everly steps inside and shivers as the cool air

hits her wet skin. Peeking out the window to ensure Asim can't see her from this angle, she strips off her wet and dirty clothes, leaving them in a pile by the hallway to the laundry room, then streaks up the stairs to her bathroom for a quick, lukewarm shower.

She puts on a clean pair of fuzzy socks, fresh panties and opts to skip the bra, instead donning a comfy, casual dress with a built-in shelf that she likes to lounge around in.

When she gets back downstairs, Asim has finished watering the newly planted garden and is coiling the hose up by the house. After sending him toward the guest bathroom with a fresh towel, Everly mixes a Manhattan with bourbon, wanting a slightly sweeter taste for herself than normal, and settles down on the couch in the living room to relax, leaning her head back and closing her eyes.

CHAPTER TWENTY

Another thing Everly hadn't accounted for was Asim not having any dry clothes to wear. He steps into the kitchen with a towel precariously wrapped around his waist, looking as though one quick turn would drop it to the floor. Everly's breath stutters and she pauses, having just been walking into the kitchen herself from the other direction, and eyes it with anticipation, brain screaming for the towel to do it. *Just let go.* Fall to the floor, it'll be more comfy there anyways. That towel doesn't even know what it has; it certainly can't appreciate it the way Everly could.

A throat clears above her, interrupting her silent argument with the towel, and Everly's eyes flash up to Asim's, her face already burning. He keeps catching her staring at him, and although it's embarrassing, she obviously doesn't care enough to learn a lesson from it. His mouth captures her attention next as it curves into a playful grin, and she licks her lip, remembering what it felt like to kiss him just a few minutes ago.

They snap out of it when a wet plop splits the air. Everly forgot she had her soaked clothes in her hands; she was on her way to put them in the washing machine when Asim walked in and her fingers ceased functioning. He looks down at the muddy mess and his smile grows wider. Bending down, he scoops them up and adds them to his pile, not at all bothered to be touching her wet, very dirty, clothing. Everly blinks in consternation; no one she knows would ever do anything that has happened to either of them so far today, except maybe Frankie who can be unpredictable at the best of times, and she's not sure what that means about her life.

"Washer?" he asks.

"Yeah," Everly's voice croaks, sounding more like a frog than a word, and she swallows hard. Waving him to follow her and taking the excuse to compose herself with some steady breathing, they walk to the laundry room and toss the whole wet mess in, then start a quick wash cycle.

Everly turns and eyes Asim up and down, he cocks one eyebrow at her.

"I don't think I have anything that will fit you," she says. "Except maybe my robe..." She trails off, imagining for a second him wearing her robe, which results in a very unladylike snort emanating from her nose as she tucks her lips into her teeth.

Now both of his brows go up. "What, you don't think I could pull it off?" he jokes.

"I mean..." Everly lets the sentence hang, silently challenging him.

"Let's see it then," Asim says, crossing his arms over his chest and jutting his chin back the way they came, indicating for her to lead the way.

Everly laughs, telling him to wait in the kitchen while she runs back upstairs to grab it. As she brings it back down, she schools her face into what she hopes is an innocent expression and passes it over to him.

"Turn around," he says, voice rumbling as one hand waits, resting on the towel.

Everly really doesn't want to, but she gives him the privacy he asks for. A moment later, she hears his "okay" letting her know he's changed. She takes in a breath as she slowly twists, intending to be a mature adult about this, but as soon as she gets an eyeful of him wearing her fluffy pink robe, she absolutely loses it. Everly's lips pinch shut for a split second before she snaps and howls her laughter, and Asim cracks up too.

"Yeah, I'm not sure this covers more than the towel," he says.

At six feet tall, he's got eight inches on her and at least a hundred pounds. He's taller, wider, and significantly thicker than she is. As a result, the long-sleeved pink robe that hits her just above the knees looks absolutely ludicrous on him. The shoulders don't fit, the sleeves only make it to the middle of his forearms, it barely ties closed around his hips, and it definitely hits above mid-thigh, hardly covering that ass she would so very much like to see.

Everly covers her mouth with both hands, attempting to stifle her laughter. Asim waves his hands in a circle at her, signaling she should get it all out now. He rolls his eyes, but his expression is all amusement. When she's able to compose herself, Everly wipes the tears from her eyes and beckons him over to the counter.

"Wow, sorry," she says. "I knew what I was getting into, but I didn't really know—" She flings her hand out at him, eyes jumping from one ridiculous view to the next, but she manages to stop the laughter before it can begin again.

"Luckily, my masculinity isn't threatened by a beautiful woman laughing at me for wearing a very pink robe." Asim jokes and Everly bites her lip while smiling back, silently agreeing with him. Too many men would have been offended by that reaction.

Everly offers him a drink, making her signature Manhattan for him as well and snagging hers from earlier. They meander into the living room while they wait for their clothes to finish in the wash, setting their drinks on the coffee table by the couch. Everly lights a candle and brown sugar, coconut and soft vanilla emanate through the room with a hint of charred wood. She inhales, letting the calming scents wash over her.

Asim lounges on the couch, and Everly makes to sit on the cushion next to his, intending to leave a polite amount of space between them on account of his awkward clothing situation, when he leans over and captures her hips, pulling her close and snuggling her in right next to him. Everly sighs, happy and content, warm and comfortable as she tucks her legs up underneath her and leans into his solid strength.

"Ever," he says, capturing her attention. "I really like you." Asim pauses, eyes searching hers. Everly swallows hard, but doesn't look away. "I haven't had a serious relationship in a while, but I want that with you. Whatever you want to call it—dating, boyfriend, I'll be anything you want me to be, but I want to be yours."

Everly stares. She forgets to blink, forgets to breathe,

forgets to think.

"Everly," he says her name again, stern this time as he tips her head so he can look at her more directly. She remembers how to blink, but the rest doesn't come back quite yet. "Don't panic. Take a breath. I think you feel the same way, but even if you don't, whatever you're feeling is okay. I don't want to put any pressure or expectations on you, but I do want you to know how I feel."

Taking a shaky breath, she looks away from his mesmerizing eyes so her brain can hopefully start to function again, and they catch on the soft pink color of the robe he's still wearing. Cracking up at the absurdity of the situation, of being told by a very attractive man in a very serious tone how much he likes her while said man is dressed in her tiny robe, she wraps her arms around her waist and folds herself over her knees in an attempt to contain the intense dichotomy of emotions going through her.

Is she laughing or crying right now? Hard to tell, probably both. It's like tossing boiling water into dry ice, or hearing a rooster call at bedtime. They just don't go together, and yet somehow that's her reality right now.

"It's the robe, isn't it? Kinda distorted the message a bit?" Asim says after she's started to catch her breath again, wry amusement lacing his tone.

"It's just," she pauses, unsure of how to put her chaotic feelings into words, "everything, I guess." It's a cop out, but she's beyond anything more at this point.

Everly takes a slow breath and feels him match her action. She turns inward and reflects on his words, realizing when he said whatever she's feeling is okay, that somehow those words penetrated her foggy brain when nothing else did. She does feel the same, and she wants him to be hers. She also wants to be his.

Everly looks back up at him.

"I want to be yours too," she says, and his entire being lights up.

He cups her face in his hands and leans down, gifting her with a tender kiss, then tucks her up against him again while he pulls his phone out and orders dinner to be delivered.

~~~
~~~

* * *

When the washing machine buzzer sounds, Asim untangles himself from her.

"Stay there, I'll toss everything in the dryer and be right back," he says.

Everly doesn't mind the view of him walking away, especially in that short robe. His taut thighs are on display, and her eyes run down his legs. Does he have to have amazing calves too? Everly scoffs, wondering if there is anything about this man that isn't attractive. Naturally, this leads to thoughts of what lies beneath the bathrobe, and she'd be willing to bet that's just as gorgeous and enticing as the rest of him.

She smoothes out her face when he returns, pretending she wasn't just thinking about the few parts of him not covered by the robe. Asim holds up two bags; their food arrived while he was changing the laundry. They unload box after box of food onto the coffee table and Everly turns skeptical eyes on Asim.

"Did you get one of each?" she says, eyebrows aiming for her hairline as she scans the plethora of Chinese take-out.

"I didn't know what you like, so... yeah, kinda." Asim scratches the back of his head, and Everly sighs at how adorable the bashful look is on him.

"Okay, well, I was kidding, but that's very sweet. Next time you could just ask, though." She pokes his ribs and he snatches her fingers, bringing them to his mouth and nibbling on her fingertips.

"Or I'll skip food altogether and taste you instead," he says, eyes darkening again as he intentionally flicks them down her body.

Everly's face heats and she splutters before turning away, pleased with his attention but unsure of how to respond to it. She continues her quest of unloading the entire restaurant onto the coffee table when Asim's arms come around her and he nibbles along her ear next, before pushing her hair to the side and nuzzling his nose into her neck.

"Is this okay?" he asks, lips moving against her skin, and Everly nods, not trusting that her voice won't sound like a frog again. She angles her head to give him better access.

"You wreck me, you know that?" His voice is low, suggestive.

"What do you mean?" Everly pauses again, tensing in anticipation against him.

"Everything you do turns me on, Ever." He growls, his husky voice a rough whisper against her ear. "When you blush, I want to strip your clothes off to see how far down your body it goes. Your beautiful eyes smoldering at me, your silken hair that I want to tangle my fingers in, that laugh. My god that laugh. I could be happy hearing only your laugh for the rest of my life. The way you throw yourself into things whole-heartedly with full dedication. And your body." He groans, readjusting himself behind her.

"I could keep going, but let's leave it at that for now, yeah? I've already nearly scared you away once today."

Everly's breathing is jagged, and she feels his deep inhale before he strokes her hair once, then pulls away. She doesn't know what to say because her brain is misfiring again, but she feels all those same things about him. His smile, his laugh, his stunning eyes and gentle soul. She wants to drown in him, but she doesn't know how to put it into words like he can.

Asim takes some sort of hint from the undoubtedly desperate look in her eyes.

"You need me to ask?" he says, referencing their conversation about her anxiety from the boat date. Everly nods.

"Do you like what I said? How I feel about you?"

"Yes," she whispers. "I do."

"And do you feel the same way about me?"

Everly bites her lip and nods again. "I really do, I just don't know how to say all those nice things like you did."

Asim doesn't seem to need that type of response though; he scoots around next to her, kisses her temple, then helps her dish out the food, sending a sideways smile her way as he does so. Everly's lips twitch up in response, and they dig in.

"So, crab rangoons are the winner here?" Asim asks a few minutes later.

Everly laughs. "I do love rangoons. Only if they have crab meat in them though, the plain cream cheese ones aren't worth the calories."

Asim squints at her when she mentions the calories, a spring roll hovering halfway to his mouth. Quickly she moves on, because that's not a conversation she wants to have with him tonight. She likes her body, but that doesn't mean she isn't mindful of what she puts in it. Most men just don't get it.

"What's your favorite?" she asks.

"I'm partial to egg rolls for an appetizer, but I love egg drop soup and a classic Kung Pao."

"What about your native foods?" Everly has been curious to learn more about his culture.

"Which are my favorites?" Asim clarifies and she nods, mouth full of rich peking duck. "That's an impossible question." He laughs, one hand flaring out like a stop-sign.

"If you haven't had Middle Eastern food, you probably won't recognize any of them," he warns, but Everly doesn't care. She wants to learn, so she looks at him patiently, eyebrows raised.

"Let's see, if I had to pick one it would probably be tepsi baytinijan, it's different depending on who makes it, but it's similar to a casserole crossed with stew. My mom's recipe has lamb meatballs and veggies, it's very good with the spices she adds. For sweet foods... that one's tough." He pauses, thinking. "Maybe daheen, or muhallebi. Daheen is textured, kind of like a fudgy cake, but flavored with dates and nuts, very sweet. I like it best with coconut on top. Muhallebi is a cold dessert. It's made with milk and sugar, like pudding with fruits or nuts on top. Zerde is good too, it's normally reserved for special occasions though."

"You have a sweet tooth?" Everly asks, laughing. She didn't picture him as the type of guy to enjoy sweets so much, but based on the sermon he just gave, he definitely does.

Asim grins back at her. "I always have. My mother used to despair that I'd never grow big and strong, but I don't think they held me back all that much." He gives himself a pointed look and raises an eyebrow at her questioningly.

"No, I don't think they did," Everly agrees.

They finish only a small portion of the food he ordered and when the clothes are dry, Asim gets dressed, returning her robe to her. He helps her pack up the leftovers and Everly insists he take some home with him, on account of the fact that there's no way she can eat that much food on her own in the next few days.

Asim treats her to a toe-curling good night kiss before he steps outside, waiting on the porch again until he hears the lock click behind him. Everly leans back against the door with a dreamy sigh, fingers touching her lips as though she can hold his kiss there forever.

CHAPTER TWENTY-ONE

Although the planting is finished, they still need to add the final touches to the terracing. Just as Everly wonders if she was supposed to reach out to him about the ground cover, his name pops up on her phone screen.

Her heart jumps, and she fumbles her phone, snatching it off the counter.

"He-hello?" Everly says, steadying the phone in her hand and leaning against the cabinets behind her, carding her fingers through her hair. Her stomach flips in an uncomfortable amalgamation of nerves and excitement.

"Hey, it's me." Asim's voice comes through short and surly, and Everly straightens, on alert. "I have some bad news… I don't think I'll make it to your place today."

"Oh. Kay." Her brows furrow, and her thoughts are ready to start spinning.

"I'm really sorry. I'd love to, but I've been neglecting some upkeep on the wiring in the shop and it's on the fritz even more than usual this morning. I really need to take a closer look and get it fixed up," he says.

"The wiring, right." Relief that he isn't ditching her washes through her, but she's also a little concerned he hasn't mentioned any issues like this before. "No problem, of course you have other things you need to do, I shouldn't have assumed. Just let me know when you have time again and we can figure it out."

Everly's voice rises in pitch the more she talks, until she sounds entirely unlike herself. Has she been taking up too much of his time? He's an entrepreneur, a business owner, and his job is much more hands on than hers. She hasn't once considered what that means for his responsibilities in light of the many hours he's been spending at her place, working on her project instead of his own. Everly starts to wonder if she's been unreasonably self centered, when he interrupts her thoughts.

"Everly," Asim says, his voice firm in her ear. "It's not a big deal, I've been happy to spend time with you and we'll get the terrace finished up before you know it, okay? This isn't on you. I'm the one who has been procrastinating over here."

She can practically see him—talking with his hands and the wry look on his face with those last words. Everly takes a calming breath, and nods. Then remembers they're not on video and he can't see her.

"Yeah," she says, "okay."

"Thanks, I owe you one," he says. "Let me know how I can make it up to you."

Everly cocks her head at that, her mind already racing with possibilities. She absolutely will.

~~~

Now that her day has opened up, Everly momentarily considers calling Addison, but then remembers how cranky she was at nine am and considering it's an hour earlier in San Diego than it is in Arizona, she decides to wait. She texts Frankie instead, asking if they want to meet up.

An hour later, they're walking out of Roasted, tightly covered travel mugs in hand. Frankie recently hired a couple of the local teens to help out—so they can take off and do other things during the day without having to close down and risk a violation—though it's just a matter of time before their nemesis comes up with something else to hassle them about. Frankie waves to the two teens through the front windows as they walk the few feet to Crooked Books next door.

Mrs. Langdon's head pops out from behind multiple stacks of books on the counter when they step in, and she barks at them to leave their drinks by the door. Everly and Frankie exchange a glance, smothering their laughs at her snarky attitude.
~~~

"Yes, Mrs. Langdon," they sing-song in reply, and she narrows her eyes at them before letting out a 'hmph,' twitching her nose and disappearing behind the stacks again. Everly and Frankie view this as further evidence of her secret fondness for the two of them; they're fairly certain she'd have kicked out anyone else already and they haven't even stepped a toe off the welcome mat yet.

Leaving their drinks by the door, they both take a deep breath of the musty, papery book smell, tipping their noses up to the ceiling. When they realize what the other is doing, they pause and look at each other, laughing when they both say "jinx" at the same time, followed instantly by "you owe me a book!" in the same breath too.

Frankie cackles, and Everly shrugs.

"Sounds good to me," she says. "Pick out two, I owe you one anyways for neglecting you recently."

Frankie just grins before weaving their way to the back corner where Mrs. Langdon keeps all the raunchy pirate smut. Everly smiles and follows in their wake. She's not looking for anything in particular, but browsing a good bookstore is one of her favorite hobbies so she happily sets to looking around. They pull books off the shelves, snicker together at the lewd covers, ooh and aww at the cute ones, and create their own little corner of quiet chaos in the back of the store. They've learned to keep their voices down to avoid Mrs. Langdon's infamous wrath, so most of what they do and say is done in hushed whispers with exaggerated hand gestures and facial expressions to compensate.

"So how is business going?" Everly asks, her voice soft. "Has you-know-who made any more threats?"

"No, thank goodness. I ran into him at the store again last week, but he just gave me a nasty death glare." Frankie rolls their eyes.

"So you served him one right back, I assume." Everly smothers her giggle in the crook of her elbow, since she currently has books in both hands.

"Obviously, and you'll be proud to hear I've only closed during "regular business hours" twice since we last talked about it." Frankie tucks a book under their arm and uses their fingers to make air quotes around the words, clearly displaying their ongoing skepticism regarding the concept of regular business hours.

"That's actually very impressive for you!" Everly whisper shouts.

Frankie snorts, and Mrs. Langdon rounds the shelves, eyes already slitted like she was just waiting for them to do something wrong. She eyes them both up and down, and Everly freezes, looking at Frankie from the corner of her eye to be sure neither of them are breaking any rules at the moment.

Mrs. Langdon lets out a loud sniff as she shuffles past them to the back room. They don't move for a few seconds, waiting until they no longer hear her footsteps, then they turn to each other at the same time, Everly's wide eyes meeting Frankie's.

"Close one," Everly mouths to Frankie, and they nod, hunching their shoulders and pretending to shrink in on themself.

They go back to browsing, picking out a couple books each. There's no sign of the cats, much to Everly's disappointment. She's not holding onto the idea of getting a pet quite as strongly as she was before, but she does like to see Luna and Harriet, and was hoping Luna would let Everly pet her again. Everly keeps her eyes peeled for a flicking tail or bright eyes as they meander up to the counter, but no luck on the cat front today.

Mrs. Langdon meets them there, eyeing the books they both place gently in front of her. Everly could swear she catches a glimpse of an upward lip twitch when Mrs. Langdon sees Frankie's choices, but it comes and goes so fast she can't be sure.

Everly pays for all of them, insisting on it when Frankie protests, and Mrs. Langdon slides them into a paper bag. They thank her, and Everly is even more certain this time of the sparkle in her eyes, but her voice is gruff when she tells them to "Be on your way then, I've got enough to do putting your mess back together." while shooing them out the door.

"She *loves* us," Frankie says, as soon as they scoop up their drinks and step outside.

Everly throws her head back and laughs. "The only things Mrs. Langdon loves are her books and her cats."

"No way, did you see, she smiled at me!" Frankie's eyes are alight and they throw their hands out as they talk. "And I left the romance corner a mess on purpose. I knew that old bat was spying on us and I wanted to see if she'd be mad. She totally wasn't."

"She absolutely was, you're delusional." Everly can't stop laughing. "I did see a hint of a smile though, so you've got me there."

Frankie smirks and they come to a stop outside Roasted. Everly opens the bag on her arm and passes Frankie's books to them.

"Come over soon? I want to show you the terracing," Everly says.

"You tell me when and I'll be there."

Hugging her friend a quick goodbye, Everly veers toward the park along the river, intent on starting one of her new books.

~~~

She's just finishing up the first chapter, already hooked by the thrill of a mysterious death and hints of a cult, when her phone buzzes with a text. Everly opens it to see a picture of Moose giving serious puppy eyes, with a hole in the wall behind him full of wires and tools.

Asim: Moose isn't nearly as fun to work with as
    you are.

Everly: Awww, he looks like he really wants to
    help though!

Asim: More like he wants to eat. You'd think I
    never feed him, the way he begs.
Asim: How has your day been?

Everly: Good. I met up with Frankie and we
    went book shopping.

Everly snaps a quick picture of her book stack
    with the river in the background and sends it
    to him.

* * *
~~~

Asim: Not quite the view I was hoping for, but
    still looks nice.

Before she can second guess herself, Everly picks up the
book she was reading and opens it, angling it in front of
her face with just her eyes peeking out over the top and
snapping a couple selfies, then sorting through for the
best one and sending it to him.

Everly: Better?

Asim: Better...

She can practically hear the growl in his voice and she
smirks to herself, surprised she isn't feeling more upset
that he had to cancel their plans. Maybe she didn't react
more strongly because he has a valid reason. Whatever it
is, she's grateful today is turning out to be a pretty good
day, despite the last minute change.

Everly: How's the wiring?

Asim: Frustrating. I think I've got it but I might
    need to hire someone to come take a look if
    this doesn't fix it. It'll be at least a couple
    more hours before it's good enough for now
    though, if I'm lucky.

Everly: I wish there was something I could do to
    help.

Asim: Chatting with you is enough, and seeing
    my favorite brown eyes has already
    brightened my day. You're perfect.

Everly blushes, glad she could do something to brighten
his day too. He returns to work and she returns to her
book, reading for another half hour before packing up
and heading home. Everly walked downtown from her
house to meet Frankie earlier, so she walks the paved
trail along the river before cutting through downtown

again toward her place. She hasn't had a day to relax and enjoy herself like this in ages.

As she walks, she reflects on how her body feels lighter, like a weight has been lifted from it. She takes in the blue sky above her, the chatter of birds in the trees, and tips her face up to feel the sun on her skin. Placing one foot in front of the other, she takes slow breaths, savoring the sense of peace and contentment in her soul.

Everly decides now is as good a time as any to try Addison, so she gives her a call and it connects after the second ring.

"Hey, sis," Addison says.

"Hi," Everly smiles, marveling that this is her life now. "How are you?"

"Bleh." Addison makes a noise similar to a cat spitting up a hairball, and Everly recoils from her phone in disgust.

"What... what?" Everly says.

"Just, you know. Life! It's happening, and I'm not loving it at the moment."

"What's going on? I thought things were good last time we talked." Everly looks around in confusion, as though the manicured lawns surrounding her are privy to Addison's secrets.

"It'd be easier to tell you what isn't going wrong," Addison mumbles, sounding forlorn. "Work is stupid, girls are dumb, boys are dumber, and my favorite fish died!"

"You have a favorite fish?"

"Had. I *had* a favorite fish. I no longer do. Because it's dead," Addison says.

"Right, I'm sorry." Realizing she stopped walking at some point, Everly shakes her head and pointedly starts moving her feet forward again. "Uh, do you have... other fish?"

"No. It was a betta fish. They don't like other fish."

"Oh, um." Everly is at a loss. This is new territory for them and she isn't sure what Addison needs or wants from her. "Do you want to talk about it?"

Those must have been the magic words, because Addison goes off. Everly does her best to listen, but she has a hard time following along with the many names Addison is throwing out. Apparently there's drama between some co-workers and her boss which is making her life infinitely harder at work, as well as some sort of love triangle that happened with a girl she was most recently dating (Everly wonders if this is the one Addison broke up with right before Christmas) and a boy she dated before the girl (maybe?) and Everly has never been so grateful to see her driveway and the comfort of home.

She tries to interject the appropriate "hmm" and "oh my gosh" and "no" responses, and that seems to be all Addison needs at the moment. Everly props her phone against her shoulder as she unlocks the door, then drops her keys on the table in the foyer and grabs water from the fridge.

Finally, Addison takes a breath.

"Wow, that's a lot," Everly says.

"I know, right?!" Addison sighs, fuzzing the line for a moment.

"So, this girl, she's the one you broke up with before Christmas?" Everly asks, tentatively dipping her toes into what might be dangerous waters.

"Yeah, to be honest that whole debacle is why I needed to get away. I spent the last two Christmases with Sabrina and her family and it was amazing, but when I caught her cheating with my other ex... I just couldn't face the idea of being alone for the holidays, you know? Then on top of it, Benji had to get involved and start talking to me again too, as if I had any desire to hear from him when he knew Sabrina and I were together the whole time he was sleeping with her. Ugh. I couldn't deal with them going behind my back like that, and apparently they're on again/off again now and they both keep reaching out to me and yeah. It's just too much." Addison pauses for a breath again, and Everly can practically feel the dejection seeping through her phone. "Sorry to unload all of that on you, you probably didn't even follow half of it."

"That's okay, I'm glad you told me anyway. I want to be there for you Ad, and yeah, it sounds like way too much for one person to deal with. I can't believe you've been carrying that around this whole time." She thinks she hears a sniffle, but doesn't want to call her sister out on it if she's crying. "Is there anything I can do? You need me to come out there and beat somebody up?"

Addison lets out a weak, watery laugh, confirming Everly's suspicion. "You think you could beat someone up?"

"Hey! I'm tough," Everly says, flexing her arm and pretending to feel more indignant than she really does in hopes of getting another laugh out of her sister.

"Oh, I know you're tough. Tough doesn't mean you have any sort of skill for punching someone though," Addison says.

"Okay fair point. I could still come out though, if you want me to."

Although her voice is tentative, the thought is sincere. She would fly out there in a heartbeat if Addison asked her, but she isn't sure if they're at a point where it's okay to offer that kind of support. Everly doesn't want to come off too strong and scare Addison away from confiding in her in the future.

"No, you don't need to. I'm okay, I think I just needed to get it all out."

"The offer stands, if you change your mind."

"How are things with you? Are you done with the landscaping? How's Asim?" Addison fires questions at her, and Everly allows her sister to change the subject.

"Good, actually. We were supposed to finish up today, but he had to take care of some other stuff at the greenhouse."

Everly updates her on all things gardening, Asim, their date, and moving forward. Addison squeals when she hears about the romantic river boat dinner, and asks if they have another date planned. This gives Everly an idea, and as soon as they end the call, she follows up on it.

Everly: I know how you can pay me back for
    today.

Asim: Name it and it's yours.

Everly: Valentine's Day. I'd like a second date.
    On the motorcycle this time.

Asim: I'll pick you up at 7

* * *

She closes her phone, face stuck in a smile that may well be permanent at this point. Valentine's Day isn't far off; she has just under a week to prepare. Everly feels unexpectedly proud of herself for going for it and texting him like that, not letting herself doubt or second guess her decision.

She wanted a second date, and now she has it.

CHAPTER TWENTY-TWO

"Your ass could not look better if you paid for it." Frankie's voice echoes through the room from the laptop on Everly's bed where she has them on a video call while she gets ready for her date with Asim.

"You don't think the heels are too much? Maybe sneakers would be better." Everly eyes the black ankle boots she's wearing. They're sexy as hell, with pointed metal toes and a sleek silver metal heel, but she's not sure how smart it is to wear them on a motorcycle. Not to mention, this entire outfit is... a lot.

"They make the outfit. If you take them off I won't speak to you for a week," Frankie says. "And leave that zipper where it is!"

Everly glances at her laptop as she releases the jacket zipper she was about to adjust, seeing Frankie fanning themself dramatically and making an "O" face. Rolling her eyes, Everly fixes the bottoms of her jeans, tucking the ends into her boots, then leans over the bed to the laptop.

"Bye!" Everly hangs up on Frankie's cackling, having had enough of the peanut gallery, and walks back to the full-length mirror.

She twists and turns, running her hands down her sides. She's paired the dark jeans and boots with a black leather jacket, zipped up halfway over a semi-sheer floral black lace bodysuit. Her cleavage looks incredible peeking out above the zipper, and she isn't ashamed to admit she can't wait for Asim to see her outfit. She's never worn anything like it before, and although it's nerve wracking, it also feels good. Old Anxious Everly would have worn a simple but elegant sweater, maybe cashmere, something sophisticated and expensive. But this Everly, the Everly she's discovering, wants to be more daring. She wants to wear lace, and leather, and dark red lipstick. She wants to take risks, and Asim is the person she wants to do those things with.

Everly feels free to be herself with him, and she giggles when she thinks about the fuzzy red socks she has on inside the boots. If they're going out at night, she doesn't want her feet to get cold. She may also be secretly hoping they lose their clothes at some point tonight and he discovers them in the process. Everly needs his laugh like she needs to breathe.

Right on time, the rumble of his bike rounding the corner onto Poinsettia Lane reaches her ears. Everly flips off the kitchen and foyer lights, then steps outside, fingers trembling with excitement and nerves as she locks the ornate wooden door behind her. When she turns around, Asim already has his helmet off and was very clearly staring at her backside. Frankie was most definitely right.

She clears her throat, and his eyes jump up to hers. Everly smirks at him and cocks her hip, hand on her waist, relishing this moment as she turns the tables on him.

Asim swipes a hand down his face, seeming to be lost for words. Then he chuckles, acknowledging that she caught him, and swings his leg over the bike.

"You clearly already know this, but just in case," he says, prowling up to her, "you are stunning, Ever."

Before she can respond, he leans down and places a sweet kiss on her lips. Everly grins as he pulls away, and Asim turns back to the bike. He flips open the storage compartment, pulling out a second helmet. It's a deep, rich red color, matte instead of shiny, with a charcoal visor. Darker than wine, it's a near perfect match for the color of her lips tonight.

Everly loves it.

"Did you get this for me?!" she gasps.

"Of course. I can't have you riding without a helmet," he says. "And I'm glad to see you're wearing leather and denim too, good choices if you're going to be on a bike, even if they are designed to torture me." He gifts her one of his playful winks, and she bites her lip as the grin threatens to take over her face.

Asim fits the helmet over her hair and secures it in place. Stepping back, his gaze fires along her skin. It's a thrum through her blood as his eyes sweep up and down her body, and he lets out a soft whistle.

"You just might be the death of me." His voice is low and gravely, hands fisted at his sides. Flexing his fingers, he pulls leather gloves from his back pocket and focuses intently on putting them on before bracing himself and turning back to her.

"Ready?" he asks.

Everly nods, her tongue stuck to the roof of her mouth.

Asim straddles the bike to stabilize it and offers her a hand to hop on behind him.

"Snuggle in close," he says, pulling her arms tight around his waist. "Hold tight, lean into the turns with me, and if you would like to stop, tap my side three times."

Everly listens intently, committing everything to memory. Secretly she's always wanted to ride a motorcycle, but her parents would never have approved, and she hasn't had an opportunity before now.

As she settles onto the seat, his heated palm meets her right calf and he guides her foot into place, pausing for a moment as his gaze snags on the image of her booted foot on his bike, then he does the same with her left. Everly's stomach tightens as she imagines his hands traveling further up her legs.

Unfortunately, he lets go instead.

Asim secures his own helmet, then reaches for her hands on his waist, pulling them more tightly around him so her breasts are pressed into his back, not even an inch of space between them. He pats her hands, indicating she should keep them there, and Everly gulps, her blood thrumming with nervous excitement.

Asim kicks the stand up and starts the bike with a thundering growl before it tapers off to a steady purr that shoots through her body. For once, Everly's grateful for the obnoxious sound, because it covers her gasp of surprise.

She knew it was coming of course, but she didn't

expect the vibrations. Everly was already feeling flustered; between Asim's hands on her and how confidently sexy he is sitting on the bike, she's feeling more than a little aroused. Add the steady vibration running straight up between her legs and she's about to completely lose her mind, and they haven't even left the driveway yet.

Asim angles his head over his shoulder, and although she can't see his face through his helmet, she knows he's asking if she's ready. She nods her head against his back and he pats her hands once more, then twists the throttle.

Everly inadvertently squeezes a little tighter as they take off and she feels him chuckle against her. She's already grinning too though, and as they twist and turn out of her neighborhood to the more deserted back country roads, Asim starts to pick up speed. Everly clutches his jacket in her fists, arms wrapped tightly around him. A giddy laugh is bubbling up in her chest and instead of holding it in, she lets it belt out of her, throwing her delight to the darkening sky above them.

Asim ups the speed when he hears her and Everly shrieks with glee. She has not felt this alive in years, maybe ever, and she's determined to embrace every moment. Everly isn't paying any attention to where they're going, instead she focuses entirely on the live wire that is her body right now.

She's electric and invincible.

All too soon, the bike starts to slow and she opens her eyes, not aware until that moment that she had closed them. Everly looks around, seeing no buildings or vehicles or any hints of humanity at all, and she has absolutely no idea where they are. She braces for the anxiety to set in, but it doesn't come.

Asim parks off the dirt road near some large boulders and kills the engine. She loosens her hold on him with a sigh as he pops his helmet off before gently shifting her feet to the ground on either side of the bike. Everly isn't sure she can move on her own; the vibrations felt good initially but now her whole body feels like jelly and her legs are almost numb. Asim twists toward her and she shrugs her helplessness, flailing her arms at her sides in emphasis.

Chuckling, he places a steadying hand on her shoulder and swings himself off first, keeping his hip against the bike to steady it, then turns and circles her waist with his hands, lifting her clean off the seat and standing her in front of him. He wraps one arm around her, and loosens her helmet with the other. Everly reaches up to pull it off, shaking her hair out as she does so and eliciting a groan from Asim.

"You're really trying to do me in tonight, aren't you?"

"I could say the same to you," she grumbles in return, biting her tongue and pinching her lips to hold in her smile at the crooked grin on his face as she hooks her helmet on the handlebar.

"Cheeky little thing," Asim says under his breath.

"So where are we?" she asks.

"About thirty minutes northeast of town."

"And we're doing what out here, exactly?"

Asim smoothes her flyaway hairs, then turns back to the bike. He's so casually tactile, it's a new experience for her and she revels in it.

Everly hadn't noticed the extra bags on either side of her seat when they set off, but now he starts pulling out one thing after another and she's beginning to suspect he managed to somehow replicate the Undetectable Extension Charm Hermione used on her handbag. He passes her a woven Mexican blanket, two metal mugs, and a large insulated water bottle. From the other side, he pulls out a cooler bag and a couple other random things that she can't see clearly in the dim evening light.

She learns soon enough one is a collapsible solar powered lantern. It gives off a soft glow when Asim expands it, and he holds it up as he walks toward the large boulders a few feet away, setting it on top of one so it lights the area around them. Asim sets everything down, then gestures for the blanket, spreading it out next to the boulders. It's then that Everly notices this area specifically is cleared of brush and debris.

"Did you... You planned all this," she says, a touch of wonder in her voice.

"I did." Asim glances at her, seeming almost nervous.

"That's really sweet," she says softly.

No one has ever put this much effort into a date for her before. She knows he's busy too, so she can't imagine when he found the time to drive out here and clean up this spot for them.

Asim's cheeks puff as he blows up an inflatable pillow, which he props against the large rock. He toes off his boots and lowers himself to the blanket, offering her a hand down as well, then unpacks the cooler. Sliced meats, cheeses, fruits, honey, nuts, crackers, and a salad are displayed in front of her. He takes a paper plate and tops it with a bit of everything, then passes it over to her with a napkin and fork, before turning to the water bottle.

He pours hot chocolate into the two camp mugs, then raises an eyebrow in question while holding up a hip flask. She shrugs with a smile, nodding her consent as he adds a splash into each and passes one of the mugs to her. Everly takes it with wide eyes, speechless as he proceeds to drop some marshmallows on top. No one has ever come close to doing something like this for her before. She's dreamed of a romantic picnic, sure, but never has she thought it would be a reality. This is the kind of thing that only happens in movies.

Sniffing her mug, she notes hints of coffee and Irish cream, and she closes her eyes in appreciation as she inhales the comforting scent, cupping the warm mug between her palms.

Asim leans back against the pillow, setting his plate and mug next to him, then spreads his legs and carefully maneuvers her between them with her side to his front. He shifts and angles her slightly, then picks up his mug and taps it to hers.

"To a night to remember, my darling Ever," he says.

"A night to remember," she whispers.

~~~

When she's eaten her fill and their charcuterie board is nothing but scraps, Everly sits closer and Asim holds an arm out. Everly tucks herself against his side and leans her head back on his shoulder to look up at the stars.

"So beautiful," she says, staring at the Milky Way glimmering above them.

"Stunning," he murmurs into her hair.

Everly peeks at him through her eyelashes, seeing he's
~~~

already looking at her, and the breath whooshes from her chest at the naked desire in his eyes. They've each only had one drink; she feels drunk anyways.

It's him. Having his full attention is dizzying and addicting.

Everly turns in his arms and he lifts her, readjusting her legs to fall on either side of his hips as her arms snake around his neck. They pause for a moment, breathing each other's air, eyes flitting up and down, the tension building until Everly isn't sure who moves first. One second she's staring into his green eyes, pupils blown wide, and the next he's devouring her. She loses herself in his lips, the feel of his tongue stroking hers, his stubble rasping against her skin as he kisses along her jaw and down her neck.

Asim's hands move from her waist to her hips, and he rocks forward while pulling her harder into him. Everly gasps at the sensation, clenching her hands in his hair and as his hardness presses against the seam of her jeans, right where she wants it. His mouth comes back up to cover hers as he obliterates any lingering thoughts in her head.

He pulls away too soon and an involuntary whimper comes out of her mouth at the loss of contact. Asim smoothes a hand up her back and hushes her.

"Shhh, my darling, I'm not going anywhere," he whispers into her neck, lips grazing her skin as he readjusts their position.

He leans to the side and flips her onto her back, snagging the pillow from behind him and sliding it under her head as he follows her down, settling his weight between her legs. Everly arches up into him, greedy for more of his drugging kisses, but he places a firm hand on her chest as he looks down at her before he moves his fingers to toy with the zipper of her leather jacket.

"Yes," she says, nodding in emphasis, and he unzips it slowly, eyes searing into every inch as he bares her breasts and midriff. She's only wearing the black lace bodysuit under the jacket, and Asim groans as his eyes devour her, sending a flood of heat to her core. Her nipples are visible beneath the lace, and he palms her breast with one hand, pinching her pebbled nipple through the fabric and she arches into his touch again as they harden even more. Their bodies are tangled together, one leg entwined between his, her other hitched around his hips and as she shifts against him, she can feel the hard bulge pressing against her inner thigh.

"I have to taste you." He barely gets the words out before his tongue curls around her peaked nipple. She twists her fingers into his hair, pulling him even closer while grinding against him. His mouth closes over her, teeth scraping, and she moans into her arm, biting down in an attempt to stifle the embarrassing sounds.

"Let me hear you," he growls. "Don't hide from me."

Everly looks down her body and meets his smoldering eyes as he moves to the other breast, then gently bites down. She doesn't hide this time, she sings her pleasure to the stars above.

~~~

His fingers are magic. His tongue and mouth are divine. Everly can only imagine what it will feel like to finally have all of him, but before she can move things in that direction, Asim puts a stop to it.

"Not here," he says, stilling her hands as she reaches for his zipper. "When I finally have you, it won't be on the side of a road. It'll be in a bed where I can take my time, and not worry about you being cold, or uncomfortable, or anxious. Where I can easily get anything you might need or want, and you won't have to think about one single thing except the pleasure I wring from your tight little body."

Everly's eyes widen, her skin flushes hot from her ears to her curling toes, and her head stutters a nod up at him.

"Can we do that now?" she says, her voice husky with want, lower than she has ever heard it.

Asim chuckles. "Let's get this picked up and we can head back, then you let me know how you feel."

He doesn't move off of her yet though. Instead, he strokes his fingers down her lightly, almost like he's petting her. He touches her face, her hair, down her neck and across her breasts, memorizing every inch he can reach through touch. Everly's skin breaks out in
~~~

goosebumps all over again and she groans dramatically.

"You have to stop touching me if you're going to make me wait," she complains, and one side of his mouth quirks up.

"You're just so touchable, I can't help it." His voice is soft and tender, bathing her in warmth. "Let's go then."

Asim rises fluidly to his feet and Everly gapes at him. She has no idea how he can be so graceful and move that easily after lying on the desert ground for what felt like an entire lifetime. She holds both hands up and waves them at him in a silent request for assistance. He obliges, grasping her forearms and effortlessly lifting her to her feet. His eyes twinkle at her beneath thick lashes and it takes every ounce of willpower she possesses not to lean into him for another kiss.

She steps back and looks around, taking stock of the situation, then starts collecting their trash. Before she knows it, everything is back on the bike, she has her helmet on, and her arms are wrapped around Asim's waist again.

Everly eagerly presses her body into his this time, wiggling to get as close as she can and hugging his legs with hers in anticipation. Asim smiles at her over his shoulder before pulling his helmet on, then he checks her feet, squeezing each calf in turn, and finally taps her hands again in warning before they take off into the night.

CHAPTER TWENTY-THREE

They get back later than she expects, and as much as she wants to finish what they started in the desert, Everly can't stop the massive yawn that threatens to unhinge her jaw right as she takes her helmet off. Asim catches it, of course, and quirks a tender smile.

"I think maybe we should call it a night here," he says.

Everly frowns, and he glides his hand down her hair to her waist, tugging her into him.

"Remember what I said?" He breathes the words into her ear, and the skin on her neck breaks out in goose-bumps. "I want to take my time with you. I promise to make it worth the wait."

Asim cups her face in his hands as he pulls back, a moment and an eternity passing as they get lost in each other's eyes. When Everly blinks, slow and lazy, he seems to pull out of whatever haze they've fallen into. Asim leans forward and softly kisses her forehead, then pulls her into the coziest hug she has ever received, tucking her head under his chin and holding her close.

"I had an amazing night, Ever." His voice rumbles under her ear.

She smiles and closes her eyes, nuzzling her face into his chest and trying not to be too obvious as she inhales his earthy scent.

"Thank you for coercing me into a second date," he says.

"Hey!" she protests, her eyes popping open as she smacks the middle of his back lightly.

He chuckles and places a quick kiss on her nose.

"I'm kidding. If you hadn't asked, I would have. I'm

glad you feel safe enough to tell me what you want though, that feels really good, having your trust in that way," Asim reassures her.

He's giving more weight to the vowels again, drawing them out so they dance like a caress across her skin as he speaks.

Everly feels like a helium balloon. So full of light and happiness that she might pop or float away at any moment as they say their goodnights.

She drifts up the stairs to the shower after watching Asim drive away, her heart fluttering in her chest.

~~~

A looming stack of paperwork waits for her at the Sioria the next day and Everly meets it with a grimace, annoyed that most of her job is simply signing her name next to yellow arrow sticky tabs. She checks in with her assistant as well as the managers who report directly to her, but everyone appears happy and everything seems to be running smoothly, so she's not needed for more than a few hours that day. Normally she would find more to do, putter around and make herself useful.

Leaning back, she spins her chair around to face the gorgeous view out over the river. Everly studies the hilly landscape with massive boulders along the water and pockets of greenery and trees here and there, but largely covered in cacti and smaller brush. It's at the tail end of the rainy season, which means everything will be blooming soon if it's not already. It's one of her favorite times of the year, when the desert turns green and colorful and everything is so alive.

As she enjoys the desert view, swinging her chair back and forth with her feet, Everly's mind wanders to the night before. She marvels at how comfortable the date was, even though every single thing was a new experience. From what she chose to wear, to riding a motorcycle and being lost in the desert, to the snack picnic and frenzied making out.

It felt like she was in high school again—if she hadn't been a perfect goody-two-shoes, straight-A student who never stepped a toe out of line and wasn't way too shy to let herself feel so openly like that. The most she ever did
~~~

in high school was some very PG-13 kissing after prom.

Her parents were always emphasizing how important it is to maintain the proper image, that you never know who might be watching, and it became so ingrained into her psyche that Everly can't remember a time when it wasn't at the front of her mind. She loved her parents, still does even though they're gone, but looking back she can admit that wasn't the most healthy way of parenting two daughters.

Reflecting on last night, Everly can't think of even one instance when she was worried that someone might see her. Carrie has explained how much of the way she was raised has impacted her view of herself, so Everly has a clear understanding on where much of her self-doubt and anxiety in social situations comes from. This is why she's so surprised at her behavior with Asim. She's been *literally* covered in dirt and mud, for crying out loud. It's unfathomable, out of character, and entirely amazing.

She feels more herself than she ever has before, in large part thanks to Asim's steady and soothing demeanor. It's a precious gift she never knew she was missing until now.

Everly thinks back to how Addison mentioned feeling like she can't truly be herself, that she doesn't know who she is. Everly is struck by a bolt of guilt, realizing she wasn't there for Addison when she probably most needed a big sister. Since Addison is a few years younger, her experience with their parents was different. Everly determines to make up for it now as best she can.

Checking her phone, she sees it's almost time for their video call. Addison had texted her that morning asking if they could schedule a time to talk, assuring it was nothing bad, but she wanted to chat face to face. Everly is a little nervous, having no idea what it's about, but knowing it isn't bad eases much of the anxiety she would have otherwise felt.

Her phone rings a few minutes later and she connects through her laptop. Everly smiles at her sister's face filling her computer screen. They make the usual small talk, chatting and laughing about the crazy trends they've seen online, what the youth are up to these days, random other small things, until Everly can't wait any longer.

"So what's the big deal? What did you want to talk

about?"

Addison looks down, and Everly gets the sense she's fidgeting with something out of sight.

"Whatever it is, you can tell me," she says, trying on what she hopes is a comforting, sisterly smile.

"Well, you remember how we talked about me coming back to visit again..." Addison trails off.

"Of course, I'd love that." In her head, Everly is already planning possible outings, including the spa, cocktails in hand, of course.

"Okay, cool. Well, yeah. That's what I wanted to talk to you about."

Everly tries to hide her confusion; her normally chipper, bubbly sister is acting odd in a way she can't quite figure out.

"Alright, did you want to check dates or something?" she asks.

"Sure, that'd be great." Addison's voice is still too high. They compare calendars, and Addison checks flights while they do so. They land on a weekend about a month away at the end of March, but something still feels off. Addison is avoiding the camera, and isn't nearly as talkative as she usually is.

"What's going on, Ad? You're worrying me," Everly says.

"It's just..." she trails off, taking a breath before looking up and starting again in a rush. "I was wondering if I could stay with you?" Her eyes flare wide and she drops them, looking back at her lap.

Everly realizes this was the hard part for her. Addison was worried about asking to stay at the house instead of the hotel.

"Of course! Please, stay with me! Of course you can, Ad. Oh this is going to be so fun." Addison's head snaps back up and a smile stretches across her face when she sees Everly's excitement.

"Yeah?" she asks.

"Hell yeah! I'd love that." The sisters are beaming at each other, excitement radiating through the screens, a beacon strengthening the connection between them.

"Okay, let's do it." Addison clicks around on her computer before turning back to Everly. "It's done. Flights are booked and car is rented."

"I can't wait. We can do all the girly stuff we never got to do..." Everly is the one to trail off this time, her face falling. Addison's smile falls too as they both realize what she was about to say.

"Ad. I'm really sorry," Everly says. "I'm so sorry I wasn't there for you. I regret it so much, I don't know what to say or how to make it up to you but I'm so incredibly sorry." Her eyes turn glassy with unshed tears. She wants her sister to understand, but there simply aren't words for it.

"It's okay, Ev," Addison says, her voice soft with aching sadness. "I'm sorry, too. It takes two, and neither of us reached out. I regret it, too. I missed you every day. We both lost mom and dad, but we also lost each other, and that hurt just as much."

Everly is nodding along with her, matching tears streaking down their cheeks. They feel like good tears, though. They're purging, renewing, making way for the healing and love that she senses is coming now that they've reconnected.

"I want to be there for you now, like a big sister should be."

"I want that too. From now on, we will always be there for each other, pinky promise." Addison gifts her a watery smile, and Everly does her best to return it. The guilt and remorse are still there; the regret and hurt aren't gone, but she senses the burden lightening.

"Thank you," Addison says, after a few beats of quiet. "I wish I could give you a hug."

Everly sobs a half snort, her emotions an absolute mess, and thankfully her nose was already covered by a tissue or she'd have snot on her keyboard.

"I wish I could hug you too," she says. "My therapist says we get some happy chemicals from hugging ourselves. Maybe if I give me a hug, and you give you a hug, we can still kind of be hugging each other?"

"Yes," Addison says, "I like that." She wraps her arms around herself and Everly follows suit, squeezing tightly and rocking herself back and forth.

When they let go, they both grab fresh tissues and swipe under their eyes.

"We are a mess." Addison laughs, pointing out some mascara that has somehow made it onto Everly's chin.

They clean up as best they can through the video.

"I'll have your room ready. It probably needs a clean," Everly says.

"Sounds good." Addison is smiling again. "Can't wait to see you in person again."

They hang up and Everly heaves a sigh to rule all sighs, tipping her head back against her chair and closing her eyes. She takes a moment to try to sort through her feelings, not having anticipated that emotional rollercoaster when she got up today. Letting out the emotions and thoughts that had been festering for the last eight years hurt, but it was also cathartic. She feels lighter, and with a pang of worry, she wonders how much lighter she can feel before she dissipates entirely.

Everly pushes that bizarre thought aside. Feeling lighter must be a good thing. She's heard it's a good thing, anyways, but figures this is another anxious thought to add to her list for Carrie. Between Addison and Asim, her emotions have been completely foreign the last few weeks, and although that's scary, it also feels good. She likes herself for the first time in years, and she's happy with the choices she's making with those around her.

Opening her eyes again, she checks her phone to see a message from Asim.

Asim: Hey, what would you like to do for the
    ground cover on the terracing? I have mulch,
    if that's what you want, but personally I
    think river rocks or even pea gravel would
    look nicer. Here are a couple examples.

Everly scans her eyes down and sees that he has attached a few images from landscaping websites and her heart swells, grateful for his thoughtfulness to include them so she doesn't have to google river rock or pea gravel. She swipes through the sample photos he linked before replying.

Everly: I think you're right, I like how the river
    rocks look. Would it be possible to do a
    couple bigger ones too? Like accent

boulders?

Asim: Yes, great idea. I'll reach out to my
    supplier and see what we can do.

Everly sends him a quick thanks and closes the text
thread, knowing he's at work and not wanting to distract
him further. She's taken up enough of his time lately.
She stands and stretches, rotating her shoulders and
craning her neck to release some of the tension from her
body before getting back to work on the stack of papers
that has somehow grown bigger in the last few hours
she's been there.
    To her surprise, she gets another text from Asim about
an hour later.

Asim: Good news - he has plenty in stock and
    can deliver it later this week. I asked him to
    bring some guys with him and get it laid out
    for you when they deliver. Our work is done!

Everly: Wow, that's awesome! Thanks! How
    should we celebrate?

Asim: I think we both know the answer to that...
    I'll confirm delivery for Friday then?

Everly: Sounds good. Thank you!

Asim: Happy to help, Ever. Talk to you soon
    winking emoji

Everly bites her lip, then her eyes crinkle, and then her
whole face smiles. She's really proud of the work they've
done together. Once the rocks are delivered, she wants to
have him over for a proper dinner date on the patio so
they can enjoy the fruits of their labor and take in the
beautiful new terracing—without being covered in dirt.
    Instead of getting back to work, Everly sets to
planning.

CHAPTER TWENTY-FOUR

The delivery guys—or rather, individuals, as there was also a well-muscled woman who lugged a boulder with surprising ease—have come and gone. The decorative rocks have been unloaded and spread evenly across both terraces, and Everly proudly snapped a picture of the finished project to send to Asim as soon as it was done, eager to share her joy with him.

That was two days ago.

She glances down at her phone for the hundredth time to see if Asim has replied yet. She's barely heard from him since they texted about the delivery, only a couple short replies here and there, and it's been radio silence for the last two days since she sent that picture. She assumes he's busy, but he hasn't even replied to the silly photo of the accent rock that reminds her of Moose, if you squint and tilt your head just right. She thought for sure that would get a reaction out of him.

Tapping the back of her phone with her index finger, she texts him again to check in, anxiety hounding her while she does her best not to give in to it. Bouncing her legs in anticipation, she looks through the steam over her mug of tea at Frankie working behind the counter of Roasted as she takes a sip.

Frankie senses her gaze and they quirk an eyebrow in her direction. Everly sends them a strained smile, lowering her mug to the worn wooden table in front of her, then looks back down at her phone. She tries to tell herself he's just busy, rationalizing the thought as best she can. The spring must be a busy time of year for plant related things, and he probably isn't ignoring her on purpose.

She pushes the worries out of her head as much as she can. Tonight she's having Frankie over for dinner and drinks, to show off her hard work. Whether her relationship with Asim ultimately works out or not, she is happy with the changes she has made in her life so far. These are the thoughts she's trying to hold on to and keep at the forefront when, for some reason, it feels like she's on the edge of something, like her life could change at any moment and she isn't sure if it would be for better or worse.

When closing time hits, she hops up from her seat, then pushes it under the table and snags a rag from behind the counter. She wipes down the tables and counters while Frankie closes out the register, having already dismissed their other worker for the day. Thankfully it's Sunday, so it's still light out when they lock up and head out.

As they stroll down the street, they pass by José, who tips his hat at her in greeting, and Everly blinks before smiling and nodding back at him, surprised he remembers her. To her consternation, Chantel, the owner of the cute little locally made shop who she also met while dropping off poinsettias, acknowledges Everly too. She's also closing up for the day and is just locking the door when they pass by and she smiles at the two of them, greeting them both by name.

Frankie gives Everly a strange, sideways look in response to these interactions, which Everly promptly ignores, because she has no idea what she would even say. Being recognized with friendly greetings around town isn't something she has much experience with. The two of them walk back to Everly's place, trading stories about their busy weeks and joking about a spicey romance book they both recently read.

When Everly dramatically flings open the back doors to the patio, leading Frankie out and throwing her arms wide with a theatrical "ta-dahhh", Frankie claps good-naturedly.

"Honestly, I can't believe you did any part of this," Frankie says, laughing as they walk down the steps next to the terracing and leaning over to smell the flowers. Their eyes are wide as they consider the new landscaping, and they truly look both surprised and impressed.

"I can't believe you doubted me," Everly says. When Frankie quirks an eyebrow and tips their head at her, she relents. "Okay same, I kind of can't believe I did this either, but it looks great, right?!"

"It really does. Looks amazing."

Everly lifts and drops her shoulders in a satisfied bounce, a small smile on her face.

"Want to order or cook?" she asks. Everly and Frankie have an unspoken agreement not to wait on each other. Either they cook together, helping out no matter whose place they're at, or they order in, and they always clean up together.

"Hmmm." Frankie meanders back up the stairs and plops into a patio chair. "I'm feeling pizza. Can we do pizza? Order or make, doesn't matter to me."

"Pizza sounds divine. Let me check what I have in the pantry, we may need to order."

Frankie nods their agreement, calling that they'll be in shortly as Everly tromps inside, poking through her cabinets and determining that no, she does not have even half the ingredients they'd need for homemade pizza, so she places an order to their local pizza joint.

"It'll be here in forty five," she calls out the door to Frankie.

"Perfect, how about a drink?" Frankie hops up and joins her inside, making their way to the kitchen and helping themself to her alcohol stash before the two settle out back on the patio again, bringing the whole bottle with them.

"So, I met this girl..." Frankie begins.

"Hold, please," Everly says. "I have a feeling I'm gonna need a refill for this story."

"That's for sure." Frankie drains their glass and holds it up for a refill too, before proceeding to tell Everly in excruciating detail about their latest love interest, who they went out with a few times, until it came to light that she was just "experimenting". Everly cringes, hiding behind her half-full glass while Frankie continues, telling her how in the middle of the last date, she decided the bisexual lifestyle wasn't for her after all. The dramatic exit sounds movie-worthy and Everly's heart aches for her friend.

Hours later, the pitcher plus two bottles of wine sit empty on the table, and neither one of them is able to stand up straight.

~~~

Everly wakes with a pounding headache and pats around her body in search of her phone. Finding it under her pillow, she squints her eyes in an effort to minimize the light beaming into her tortured retinas and taps it, then flips it over and looks at the back for some reason, not comprehending why the screen is remaining black.

Throwing it back down, she flings her arm over her eyes and groans.

"Aspirin," she croaks, and then nearly startles right off the side of the bed when she hears an answering groan from the floor next to her.

"Frankie?" she says. "You didn't go home?"

"Apparently not," Frankie mumbles, sounding like their face is buried in a pillow.

"Why are you down there?" Everly's brain isn't quite working yet, and she can't figure out why Frankie wouldn't have shared the bed with her like they've done on countless other sleepovers.

"How should I know."

Everly closes her eyes again, mind blank. Obviously, neither of them is vibing well with the concept of functioning right now.

"About that aspirin?" Frankie's voice is still muffled, and very cranky.

Everly doesn't blame them if they're feeling even half as bad as she is right now. She's absolutely never drinking again.

Everly heaves herself out of bed, stumbling to the bathroom with her eyes closed and hands outstretched in front of her, then fumbling in the medicine cabinet until she finds the right bottle. She shakes a few pills into her hand and dips her mouth under the faucet to suck up some water like a classless heathen, then brings the other two to Frankie, shooting them a glare when they tell her to shhh.

She wasn't even being loud.
~~~

Clearly, the alcohol was too much for both of them last night. Everly doesn't have the foggiest idea how they ended up in her bedroom, but it's better than waking up on the patio or couch. Hopefully Frankie isn't too stiff from the floor.

"Do you want me to call you a ride?" Everly whispers, picking her phone up again. She taps the screen, then remembers it's not turning on and flings it back down. "Dead. Never mind, you're on your own."

Everly turns back to the bathroom and strips out of her pajamas. By the time she steps out of the steamy shower and brushes the cottony gunk from her mouth, the aspirin has kicked in and she's feeling marginally better. She pulls on her robe after hesitating for a split second when reaching for it, trying her best not to think about Asim wearing it, and wanders downstairs for some tea. She hears the guest shower running, and Frankie walks out in a pair of her sweats a few minutes later.

"Coffee," they mutter, then flop onto a barstool at the counter and lay their head on their forearms.

Everly starts the coffee machine, having already prepared it in anticipation of the request. Frankie is the only reason she even has one; they can't function without their morning fix. Now would be a very bad time to not give Frankie their coffee.

When they've both recovered a bit and nibbled on some food, a slice of plain wheat bread for Everly, not even toasted, and cold, leftover pizza for Frankie, her friend breaks the silence.

"I know why I got hammered last night. Pretty sure I ranted to you about it for at least an hour. But why the hell did you drink so much?"

Everly knew it was coming. She still doesn't want to acknowledge it, though. Steam from her mug curls in front of her face as she takes a fortifying breath.

"I haven't heard from Asim."

"What does that even mean," Frankie says it as a statement rather than a question, their voice muffled by the hoodie sleeve from laying their head back down on their arms.

"I mean, he stopped texting me. He was short with me for a couple days, and then once the landscaping was done, he just ghosted me. I haven't heard anything since.”

“Wait, for real?” Frankie picks their head up and looks at her directly for the first time all morning.

“Yeah. For real.” Everly flattens her lips, eyes on her finger tracing the fine lines in the marble countertop in front of her. They look like cracks. It looks how her heart feels. “I don’t know what happened. Things were good. Great, I thought.”

“Nothing happened?”

“Nothing happened.”

“But... you two totally hit it off. I could tell. You didn’t talk to me for days. That has never happened, and then when I did see you... You were happy. Like. Happy, happy.” Frankie’s brows are furrowed.

Everly doesn’t reply. She doesn’t have anything to say. She was happy. She was really happy, and she fell for him. Hard.

“Is this real.” Again, Frankie says it as a statement rather than a question, almost accusatory.

“Yes,” Everly sighs, “unfortunately, this is very real.”

Frankie looks away and squints their eyes, staring into the distance. They sit in silence for an eternity, and Everly can no longer hold back the swirling thoughts.

She wonders if she did something to turn him off. She thinks back to all the time they spent together, inspecting every moment for a mistake, a misstep, something she said or did, or didn’t say or do that she should have. She even has the thought that it was because they didn’t sleep together, but she dismisses that one. That was entirely on him, not her. He was the one putting the brakes on when Everly was ready to strip him naked in the desert. That’s when the most mortifying thought so far crosses her mind. Maybe he didn’t want to sleep with her, or maybe he felt pressured. Now she’s wondering if she made him uncomfortable or if he thought she expected or wanted certain things he wasn’t willing or able to give. As the chaos starts to spin out of control, Frankie interrupts her inner turmoil.

“Nah. I don’t believe it,” Frankie says. It takes Everly a moment to catch up. She thinks for a second she had said her thoughts out loud, but then realizes Frankie is referring back to their earlier conversation. “Something must have happened.”

"Nothing happened. I've been spinning every moment over and over in my head, and I can't find anything. Nothing happened, Frankie."

"Not between you two," her friend says, exasperated Everly isn't somehow on the same wavelength as them. "I bet something happened on his end. Maybe a family thing, isn't he close with his family? Or something, there has to be *something*." Their words taper off, and Everly cocks her head.

She hadn't thought of that possibility. She can't think of anything she did wrong, so maybe she *didn't* do anything wrong. Enormous relief fills her lungs for the first time in days.

Maybe it's not her fault.

Then everything comes crashing down again, because if it's not something with her, or them, then it's something else. What could keep him from contacting her? It must be serious, and Everly's mind starts spiraling in a whole new direction. She jumps up from her seat and spears her fingers into her hair, still damp from the shower.

"Oh my god. Do you think he's okay? What if he's hurt? He could be in the hospital!" Everly's voice rises frantically, her pitch increasing and Frankie claps their hands over their ears.

"Ugh, Everly. Stop. My head." Frankie ignores her crisis and grabs their coffee, then stumbles to the couch in the adjoining room and curls up with a blanket.

Everly follows and rips it off, causing Frankie to growl and curl into a tighter ball.

"I'm serious, Frankie. You said it. Something happened. What if he's..." Everly can't say the words. She hasn't heard from him in days. What if he can't answer, or even worse, what if he's not answering because he's not around to do so anymore. Everly can't even think the words she's afraid of.

She flashes back to when she received the news her parents had been in an accident. It was the worst phone call of her life, and she still has nightmares about the voice, the words. Sometimes it's just a phone ringing and ringing and ringing and she knows what will be on the other end of it. She can almost hear it again now, and she stumbles, her back hitting the wall. She slides down it and her legs tangle in the stolen blanket puddled around her feet.

Everly doesn't know how long she sits there, eyes blank, staring into the void of her parents' funeral and the loneliness that took over in the days, weeks, months following. She isn't aware of anything, not her breathing, or her empty thoughts, or Frankie crouched in front of her gripping her hand.

It's just darkness, and ringing, and emptiness.

Gradually, she becomes aware of a hand stroking her arm. Everly blinks, takes a gasping breath.

"Hey, I'm here, you're okay," Frankie says, their hand tightening around hers. "Just breathe."

Everly breathes, sucking air into lungs that feel starved and panting it back out again. Her mind feels like it went from empty to overdrive, and she can't pick one single thought apart from the others.

"You told me once it helps to focus on one thing," Frankie says, their voice quiet and slow, eyes steady on hers. "How about you focus just on my voice for a sec, okay?"

Everly nods. Frankie's voice, she can do that.

"I'll just talk to you for a minute. You can focus on my voice, my words, and just listen. You don't have to do anything else." They speak slow and calm, and Everly's eyes start to refocus. "You're okay, we're here in your living room, with a blanket, sitting on the floor. You have a surprisingly plush rug, I've learned. We should sit down here more often."

Everly's lips twitch at the wry note in Frankie's voice.

"I know that was scary, but we don't know anything for sure. Don't get stuck in what ifs. What would Carrie tell you right now?" Frankie asks.

"She'd say..." Everly thinks for a moment about Carrie, and her thoughts start to slow and coalesce. "She'd tell me to use my senses."

"Your senses, okay," Frankie looks around. "Like, what you see?"

Everly nods. "I see you. The blanket." She reaches her free hand out and strokes the blanket, noticing how soft it is under her fingers. "It has a textured pattern on it. I see the hard floor, and the rug." She blinks up at Frankie.

"It's a nice rug."

Everly exhales sharply through her nose, almost a laugh.

"What else?" Frankie says.

Instead of answering, Everly leans forward and pulls them into a hug.

"Thank you," she mutters, cherishing Frankie's arms around her and their hand rubbing comforting circles on her back.

CHAPTER TWENTY-FIVE

When she feels like she can move again, Everly and Frankie clean up from the night before, finding empty glasses and bottles scattered throughout the kitchen, living room, and patio. Everly snags her phone off the charger, avoiding the fact that there are no missed calls or messages, and offers to drive Frankie back to their place across town.

Everly pulls into the driveway and shifts the car to park, sitting back in her seat with a sigh.

"What are you going to do?" Frankie asks.

"I don't know. I guess maybe I'll go to the greenhouse?" Everly's voice tips up at the end, not entirely sure if that's the right choice.

"I mean, stalking worked once, right?"

"Frankie! You're the worst," Everly says with a groan, but she can't help the stupid smile in response to her friend's jibe.

"Real though, you should go. Just swing by and check, then at least you'll feel better knowing. Whatever the outcome is, it's better to know," Frankie says.

"You're right. I know you're right."

"Say that again? Not sure I heard you."

Everly slaps their arm lightly and rolls her eyes. "Get out of my car."

Frankie cackles, then groans as it triggers their hangover headache, pulling the car door open and stumbling out with their hand shading their eyes.

"Good luck out there," Frankie says, then slowly shuffles their way to the front door and disappears inside.

Everly is left alone in her car, and she lets it idle in Frankie's driveway for a minute while she takes a moment to herself. She doesn't feel as terrible as she did a few hours ago, but she still doesn't feel great physically or mentally.

Despite that, she's determined to get some answers today. Everly works best off a solid plan, so she takes a few minutes to think about it. Her first step is to go home and change. Maybe also take some more pain killers, chug some water, and grab a bite to eat, if she can stomach it.

She thinks about the rest of her plan for going to the greenhouse while driving home, mentally fortifying herself for bad, worse, and *worst*.

~~~

Everly is idling in her car again, this time in her driveway instead of Frankie's. She's washed, changed clothes, and checked everything off her list, as well as a few random extra things, and there's nothing left to procrastinate with. It's now or never, but she can't get her hands and feet to work together properly to shift the car into drive.

She's been trying not to let the spiraling, negative thoughts take over, but that's nearly impossible at this point. Reflecting that the pounding in her head stopped over an hour ago, she decides if she can't block them out, she'll drown them out. Pulling out her phone, Everly connects to her car's bluetooth and pulls up her "dance" playlist, the one she mainly uses when cleaning. Blasting it as loud as she can stand, she inhales a fortifying breath and takes the plunge.

On the drive to Magnolia Nursery, she focuses entirely on the music. Singing along, belting out the lyrics, head bopping and shoulders shimmying, she is in absolute denial and avoidance of any negative, anxious thought that might try to pop into her head. It works perfectly, until it doesn't—the moment she turns onto his road.

Everly wonders why someone like Asim would want to be with her anyways. She's boring. She works in an office, has no hobbies besides reading and sitting at the coffee shop, and barely has a personality, unless you count crippling anxiety. Everly braces herself for the
~~~

likelihood that she will be dismissed, rejected, that he doesn't want to see her and doesn't care for her like she does him. Luckily, she manages to stay away from any thoughts more dire than that.

When Everly is close enough to see the greenhouse though, her mouth falls open and she gapes at the sight. Everything in her freezes, her body failing to respond to the signals her brain is sending, and she nearly sends the car careening off the side of the road. She overcorrects, wrenching the steering wheel the opposite direction, and a car behind her lays on the horn.

Everly makes it to the empty parking lot and parks haphazardly in the middle, her whole body trembling. Her mouth is dry, mind blank, and she feels like her heart fell out on the road and got ran over, twice. She can't even speak, she's just mouthing the word *"what"* over and over, trying to comprehend what she's seeing.

The building is gone. Glaring yellow caution tape surrounds what used to be the main sales area, the part of the building Asim lived above. All of it is gone. Instead, she's faced with charred rubble. Black, soot stained beams, piles of debris, and endless ash.

She can't fully grasp what she's seeing. Everly hesitantly turns the engine off and steps out, not even fully closing the car door behind her. How did she not hear about this? How did Frankie not hear about this and tell her? The rumor mill in their town is wild, and Everly is kicking herself for being such a recluse and hogging all of Frankie's time the last couple days. Maybe if she hadn't, she would have heard something and been here sooner.

She walks toward the remains, a few scorched beams still standing, one blackened wall along the back right corner, but the rest of the structure is crumbled and incinerated on the ground.

It smells like a bonfire, and she hates it. That's not how Magnolia Nursery is supposed to smell.

Realizing she's still gaping, Everly snaps her mouth closed and looks around, searching for Asim. She doesn't see him anywhere, but there's a canopy set up to the right side of the building's remains, a camp chair and folding table underneath it.

She convinces her feet to walk in that direction, heart

in her throat and dreading what or who she will find—and who she won't. As she gets closer, someone rounds the blackened corner, and her breath catches, moisture flooding her eyes.

Asim.

Everly freezes in place, afraid to move and shatter the image of him, alive and well. He's talking on the phone and hasn't seen her yet. She only catches snippets of what he's saying as he walks closer, eyes on the ground and one hand shoved into his hair. It sounds like maybe a claims or insurance company, something about the property and its value. When he hangs up, he walks under the canopy and drops his phone on the folding table, falling into the chair. She watches, a lump forming in her throat as he leans forward, forearms on his knees, hands clenching together with his head dropped low, and Everly's heart breaks.

She forces herself to step closer, when Moose, who she hadn't noticed lying tethered beneath the table, picks his head up and whines plaintively, his big brown eyes meeting hers. Asim's head snaps up, eyes finding her instantly, and time lurches forward. She rushes to him as he stands; she wants to run into his arms, but despite the relief radiating from him at seeing her, he seems unsure. Of what, she doesn't know, but it makes her hesitate.

Everly stops in front of him instead, just under the canopy overhang, and searches his face. His beard is longer than normal, unkempt, and his hair is disheveled, likely from constantly running his hands through it. There are dark circles under his eyes, but no cuts or burns. Her eyes scan him from head to toe, searching for hidden injuries.

Finding none, she releases the breath she was holding.

"You're okay." She breathes out, relief flooding her veins.

Asim clears his throat, swallowing hard before replying. "I'm okay." His voice is hoarse, and his eyes flick behind her to Moose. She turns, crouching down to see him under the table, and then gasps in shock, falling backward onto the ground.

"Oh my god," she cries. "Moose! Is he okay?! What happened?" She reaches a hand out, then pulls it back to her chest, afraid to touch him. "Asim, what happened?"

Everything is moving too fast now. Moose is lying on a bed of puppy training pee pads. His fur is patchy, and there are raw red areas of skin showing. His back left haunch is entirely bandaged, and now the tears do spill over. Sweet Moose, what happened to him?

Asim sits down on the ground next to her about a foot away, keeping his distance. She wants nothing more than to pull him close or crawl into his lap, but he's so closed off, giving her no signals, and she doesn't know how to read this situation.

"Asim?" Everly whispers.

He nods, resigned, and begins talking.

"Moose is okay." Asim's voice is scratchy and strained. "He was inside when the building caught fire, but I was able to get him out. He has some burns where something fell on him, and likely some areas his fur won't grow back, but overall he should make a full recovery."

Everly is so relieved to hear this, the tears resume again in earnest.

Then he tells her about the fire itself. Everly listens quietly as he tells her he lost everything in the main building, including most of his personal possessions from his living area upstairs. Luckily, the fire was contained quickly enough that it didn't spread to any of the greenhouses, and the majority of the plants are okay.

She's glad he's updating her, but he isn't telling her any of what she wants to know. Where has he been staying? Is he really okay? And, selfishly, why hasn't he contacted her? Everly tries to put these questions aside for now, respecting the boundary he has set for the moment.

"What caused it?" she asks, and Asim visibly flinches, looking away from her. Everly pulls back, confused by his reaction.

"The wiring," he mutters.

"The... wiring?"

"It was an electrical fire. I've been working on replacing large sections of the wiring, parts were damaged and faulty. The original contractor cut corners and I was fixing it, but I didn't get it all done when I needed to. It should have been done months ago. I guess it's too late now..." Asim trails off, palming the back of his neck and looking over the ruins of his business and home.

Faulty wiring.

The blood drains from Everly's face. Her head swims for a moment, the sudden lack of blood and shock of her realization making her dizzy. This is why he hasn't been talking to her, because it *is* her fault. She's been taking all of his time, and he tried to tell her he had work to do, but she didn't realize it was so serious. Truthfully, she didn't even give it a second thought. Guilt suffocates her, the reality of their situation drowning her in shame.

He said months ago—that must have been what he was buying at the hardware store the day they ran into each other. The pieces fall into place and her heart begins to bruise, her chest curling in on itself. Asim cancelled on her to work on it, and she didn't ever ask if it was done or if he had more he needed to fix. Everly prioritized herself and her stupid terrace and then had the audacity to demand a date, as if she hadn't already consumed enough of his time. She just took and took and took. She took all of him, and now he has paid the price.

Everly pulls herself up on shaking legs. No wonder he didn't reach out to her, it all makes sense now. She can hardly see from the tears blurring her eyes, and swiping them away doesn't help. They just fall faster.

She starts to back away, and Asim looks up at her, still seated on the ground next to Moose. His eyes are haunted, the dark shadows ringing them piercing her soul, tension lining his body. He looks exhausted. Everly's eyes flick between him and Moose, and somehow, she hurts even more. She not only destroyed Asim's life, his entire livelihood, but she put both him and his dog in danger, and Moose is suffering massively because of it.

"I'm sorry," she manages to whisper the words, clenching the sobs inside her chest so they don't escape. "I'm so, so sorry."

Then she turns, and flees.

<p style="text-align:center">~~~</p>

She only makes it as far as her car. Everly slumps into the driver's seat, fumbles her keys as she tries to insert them into the ignition, vaguely hears them drop somewhere by her feet. She can't drive like this anyways; she can hardly see through her blurry and swollen eyes.

Pulling her feet up onto the seat, Everly hugs her knees to her chest and hides her face in them. A few moments later, the passenger door opens and she has no doubt who it is. Asim drops heavily into the seat next to her, folding his large frame into her car. They don't speak for minutes that feel like hours, and Everly hates this silence. It's always been comfortable quiet between them, but this one is deafening.

Finally, Asim speaks. "I can't let you go."

He pauses and Everly holds her breath, keeping her eyes averted. In her periphery, he rubs his throat with his hand before he swallows hard and continues.

"I tried, I really did, but now that you're here, I can't. I can't let you go, and for that I'm the one who is sorry."

Everly blinks rapidly to clear her tears, then she turns her head on her folded arms, focusing on his chest because she can't bear to see the hurt that is sure to be looking back at her from his eyes.

"I don't blame you for trying," she says. "I would have tried to get rid of me too." Everly picks her head up and looks around, staring again at the scorched rubble in front of them, then looking toward poor Moose lying uncomfortably under the table in the shade. "This is all my fault. I've cost you everything, and if you want me to go, I will. I understand."

"Wait." Asim's brows furrow and he shakes his head, clears his throat. "None of this is your fault, Everly."

He uses her full name, and it catches her attention. He rarely uses her full name since he started shortening it. She's already shaking her head in response to his statement though.

"No, it is. If I hadn't taken so much of your time, if I hadn't insisted on going out on that date, or made you spend all of your free time with me," she says. "You even told me you needed to fix the wiring and I didn't think any further about it. I should have asked. I should have given you the space you needed, but I didn't. I took everything from you."

Her eyes fill with tears again and she turns her face away from him so he won't see.

Of course, Asim doesn't allow her to hide. He adjusts

in his seat, angling himself toward her, and gently turns her face back to his.

"You didn't ask, because I didn't tell you. You didn't know it was a bigger deal, because I hid it. I chose to spend my time with you, instead of on my responsibilities. I have always had a never ending to-do list for the shop, and I minimized this one all on my own."

Asim's green eyes hold her captive.

"I was fully aware of the choices I was making, Ever. I'm an adult, and the responsibility for my actions falls on me, and me alone. I won't allow you to take any accountability for one tiny speck of this, do you understand?"

Everly nods, but he sees right through her agreement. Pinching his lips, he clenches his hands on his thighs and silence drenches them again.

"You probably have questions," he finally says.

"Are you okay?"

His eyebrows go up, apparently not expecting that one.

"I am. I needed some extra oxygen after I went in to get Moose, but nothing lasting or serious. Just some minor issues with my lungs and voice, as you can tell."

"What about... mentally?" she asks.

Asim sighs, looking lost for a moment before he swipes a hand down his face. "That is going to take some time, I suppose."

Everly nods silently.

They both look out the front window, absorbing the desolate view through heavy eyes. Everly doesn't want to see it anymore, so she looks down at her hands instead.

"I'm sorry I didn't reach out." Asim's voice is quiet and rough in the stillness between them.

"Why didn't you?"

Her eyes flick to him before her gaze returns to her hands. She isn't sure she wants the answer to that question, but it's been hammering to be let out anyways.

"I... I didn't want to put you in danger." He shakes his head, trying to sort out his thoughts. "When it happened, you were the first person I thought of, but I didn't even have time to text or call. I skipped the ambulance because I had to take Moose to the emergency vet, and then when he was stabilized I had to get myself checked out. Lungs and all that." He waves his hand dismissively, but Everly can tell his voice is going to cut out soon. She reaches into the backseat for a bottle of water.

"My phone died, I didn't have a charger at first because... well." He averts his gaze, staring unfocused out the window away from her as he takes a sip, wincing when he swallows. "By the time things started to slow down, I realized my negligence nearly destroyed everything I care about. I couldn't stand the thought that you could have been there. At any moment when you were here, it could have happened, and you could have been seriously hurt, or worse."

Both of his hands sweep through his hair to clasp behind his neck, his head pinched between his forearms. His throat bobs with a hard swallow before he speaks again.

"What if it happens again? What if I overlook something else and I continue to put you in danger? I can't risk that. That's why I stayed away. I wrote you so many messages, only to delete them. My fingers hovered over your name every day, every hour, but the horrible image of you getting caught in something like this..." he flings his hand out, gesturing to the ruins in front of them.

Asim sighs, the sound belonging to someone twice his age, then he swings his head around and meets her eyes.

"You deserve more. You deserve better than me, better than what I can offer you. You deserve the best in the world, Ever, and I'm not it."

CHAPTER TWENTY-SIX

She's floored by his words. Asim thinks he doesn't deserve her? They've both been blaming themselves, assuming the worst of themselves, when they really needed each other. It's obvious he isn't, and hasn't been, thinking clearly with everything that happened, and Everly doesn't blame him for a moment. It's her who needs to get her head on straight and fix this.

Everly inhales a long breath, drops her feet from the seat, sets her shoulders back. Then she turns to Asim and cups his face in both of her hands, forcing his weary gaze to stay on hers.

"I love you," she says, and his eyes flare wide. He attempts to jerk back out of her hands, but she holds tight.

"I love you, and I won't let you push me away. I won't let either of us ruin this. You are the best part of my life, Asim, the best thing to ever happen to me. You can try to hide, but I'm not going anywhere," she says, staring directly into his green eyes. Her favorite eyes, now dulled by trauma and loss.

His beautiful gaze turns glassy, and he leans forward, pressing his forehead into hers. She pulls him in and snakes her arms around him, giving him the best hug she can while awkwardly cramped in her small car.

Everly holds him for a moment, her thoughts spinning through scenarios, lists, problem solving and brainstorming solutions at a rapid rate. Her business brain has kicked in, and she's ready to buckle down and get to work—for him this time.

"Where have you been staying?" she asks, pulling back

from him and taking a hard look at his unkempt appearance again. It's so unlike him.

"I've got a room at a neighbor's down the road. It's fine, it's close by," he says, but Everly can see how mentally and physically drained he is, and she knows it's not a long term solution, or even a viable short-term one.

"You'll come stay at the hotel. Free of charge for as long as you need. Moose will come too." She nods in emphasis and scrabbles her hand around by her feet for her keys. Finding them beneath the seat, Everly snags the door handle and swings out of the car, slamming it closed behind her and striding back in the direction of his tent. She hears Asim scramble out behind her.

"No, I can't do that. That's too much, Everly," he says, jogging to catch up with her.

"You can, it's not too much, I promise." Everly side eyes him, noticing the pained look on his face and the tension that is back in his shoulders.

She stops and faces him, reaching up to place her hands on his shoulders and doing her best to look down her nose at him, even though he's significantly taller than her.

"Asim, please let me help. You've done so much for me." He's already shaking his head, so she pulls out the big guns. She's not below throwing herself under the bus for this.

"I told you I've been working on being authentic."

He freezes and tilts his head slightly, eyeing her with suspicion.

"I shared that with you. I told you I've been taking more risks, putting myself out there and advocating for what I want and need. I want this, Asim. I want to help, and I need to be there for you. I can't undo what happened, but I can give you a comfortable place to rest with Moose while you rebuild."

She pauses, assessing the situation. Asim hasn't protested again yet, but she can see the skepticism in the lines of his face, his reluctance to accept this gift.

"Don't you dare turn me down when I'm putting myself out there like this, Asim." Her voice is low and quiet, and she doesn't have to fake the tremble of nerves. "If not for yourself or for me, do it for Moose. Please."

Her last word comes out as a whisper. The moment he

caves, her heart lifts. It feels like she can breathe again.

His shoulders slump under her hands, and before she can pull her arms back, his slide around her waist and he pulls her into him, holding her tight to his chest. Asim lifts her off her feet, burying his face in her neck and breathing her in. She lays her cheek on his shoulder and relishes the feeling of safety resonating between them.

Asim doesn't set her back down. Instead, he takes the last couple steps to the camp chair set up under the canopy tent and lowers himself into it, taking her with him and settling her sideways on his lap. His arms don't loosen, and she has to wiggle around until he allows her enough slack to breathe properly. They soak up this moment together, breathing each other's presence and convincing themselves they are not alone.

It takes a few minutes, but they sort out the details—when he can get to the hotel, what supplies he has and what he might need, the logistics of caring for Moose while trying to handle the insurance and other pieces of this convoluted puzzle. Everly starts a list in her head of items she can bring from her place to the hotel for him, as well as other little things she can do to make his life easier the next few weeks.

Then they simply sit in silence together, and Everly has never been more grateful for the comfort of it. It's not weird, or deafening, or threatening, or confusing. It's just them; his chest rising and falling against her shoulder, his lips grazing her temple or her hair every few moments while his hands smooth and squeeze along her waist, hip, and thigh, reassuring himself she's still there with him.

Everly stands before she gets too comfy or nods off, and gives Moose some gentle pets.

Just as she's about to leave, a Prius pulls into the lot and parks right next to the canopy. Asim puts his arm around her, and she takes the hint to stay, then he murmurs in her ear.

"It's my sister, Farah, the one you met over the phone."

Everly nods and Farah steps out of the car, not seeming surprised at the wreckage around her. She must have seen it already. Asim gives Everly a quick squeeze before he lets go and walks over to his sister.

"How much did they send this time?" he asks and Farah snorts.

"I convinced them to send only two meals this time, but of course Mama made the meals fit for a family of five so I'm not sure where you're going to keep all of it," Farah replies, then softer, "They wanted to be here, too."

"I know, thank you for convincing them to stay home. I know they want to help but..." Asim trails off and Farah nods.

"But there's not much they can do, and it would just make everyone feel worse," she says and Asim's mouth pinches into a grim line. They share a look before Farah drops a large, wrapped dish into Asim's arms and turns her way.

"Everly! We finally get to meet in person." Farah walks toward her with her arms outstretched and Everly hopes against all hope that her eyes and face aren't too puffy from crying. Farah grasps her shoulders and leans in, kissing both of her cheeks before pulling her into a tight hug. Everly returns it with a smile.

"I think I can help with the food issue," Everly says.

"Oh yeah?" Farah glances back at Asim before refocusing on Everly.

"I offered Asim a room at the Sioria. It's, well, I'm not sure if you know," Everly stammers, "that is, I own it, so um, well. Asim agreed to stay there, and he'll have a full kitchen with plenty of room."

"Excellent!" Farah claps her hands in emphasis. "I'm sure you had to practically pull your own arm off to get him to agree."

Farah rolls her eyes at Everly's shrug, bypassing her awkwardness with ease. "He's not the best at accepting help, thank you for not giving up on him."

Everly isn't sure what to say to that, it's truly the least she could do, so she offers a meager sort of smile before turning to Asim.

"We can put the food in my car if you want, I'll drop it all off at the hotel. I've got a few things to do there today anyways, so I'll reserve a room for you and pop them in the fridge for later."

Farah eyes him, a slight threat in her gaze, and he agrees.

"It was nice meeting you in person," Everly says,

"despite the circumstances."

"You too, okhti," Farah says, pulling Everly into another hug.

Asim walks Everly over to her car, more than a week's worth of meals in hand, and she glances up at his sun-warmed face, so incredibly thankful she decided to drive out here today. They load the food into her backseat and he wraps his arms around her again, blocking out the world with his biceps and taking as much comfort from her as he gives.

She confirms he'll be at the hotel later that day, then heads back into town when he insists on staying and going back to work, salvaging what he can, caring for the surviving plants, and fielding a relentless stream of phone calls.

~~~

Asim texts her a couple hours later, letting her know that his sister is headed back to the city and he's on his way to the hotel. When he walks into the lobby, so very slowly to accommodate Moose's unsteady gait, Everly is there waiting. She's been doing her best to not to fidget or pace so she doesn't set her employees on edge too, but when she sees him, all the restless anxiety drains from her body.

He gives her a sad smile as she greets him, tipping up on her toes for a kiss. Everly ushers them to the elevator, holding it open for Moose to waddle his way in and collapse to the floor.

"I've tried carrying him," Asim says, "but he hates it. Wiggles around so much I'm worried he'll injure himself further."

"Doesn't want any help, huh?" Everly side-eyes him. "Sounds like someone else I know."

Asim shoots her a mock glare and she grins over her shoulder as she exits the elevator, walking down the hall and opening the door to the room she reserved.

"It's a full suite. Bedroom, bathroom, kitchen, small dining nook and living area."

"Whoa, Everly." Asim's eyes are wide as he looks around. "This is way too much. I don't need all this."

"It's standard." She averts her gaze. That might be a
~~~

small white lie, as technically their "standard" rooms don't have a full kitchen or living area, but really it's only a small step up from that. Or maybe two, whatever.

"Besides," she continues, "it's already done. I've reserved this room for you for the next two months and I've already threatened to fire anyone who allows you to downgrade."

Asim gapes at her.

"I know you. You don't think you deserve this, but you do." Then she smirks at him. "Plus, it's my hotel, and I like to stay in luxury. If I plan on spending any time here with you—which I do—I want it to be in one of our nicer rooms."

She sticks her nose in the air, putting on her most haughty expression and daring him to contradict her as she strides into the kitchen.

Asim steps up behind her and wraps her in a fierce hug.

"Thank you, my sweet Ever," he says, and she melts in his arms. It means a lot to her that she can do this for him, and she wants him to accept it, accept her.

Letting go with one arm, Asim opens the cabinet next to them and pauses, noticing that it's not entirely filled, but does have a good amount of dinnerware in it, certainly more than a two person hotel suite would typically have. He releases her from his hold with his other arm and opens the next cabinet, again taking note of the variety of pots and pans inside. Opening a drawer of cutlery, and then one of hot pads, and then the counter under the sink with dishwashing supplies, his eyes narrow and his brow furrows. When he opens the pantry to see it fully stocked with food, he turns around abruptly, and she schools her face into her most innocent expression.

Eyes wide, eyebrows slightly raised, and hands clasped behind her back, she asks, "What?"

"Are all of the suite kitchens stocked like this?" he asks. The words are slow and measured.

"Sure," Everly says with a shrug. The hotel does offer groceries as a special add-on feature, for guests who request and pay for it to be stocked ahead of time.

Asim tips his chin down and eyes her, gaze still narrowed.

"Sure." His voice is skeptical now, and she doesn't blame him one bit.

"Yep." Her lips pop and she nods decisively, then slips past him into the living area.

"Oh, I picked up a couple things for Moose, I hope that's okay." She has a memory foam dog bed laid out in each room for him. She ordered them from a pet store near Phoenix and paid extra for them to deliver right away. He's already found the one in the living area and is sprawled out on it, as comfortable as he can be considering his injuries.

Everly bends down, crooning and petting his silky ears when Asim walks over, shaking his head.

"You know I can't say no to either of you."

Standing after one final pat on Moose's uninjured shoulder, she gives Asim a quick tour, not pointing out any of the extra touches she added just for him, but hoping he likes them anyways. The cozy plaid throw blanket and soft pillows on the couch, the scented diffuser in the bedroom, the herringbone rug in the kitchen. She wants this to be a comfortable place for him to stay the next few weeks, and these things make it feel more like a home to her.

"Should we eat?" she asks, and Asim nods his agreement, eyes still taking in the space around him as he pulls a tray out of the fridge.

"Looks like margat bamia, have you ever had it?"

Everly shakes her head. "I'm down to try anything though."

He sets the oven to reheat the food, and before she knows it, the small space is filled with the scents of aromatic spices.

"What is it?" Everly asks, gesturing to the oven.

"It roughly translates to okra stew." Asim hums in thought before continuing. "Generally made with lamb, okra of course, and a tomato garlic base, served over rice, like a curry, if you've had that."

She nods and her mouth starts to water. "It sounds delicious."

Only a few minutes later, she confirms that it tastes just as good as it smells. She lets the flavors roll around her tongue, savoring Asim's sparkling gaze as he watches her enjoy his native foods. Asim lets out an appreciative moan of his own when he scoops a massive bite into his mouth and she nearly bites her tongue when she hears it.

Everly asks a few more questions about the situation with the garden center, how long until he has answers from the insurance, what rebuilding will look like. Asim has some answers but not all, and she determines to research any missing information or tips she can find to help him with these aspects too, if he accepts it. He has enough on his plate right now, so she will do anything within her power to help.

As dinner is winding down, Asim leans back in his seat and looks out the window. Although he appears to be going for a casual pose, Everly notices the exhausted tension lining his body again. Maybe she shouldn't have asked so many questions. He probably doesn't appreciate her bringing his worries up when he finally has a moment to relax.

Asim sighs, interrupting her spiraling thoughts, then turns to her, a somber look on his face. Everly's heart nearly cracks in two when she thinks about the devastation he's experienced the last couple days.

She stands and clears their dishes, taking them to the kitchen and rinsing them in the sink.

"I'm going to let you rest," she says. "I have a few things to finish up in the office, then I'm going to head home."

Asim looks like he wants to protest, but he stops himself. He slides his arms around her and settles his cheek on her head.

"Thank you for saving me," he whispers.

Everly blinks back tears, reigning in her emotions before pulling away from the comfort of his arms.

"See you tomorrow?" she says.

Asim nods, a soft, tired smile gracing his lips.

"See you tomorrow, Ever."

CHAPTER TWENTY-SEVEN

Everly forces herself to walk calmly up the flight of stairs to her office, managing to make it inside and closing the door behind her before her pent up emotions from the last few days boil over. Her back falls against the closed door and she slides to the floor, her hands tight across her mouth, holding in the sobs. The last thing she needs is any of her staff to hear her crying.

Her brain flashes images at her: Moose barely able to walk and covered in burns, Asim running into a burning building, the charred remains of Magnolia Nursery. She's been holding it all back, not wanting to put more on Asim when he's already been through so much, but her anxiety takes hold and combined with her grief for Asim and Moose, it's too much. A river of tears flows down her cheeks, and Everly can't hold in her sorrow for their loss, her fear for their safety, the terrifying 'what-if' scenarios that plague her.

She fumbles with her phone, sends it skidding across the floor. Shuffling over to pick it up with trembling hands, Everly connects it to the bluetooth she has installed throughout the office suite and turns on a random playlist to cover the sounds of her crying. Tchaikovsky pours from the speakers.

Then a harsh sob tears from her throat.

She cries for Asim's loss; his hurt and his heartbreak and his sadness. She cries for Moose and his injuries and pain. She cries because she told Asim she loves him, and he didn't say it back, and she's afraid of what that means. Her anxiety tells her that he's going to end things. That he doesn't love her, she's a liability, and he won't have time for her anymore. Fat tears slide down her cheeks and wet the top of her shirt. Everly holds her arms around herself and rocks against the door, not bothering to move to the couch or her office chair. The physically uncomfortable position feels better to focus on than her emotional pain anyways.

Her tears eventually slow, and her cries turn to hiccups, then to sporadic, shuddering breaths before they ease. Everly's body slumps against the door behind her, and she closes her eyes with her head tipped back against it. Letting all of the emotion of the last week out at once was draining, and cathartic. She feels cleansed, in a way, and it clears her mind from the emotional upheaval.

Everly places her hands on the floor next to her, taking a steadying breath as she pushes herself to her feet and walks over to her desk. She carefully sits in her chair, straightening her back and rolling up to her work space. She pulls out a notebook and a pen, and she makes a list.

A short while later, Everly sets her pen down and picks up the list, reading it over. It's a list of lies and truths. A list to prove her anxious thoughts wrong.

> Lie: Asim doesn't care about me or love me.

>> Truth: Asim has shown me he cares in a number of ways: date 1 and date 2, spending time with me instead of other priorities, helping me with a large project.

> Lie: Now is not a good time for a relationship.

>> Truth: All relationships have ups and downs, and life will always throw curveballs. Even if he is more busy now, I believe we can make time for each other in a way that doesn't put anyone in danger.

> Lie: I'm a liability. All I bring is hurt to those around me.

>> Truth: I haven't done anything wrong. I didn't hurt anyone or put anyone in danger. Asim is an adult who can make his own choices, set his own boundaries, and decide how to spend his time and money.

> Lie: I'm not good enough. I don't deserve his love or

affection.

>> Truth: I am a good person, and I deserve love. Everyone deserves love. Asim and I have a real connection, and we are good for each other. I am good enough.

Everly sets the paper back down on her desk, taking a long, slow breath as she sits back in her chair. Her heart wants to knit back together, but she's scared. Terrified, really. Her anxiety fed her a bunch of realistic-sounding lies, and although she's talked herself down for the most part, she needs to see him, *talk* to him, to solidify the truth.

Everly told him she wouldn't let him push her away, and she's not going to let herself push them apart either. She slaps her palms against her desk and stands, then strides across her office to the door.

She flings it open and lets out a piercing shriek that splits the air when she sees a hulking figure standing in the doorframe. Everly jumps back and slams it closed again.

Breathing hard and holding her hands to her chest, Everly tries to wrap her head around what just happened. She jumps again when a knock sounds on the door, right in front of her face, and a familiar voice calls her name.

Everly cracks the door open and peeks out, as though that will keep her safe from whoever is on the other side planning to murder her.

"Asim?" She pulls the door wide and tilts her head up at him. "What are you doing here?"

He shifts on his feet. "Can I come in? I'd like to talk, if you'll allow me. I think I just need to make sure you're okay. That *we* are okay."

"Of course," she says, gesturing to him to have a seat on the couch. "I was actually just about to come talk to you. Wait... How did you know where my office was?"

Asim looks away, sheepish, running his hand through his hair.

"I tried to ask the front desk staff, but it took some convincing to get your concierge to tell me. The staff are very loyal to you, by the way," he says.

Everly huffs half a laugh.

"Yes, well, I was about to come talk to you, too."

Asim angles his head in question.

Now that her emotions are more or less under control, she can think more clearly.

"I know that you're going to be really busy the next few weeks, and if you don't want to date or, you know, be romantic, or whatever," she pauses and narrows her eyes at his quiet huff. "I'm just trying to say I won't push you. I won't let you push me away, and I'm not going to let myself hide. I'm still going to be here for you, for us, but I also won't push you. I care about you so much, and I want to stick up for us. That's who I am, or at least it's who I want to be. The kind of person I'm working toward."

Asim leans forward and kisses her, cutting off her rambling nerves.

Pulling back just slightly, he cups her face and speaks softly against her lips. "I couldn't wait until tomorrow to tell you one very important thing."

"What's that?"

"I love you. I love you with my whole heart, and I won't ever let you go. Even when I am most afraid, I know we can get through it together. You're right, of course you're right. You are the light in my life and you breathe joy and sunshine into every moment. I am unmoored without you, my darling Ever. I know it's a lot to ask after I disappeared, but please, forgive me?"

Everly's arms prickle as the hair stands on end. Her head rushes with blood and she gets lost in the blur of his bright green eyes so close to hers. Their lips meet and passion explodes from every pore on her body. Every touch and slide of his fingers burns her skin. She clutches his biceps, feeling the muscles flex under her hands as he grips the backs of her thighs and lifts her into his arms. Her legs circle his waist and he moans into her mouth as he pushes her back into the closed door she was sitting against only minutes ago.

The distress of earlier somehow feels like another lifetime. The memory of a fading nightmare. Her body is waking up under his lips and tongue and teeth and hands, and she wants more.

She wants it all.

Spearing her fingers into his hair Everly drags at him,

attempting to pull him closer when the opposite happens. Asim lets out an awkward chuckling groan as he tips his head away from hers and looks around the office. His eyes light on her couch, but then he shakes his head as his eyes travel the length of it.

"Remember when I told you I wouldn't rush? I'd have you in a bed and I'd take my time? I plan to have you begging for more until you can't, but I won't do that here. Not for our first time together," he says.

"Your room?" Everly doesn't want to wait even the few minutes it would take to get back to her place. He nods and opens the door without setting her down.

"Back pocket," Asim mutters into her mouth when they arrive at his door, and she reaches down, struggling to extract his key card as his lips roam her neck. Finally she gets it, and he steps inside before slamming the door and pushing her up against it again.

As soon as they step in, Everly tugs impatiently at his shirt. She's seen the divine, carved muscles of his body before, and she wants to trace every ridge with her tongue.

Asim obliges and helps with her efforts, pinning her hips to the wall with his, then angling his torso and grabbing the back of his collar with one hand. He yanks the shirt off over his head and flings it to the floor.

Everly dives in, licking and sucking her way down his throat and he groans again, vibrating under her touch. He spins around and carries her toward the bedroom, a messy, stumbling walk around unfamiliar furniture. They don't quite make it when she nips at his neck and he pushes her against another wall, whooshing the air out of her lungs and making her laugh breathlessly at the look of feral desire on his face.

"Take it off before I rip it," he growls, low and hoarse, and although Everly isn't sure what specifically he's talking about, she wastes no time getting rid of her shirt as he starts walking again, and is working her way out of her bra when he tosses her onto the bed.

She lets out an "oof" as she bounces on the mattress, flinging the bra away and then looking up to see him frozen above her. His eyes are glued to her body, racing from her navel to her breasts, to her throat and dark hair splayed out on the cream bedspread beneath her.

"I have never seen anyone so exquisite," he says, and she flushes from the praise, her entire neck and chest turning pink.

Asim leans down and traces her blush with his tongue, peppering kisses on her skin and leaving goose bumps in his wake. He travels down her neck and circles her breasts, cupping one in his palm while tracing the other with his mouth. Everly whimpers at his teasing when he gets so close to her nipple, but doesn't directly touch it. She doesn't think they have ever been this tight and hard, and the torture of not having his tongue on them is almost painful.

He huffs out a rumbling chuckle just above the skin of her breast and she feels it puff against her.

"Impatient, my darling?" he asks.

Everly grabs his hair and yanks, pulling his mouth to her and arching up into him so there's no avoiding it; she's getting what she wants. This time, she feels the vibration of his laugh through her nipple, and she moans at the sensation. His tongue circles her, then he gently bites down, teeth scraping sensitive flesh as he pinches the other and rolls it between his thumb and finger. She throws her head back and squeezes her eyes shut at the sensation, reveling in the feeling of being here with him, with nothing stopping them this time.

Asim licks and kisses his way down to the waistband of her leggings before he pauses and pulls back, his fingers teasing along the edge and dipping under.

"May I?" he asks.

"Oh my god, please." She's desperate and she doesn't care if he knows.

Asim smirks up at her, a heated glint in his eye, then takes his time tugging and rolling the leggings down her hips as she lifts for him, slipping first one leg and then the other off before he drops them at his feet by the side of the bed. She's left in a simple, black silky thong that she put on for the sole purpose of not having panty lines this morning, and she has never been more thankful for such a convenient, logical accident.

Grabbing her hands, Asim pulls her to her feet in front of him and steps back, dropping one hand and using the other to slowly spin her around. When she's facing him again, his eyes are molten and hers widen at the intensity she sees there. He reaches down and adjusts himself in his sweatpants, and her eyes flare impossibly wider at the massive bulge tenting them.

Her mouth waters and Everly licks her lips, drawing his eyes there before he grabs her around the waist, lifting her again and yanking the thong off as he pushes her back on the bed and drops between her legs. He slides down to the foot of the massive mattress and flattens his body so his face is perfectly aligned with her core, then he throws her legs over his shoulders and uses his thumbs to spread her open to his hungry gaze.

Everly flushes, suddenly acutely aware of how bare she is. The bedspread and sheets are already a crumpled mess beneath her, stroking her flaming skin, and there is no inch of her that isn't exposed to him.

"So pretty," Asim murmurs, and then he swipes his tongue straight up her slit, groaning in satisfaction. Everly arches at the sensation and her hands scramble for purchase, fisting in the sheets. He flicks her clit once and then pulls away, looking up her body into her eyes and then perusing slowly back down.

Asim reaches up, untangling her hands from the bedding and burying them in his hair instead. Everly's fingers clench into his thick, dark locks as he licks her and she pulls him closer. She's already at the edge; she's thought of this moment for weeks, so it doesn't take much to get there. Letting her eyes fall closed as she rides the waves of bliss, her core clenches around his fingers with his tongue on her clit and his name spilling like a prayer from her lips.

When she floats back down to reality, Asim is gently kissing his way up her body again and she smiles down at him, feeling languid and hazy in a world of contentment. He crawls over her and then twists his body down next to hers. He turns her onto her side, pulling her back against him and snuggling his face into her neck. Everly sighs, happy, feeling on top of the world, and lets him hold her for a few minutes, relishing the closeness and physical contact.

Soon enough though, she wants to move. She pushes her hips back into him, feeling how hard he is against her still. His nuzzles turn more sensual as he starts kissing and sucking along her skin again, hitting a spot where her shoulder meets her neck that sends a shiver down her spine. He pauses, because of course he notices, and she feels his smirk against her skin as he stays there and teases.

Everly can play this game too, though. She reaches a hand between them and strokes up his shaft to the waistband of his sweatpants, then snakes her hand under it and palms his cock over his boxes. Asim's hips thrust into her and her lips curve into a satisfied smirk of her own. Turning in his arms, she pulls back and tugs his pants down to his knees, not bothering to deal with them any further. Asim huffs and shuffles them off the rest of the way on his own while she starts to play.

Everly pushes him to his back and straddles his hips, eyes roving over every dip of muscle, every line of tattoo, every hair on his broad chest and navel. Leaning down, she licks her lips, then her tongue darts out and she connects with his skin. She's wanted to do this since the first moment she met him. Everly traces the tattoos on his arm and chest with her fingers, and then with her lips and tongue. She tastes the ridges and valleys of his muscles, and eventually makes her way down the delicious 'V' to where tight boxers are barely containing his throbbing erection. There's a small wet spot near the waistband, a bead of precum already leaking from his tip, and the sight makes her feel more powerful than she ever has before.

Urging him to lift his hips, Everly strips the boxers off and momentarily gapes at the size of him. It's been a while for her, but she doesn't remember others being this large. Blinking, she flicks her eyes up to see he's tucked one hand behind his head, causing his biceps to bunch obscenely on the pillow, and his lips are pulled up on one side, a knowing glint in his eyes. He's truly not playing fair.

Everly swallows and licks her lips, turning back to the glorious view of his cock jutting up at her. She leans down and pauses, her breath skating over him, his cock twitching in response. Then she flattens her tongue against the vein running up the underside and looks up into his eyes as she licks him from base to tip, then swirls her tongue around his head before sucking it into her mouth. His smirk drops as his eyes darken and his hand clenches next to him, veins in his forearms and neck popping with tension.

She hollows her cheeks as she pulls back and he jerks up onto an elbow, his other hand fisting in her hair.

"Holy fuck, Ever."

She hardly recognizes his voice between the smoke inhalation causing it to be more gravelly than normal, and the low timbre it's taken on over the last few minutes. Her core clenches and she closes her eyes as she squeezes her legs together and pushes down on him again, taking him to the back of her throat.

He jerks in her mouth, and she hums approvingly. His fisted hand in her hair yanks hard, pulling her off him with a pop, and Everly looks up to see the breath sawing in and out of his lungs. They lock eyes and she freezes, her entire body clenching at the raw need on his face.

CHAPTER TWENTY-EIGHT

Before she can so much as twitch a muscle, he's scooping her in his arms and rolling her underneath him. Everly's legs spread to cradle his hips between hers, their breath ragged with need.

Asim plants his elbows on either side of her face, and somehow her wrists are in his hands, pushed into the pillow above her head. She tips her face to look up at him, seeing his eyes searching her.

"Protection?" he asks, his accent punching out, making his voice sound harsh with want, and Everly shakes her head.

"Birth control. I don't want anything between us," she says and he closes his eyes, another groan reverberating through his chest at her words.

He releases her wrists before pulling her hands up further until she feels the wood of the headboard above her.

"Hands on the headboard, gorgeous," he says.

Her body floods with desire and she can't get enough oxygen into her lungs. Asim smooths the head of his cock between her pussy lips, slicking himself up as he rubs himself against her clit.

Everly writhes underneath him, angling her hips up as he starts to push into her. She wants it all, and she wants it now.

"Patience," he says. "I'll give you what you need, I promise."

She can't help it though. Everly stills for a moment, but as soon as he starts pushing in again, she wants more and her body arches into him, trying to find the seemingly never ending length of him as she lifts her head to suck on his neck at the same time.

Her head sinks back into the pillow as his hand loosely circles the base of her throat and her eyes widen when he pins her down.

"I want to see you when I take you. I want to feel you clench around my cock, and I want to watch you come as I fill you up." His voice rumbles into her.

She swallows against his hand and his pupils dilate when he feels it. Everly's lungs stutter as he starts moving again, easing into her wet heat.

"But I will *not* hurt you, so be patient," he says, baring his teeth as he forces himself to go slowly.

Everly tries her best not to push him. She presses her hands into the headboard above her, feeling the scrape of the wood against her palms as her breasts heave with every shallow breath.

"God," he says. "You're so tight, Ever. So perfectly tight and wet for me. Fuck," he mutters obscenities in both English and Arabic as he takes her, and it sets her blood on fire. Her pulse hammers through her as his cock slides in and in and in. Every inch is torture and bliss and she whimpers when he stills.

"You can take it," he says, pulling out and then sliding in again. "Almost there."

Everly does her best to breathe and relax under him, to let him in. His weight pressing her into the mattress, his biceps flexing above her, and his hardness filling every empty space inside her is heavenly agony. She needs him to move, to pound into her, to *fuck* her.

Finally with the next thrust, she feels his hips flush against hers and his balls hang heavy against her ass.

"That's my good girl," he says.

Asim leans back, stroking a gentle hand down her body, over her peaked nipple, his gaze hot as he follows with his eyes until he's looking down at their joined bodies.

"Look at you," he says, pulsing himself in and out of her. "You're perfect."

It's all Everly can do in this moment to remind herself to breathe.

"Tell me what you want. How do you like it?" he says.

"Harder," Everly pants out, her voice hoarse,

simultaneously demanding and needy.

Asim hooks his arms under her knees and leans over her again, covering her body with his while pulling her legs up and opening her wider for him. Everly gasps at the blinding pleasure as he plunges into from a new angle. He covers her mouth with his, teeth and tongues battling between them, inhaling her gasps and whimpers of pleasure. Threading a hand in her hair he angles her head to the side, nipping and licking and sucking, and just like that, he wins. Everly gives in to the sensations, his cock pounding into her, his tongue and teeth rasping along her neck.

She surrenders, letting him own her in every way until her walls clench tightly around him. He lets out a guttural moan as her body contracts and his cock becomes impossibly harder, sending her spiraling even higher, higher, higher, then he pulses inside her as her walls tighten with her climax. She clenches and throbs around him as he rocks them through their releases together.

Through a distant, floaty haze, Everly feels Asim's arms adjust their bodies before his weight presses down on her, comforting and secure, surrounding her in warmth and safety and the earthy smell of *him*. She sighs as she comes back to reality, and her eyes blink open to see him hovering over her.

Asim smoothes her hair off her forehead and kisses it, a sweet and tender smile on his face as he looks deep into her eyes.

"You are..." He shakes his head, gaze scorching her soul, searching for words. "Utterly unbelievable."

Asim leans down again and scatters kisses along her face; across her cheekbones, the tip of her nose, her eyelids and forehead, and from one corner of her lips to the other until she's smiling so widely she can't possibly contain it.

"That was amazing." Everly breathes out, and his sweet smile angles into pure satisfaction.

He rolls onto his back and pulls her with him, so she's cradled against his side with her head on his shoulder. Asim traces light patterns with his fingertips along her side and back, sending shivers over her skin, so she does the same to him, lightly running her hand over his chest and side, down his arm, and swirling over his hip. Asim pulls her tightly into him, kissing the top of her head and holding her possessively while she drifts off, and she knows he won't let anything in the world tear them apart.

~~~

The last two weeks have been nothing short of nirvana with them working side by side as Asim straightens out the logistics of his business so he can get it back up and running again. Every day he has been taking phone calls, sending emails, ordering new supplies and fighting with the insurance company, scheduling contractors for repairs, and who even knows what else.

Everly pauses her typing when Moose starts snorting in his sleep, his paws and ears twitching like mad. She looks to the left across the desk from her where Asim sits with his laptop and they share a smile, Everly biting her lip to hold in a giggle.

She insists he work in her office and share her desk, even though he states he could just as easily work from his room or the canopy tent he set up on the property. Everly likes having him here though, his scent invading her space and permeating throughout her office every day, and his smile only seconds away at any given moment. It was a challenge at first, figuring out how to share the space effectively, and she learned he has a bit of a temper when it comes to working with "incompetent idiots" as he phrased it, also known as insurance agents. She was surprised to see this side of him, but after a walk to "cool off" he always comes back calm and collected again, ready to move forward. This impresses her even more, because she certainly could not have maintained that level of professionalism given the situation he's been dealing with.

Asim's work is endless, yet every time she looks his way, he meets her eyes and smiles or winks at her. The love she sees there is undeniable and it threatens to fill her heart to bursting every single time.

Moose gives a loud yip and startles himself awake, looking up at them with sad puppy eyes. Everly giggles and gets up from her seat, walking over to give him some
~~~

comforting pets as his tail starts thumping against the hardwood floor.

"Should we pause for lunch?" Asim stretches his arms above his head, catching Everly's attention, and her hand pauses on Moose's back. Her eyes travel from one outstretched wrist, down the length of his arm and across his broad chest to the other one, tracing over his tattoos with her eyes. She's had a lot of fun the last couple weeks learning every curve of those tattoos.

"Ever?" He's smirking now, drawing her name out as he flexes his arms, and she makes a face at him.

"Yeah, lunch sounds good."

Everly straightens and walks to the other room of her office suite, grabbing their lunches from the mint green vintage fridge she scored at an estate sale a couple years ago, along with a couple napkins and utensils on her way back.

Pulling out the vegan chicken salad sandwiches they prepared together the night before, Everly reflects on the therapy session she had with Carrie earlier that morning.

"Let's step back for a moment," Carrie said. "What changes have you noticed since last year?"

"Well, I think the most obvious one is that I'm seeing someone now," Everly replied, and Carrie nodded, but didn't speak. "I guess maybe there aren't a ton of changes. I'm not really all that much more social, and I haven't made a ton of friends, but I do feel different."

"In what way?"

"I feel... more like me, I guess. I don't know. It's hard to put into words."

"Let's take some time to figure it out. I think this is an important thing to find the words for," Carrie had said, encouraging her not to give up.

"I don't feel like I'm wearing a mask all the time anymore. It's almost like," Everly had scoffed at herself, but continued, "almost like I'm shining?"

"Shining?" Carrie's eyebrows went up and she looked to be holding back a smile.

"Yeah, like something inside me is lit up. I feel brighter."

Carrie had smiled then, but she wasn't done yet. "Why do you think you feel brighter?"

Everly sighed. Carrie never makes it easy for her or lets her off the hook, but that's why she's worth every penny. "Um, well, it could be that my thoughts are changing. I don't have as many negative thoughts anymore."

"What else?"

"I don't worry about being perfect for other people." She realized she'd had a general impression of this already, but hadn't reflected on the depth of it yet. "I haven't been anticipating people's expectations just so I can try to meet them, like I used to do. Constantly. I didn't even realize until now how much I used to do that, and I haven't been anymore. Except at work but that's normal I'm pretty sure. I think that's a big part of it," Everly said.

"What have you been doing instead?"

"Nothing?" Everly crinkled her nose up, not sure how to answer that one.

"Not nothing, you're always doing something," Carrie prompted. "Instead of being focused on what other people want from you or what others think about you, what thoughts are going through your head instead?"

"I'm just... thinking about other things, I guess. Life things or what I have to do that day or what I will say or do in the moment depending what's going on," she said.

"So you've let go of some of those perfectionistic tendencies and insecurities. You've created a new thought pattern for yourself, a much more healthy one by the sounds of it." Carrie summarized it much more insightfully than Everly did.

"Yeah, that," she said, pointing at Carrie's image on her computer screen, and Carrie laughed.

Thinking about it now, she realizes that emptiness inside her is gone too. It sometimes pops up when she's having a bad day, but for the most part she feels genuinely happy. It may be in large part due to Asim's presence in her life, but even more so, it's the internal changes she's pursued, changes he welcomes and encourages. Everly looks over at Asim again, eating his sandwich while he scrolls and reads something on his laptop. His eyes are narrowed, focused, and he's leaning forward in his chair, forearms propped on the desk in front of him.

Everly turns back to her own lunch and takes another bite, pondering what her next steps might be now that she feels more herself, when she's startled out of her reflections by Asim's finger swiping a bit of food from the corner of her lips. She looks up to see him pop his finger in his mouth to lick it off, one side of his lips twitching up at her gaze.

Her thighs clench reflexively, and she licks her lips in response. Before she can so much as take another breath, he's leaning across the table and grasping the nape of her neck, pulling her up out of her chair into a heated kiss. Everly drops her sandwich and leans into the kiss, her tongue teasing his lips, and she feels him smile against her mouth before taking it deeper. Her hand fists in his shirt and she pulls him harder against her, arching into him and wishing the desk wasn't in their way.

"UGH, MY EYES!"

Everly shrieks and nearly jumps right out of her skin as Asim breaks the kiss but doesn't lean away. He looks over his shoulder at the intruder and gives them a mock glare. Everly and Asim release their holds on each other and sink back into their seats. Frankie laughs and saunters in, pushing some papers out of their way on the far end of the desk before hopping onto it and folding their legs, criss-cross applesauce style.

"Gah, seriously?" Everly gripes at her friend. "At least take your shoes off."

They kick off their omnipresent black combat boots with a grin at Everly's muttered "freaking heathen" and then pull out their own lunch and chopsticks.

"Looks like I'm right on time. How's everyone's day going?" Frankie says and takes a slurping bite of pad Thai.

"You're obnoxious," Everly says to them, one side of her mouth twitching up.

Asim laughs at their antics while Everly rolls her eyes and they all start chatting about their mornings. Soon the conversation consists mainly of Asim and Frankie sharing the latest town gossip, gasps and wide eyes and gesticulating hands left and right.

Everly tunes them out; she's accepted that she will

never be as social or popular around town as the two of them are, and she's okay with that. She enjoys their banter and is inordinately pleased at how well the two of them get along.

Her best friends. The only piece missing is her sister, and Everly hopes to have this close of a connection with her someday as well.

238

CHAPTER TWENTY-NINE

Everly is waiting in her kitchen, cream fuzzy-socked foot tap-tap-tapping on the stone tile as she leans back against the marble countertop, arms folded across her chest, hands clenched into fists. Her eyes flit between the phone propped up on the counter opposite her and the kitchen window. Asim is on a video call with her—he's working in the back greenhouses today—and she's doing her best not to pace while she waits.

"No word yet?" he asks, his head popping into view for a moment before she hears him rummaging around off camera.

"Not since she left Phoenix. I mean, I guess I'm glad she's not texting and driving, but shouldn't she be here by now?"

"There's probably traffic, especially getting out of the airport. She'll be here soon. What are you most excited about?" he asks, doing his best to distract her from the torture of waiting. Everly appreciates the sentiment, even if it's not really working.

"I guess just to see her? I don't know, maybe going to —"

"She's here!" Everly screeches, interrupting herself. "She's here, gotta go! Love you bye!"

She hears Asim's chuckle as she ends the call and clenches her phone in her fist, watching Addison turn into the driveway and circle around in her rental, then pull to a screeching stop in front of the porch.

Everly throws the door open and dashes out.

"You made it!" she says, a wide smile on her face.

"I did!" Addison hops out and slams the door closed,

then strides around the car toward Everly. Without hesitation, Addison throws her arms around her sister and Everly's breath catches at the ease with which Addison embraces her.

Everly's arms come up and wrap around her in return, and she breathes in the moment, savoring the feel of her little sister in her arms and exulting in this epic hug of all hugs. It feels like love and joy and comfort.

It feels like home.

As Addison chatters about the flight and how she recognized a book someone was reading in the row in front of her, Everly can't stop smiling and her cheeks already hurt with how wide it is. They stow Addison's luggage for the week in her old bedroom upstairs, not even unpacking before they agree drinks are in order.

They're sitting on barstools at the kitchen counter catching up when Addison asks about Asim.

"He's definitely still stressed and has a lot on his plate, but it's coming back together. He's at the garden center, but might swing by later," Everly says.

"Okay cool, I can't wait to officially meet him." Addison's eyes twinkle as she clasps her hands in front of her.

They've said hello a couple times on video calls over the last two weeks, and Everly can't wait to see how they get along in person.

Then she surprises Everly by bringing up someone else.

"So what about your other friend, Frankie?" Addison says. She glances sideways at Everly from the corner of her eye.

"What about them?"

"Are they coming over too?" Addison's cheeks are pink and she's shifted her focus to looking resolutely at her hands.

Everly narrows her eyes.

"Ad…" Her sister's eyes flick to hers briefly before darting away again. "Do you want me to invite them over?"

"Oh, no, that's not," she stammers, "I mean, if *you* wanted to, I don't mind, is all." Addison takes a swig of her dry Manhattan and immediately starts hacking, pounding her chest with the heel of her hand and leaning over in her seat.

"Geez, are you okay?!" Everly pats her back on her way to the sink for a quick glass of water. She slides it in front of Addison, who nods her indication that she's fine and takes a grateful gulp. "If you like Frankie, that's okay. I won't be mad. But I'll be honest, I don't know if they're interested one way or another."

"Oh my god, Ev!" Addison's cheeks are more than pink now.

"I'm just saying!" she says, throwing her hands in the air in surrender.

Addison downs the rest of the water before looking back at Everly. "I don't know if it's like that. I guess I just want to get to know them."

Everly nods and decides to go easy on her for now, while a plucky trail of schemes start flitting through her brain. She holds in the maniacal laugh, but lets it ring through her mind loud and clear.

"So what happened with those other two? Your ex and your... other ex?" Everly asks, still unclear on the relationships between all of them, and Addison sighs dramatically, rolling her eyes to the high heavens, then launches into an update on what sounds like an incredibly awkward ex-love triangle which she somehow keeps getting pulled into, despite her consistent denials of any lingering interest in either of them.

Addison gets up to refill her drink, offering one to Everly as well and grabbing some snacks while she's near the pantry. As she's distracted, Everly texts both Asim and Frankie to come over, debating whether or not to warn Frankie about her sister's possible crush. She decides to stay out of it; they're both adults and can figure it out on their own.

~~~

Alone in her kitchen a few hours later, Everly leans against the counter as she looks out the sink window at the night sky and listens to the beautiful sound of her sister, boyfriend, and best friend laughing and chatting in the next room. She's filled to the brim with a sense of cozy joy, a sort of peaceful euphoria she can't exactly put her finger on. It's a new feeling for her, something that's
~~~

been coming up the last couple weeks that she's trying hard to be accepting of. Everly sighs and smiles to herself, eyes unfocused as she gets lost in the moment, then jumps when a hand lands on her shoulder.

"Good god, Frankie." Everly presses her palm against her chest, willing her heart to slow before it catapults her into an early grave. "Are you trying to kill me?"

"Wow, sorry. I didn't know you'd be so jumpy, what's up?" Frankie asks.

"Nothing, I was just getting some water." Everly turns to the purified water dispenser on the fridge, waiting for her glass to refill.

Frankie is silent for a few moments, waiting for her to turn around before speaking again.

"They're both really great, you know," Frankie says, their voice uncharacteristically serious. "I'm really proud of you."

Everly hasn't heard those words in years, probably close to a decade, and they instantly bring tears to her eyes. She blinks and scrunches her nose in an effort to keep them in. Frankie gives her soft smile, and she can see all of her own emotions reflected in it. They've been her rock for years; they know the heartbreak, loneliness, hurt, sadness, despair... everything Everly has gone through, they've been by her side, and they also know how much happier she is now.

She's more free, fulfilled. Everly has found herself and her people, and it shows. She's been practically glowing lately, not to mention she's had more motivation and energy; she's even started walking Moose and chatting with some of the other dog owners in the neighborhood.

A truly astounding turn of events.

"Thanks, Frankie," Everly says, her voice thick. She pulls them into an embrace, then swipes under her eyes to clear any tears that might have leaked before they walk back into the living area together, stopping in the doorway.

Addison and Asim are in a heated debate, and it takes Everly a few moments to piece together what, exactly, the topic is. When she realizes they're debating the reality of aliens, and that they both seem to be arguing for aliens being real rather than taking opposing sides, she shakes her head and relaxes back into the cushions next to Asim. Frankie plops onto the couch beside Addison, causing her to bounce into them and let out a tiny squeak, which instantly turns her cheeks red and effectively ends the pointless alien debate.

Asim puts his arm around Everly, pulling her close into his side. Frankie, on the other hand, is eyeing Addison up and down like she's their next snack while they take a playful sip of their drink, and Addison, for once, doesn't seem to know what to do with herself. When Frankie asks if they all want to play "never have I ever," Addison's eyebrows shoot into her hairline and Everly buries her smirk in Asim's arm.

This should be good.

"I don't think I've played that since college," Addison says.

"Were you a good girl then, too?" Frankie asks, quirking one eyebrow. Their lips tilt up in a mischievous grin that Everly doesn't want to be within ten feet of when Addison's jaw falls open.

"Close your mouth, love," Everly whisper shouts to her sister, reaching across the space between them to tap her chin with her finger.

Addison's mouth snaps closed and she bounces a narrow eyed glare between Everly and Frankie, who simply chuckles in response.

Thirty or so minutes and many drinks later, they're all out of fingers. Everly is in Asim's lap and Frankie appears to have reduced Addison to a puddle of wistful adoration with the way she's looking up at them like a lost little puppy who has finally found its way home. When Frankie decides to turn the charm on like that, she doesn't think even a cold, dead corpse would be able to resist, and poor, sweet Addison has no chance. Everly isn't surprised by her best friend's interest; people have always been drawn to Addison, and it seems Frankie is no exception.

Everly looks up at Asim, tilting her head toward the two of them and raising her eyebrows in a nonverbal question. The twinkle in his eye confirms that he sees it too, there's definitely something going on there.

Luckily, Frankie decides to take pity on all of them after destroying everyone in the drinking game. They're the one who could party for hours, but they read the room and correctly recognize it's time to call it a night. Her friend asks Addison to walk them to the door, and Everly snorts a drunken laugh at the astonishment on her sister's face.

With light fingers Asim pinches her hip teasingly in response. "That was you not so long ago, you know," he says, lips grazing her ear.

"It was not," she says, sounding petulant as the 't' snaps off her teeth like it's readying for a fight. Everly's face flames—with fury, of course—there's no way she was as transparent as either of those two.

"It absolutely was, and I loved every second of it," he says, pulling her mouth toward his with a hand on the side of her neck.

She gives in easily, accepting his kiss and lingering in the moment until they draw apart for air. They hear Addison's quick "good night" a few minutes later as she rushes up the stairs to her bedroom without stopping or turning in their direction, and they share a giddy smile.

Asim stands up with Everly still in his arms, depositing her on her feet and ensuring she's steady before gathering the dirty glasses and dishes. He tidies up, quick and efficient, loads up the dishwasher, and helps her get the place back in order before he leaves.

"Are you sure you don't want to stay?" Everly sways into him, her words coming out much more needy than she intended.

"You know I'd love to, but I have a very early morning."

Everly scrunches her nose, not pleased in the slightest with that predicament.

When they step out onto the front porch together, Frankie is long gone and the neighborhood is dark, silent and still. Asim gazes down at her and cradles her jaw in one callused palm, his eyes tracing over every inch of her upturned face.

"You're amazing, you know that?" he says, his voice soft in the night air.

"Well duh, I snagged you after all." She turns her head slightly into his hand, kissing the soft skin of his palm below his thumb, and he smiles.

"Seriously Ever, you did all this. You brought the four of us together, and we are all better for it. This night, these people... none of it would have happened without you," he says.

Everly tilts her head and thinks about that for a moment. She did bring them all together, and it feels incredible to be on the inside, in the middle of a group of people who truly know and care about her, rather than on the outside looking in and pretending to be part of something she's not. She's found her core circle, her favorite people in the world, and she doesn't feel alone anymore.

Her heart is full and her soul is happy.

She smiles up at Asim and his own smile grows wider, softer, more tender as he gazes at her, nodding slightly and twining his other arm around her waist as he recognizes that she sees it. She sees the impact she's had on all of them, herself included, and she understands the significance.

"My beautiful Ever. My Ever-after," he says, brushing his nose against hers. His voice is still low and soft, and his eyes capture hers in their gaze. Asim's hands trail reverently over her curves to lightly brush her hair back before he cups her face in both of his hands. He searches her eyes, just as she searches his, seeing everything in her heart reflected there.

"I love you," she whispers, pulling him into a kiss and realizing for the first time that she's not at all worried about who might be watching.

Their foreheads rest against each other, lips a hair's-breadth apart as they share the same air and Asim whispers his reply, his mouth brushing softly against hers as his lips move.

"And I love you, Everly. I love you as endlessly as the clouds form in the sky, and the rains fall to the oceans, and the grasses grow from the earth."

Epilogue

Asim
   One Year Later

Asim can't tear his eyes away from her. Everly is stunning in a shimmering gold dress that looks like it was poured over her, and he relishes the sense of pride and satisfaction that bubbles up in his chest every time the ring on her finger glints under the massive chandeliers spanning the ballroom of the Sioria.

He wasn't surprised at all when she broached the subject of the annual holiday party a few months ago, stating she wanted to change it this year. She's been working tirelessly on being the kind of person she wants to be, which is what led to the charity ball she's hosting this evening. Instead of a private party at her family's mansion, the love of his life decided to invite her parents' wealthy friends, as well as extend an open invitation to all the locals here in Stone Ridge, to support her chosen cause—sea turtles.

Asim thinks back to when they took their first vacation together over the summer, when he proposed. He needed a break from the frustrating process of rebuilding, and his contractor said there was nothing he could do in person anyways, so they took a week off and escaped to a literal paradise.

They stumbled upon a beach that was blocked off, with signs warning it was a protected area for hatching sea turtles. Naturally, Everly turned her irresistible, big brown doe eyes on him and asked if they could stay to watch, and he couldn't say no. He carried beach chairs and towels and set them up a short distance away from the protected area, and while her eyes were fixed to the sand, he couldn't take his off of her.

Asim smiles to himself, remembering the tingle in his chest when he saw her face light up at the first tiny sea turtle she spotted waddling across the sand toward the water.

He's pulled out of his thoughts and back to the charity gala by Everly's hand on his lapel.

"What are you smiling about?" Everly asks, pulling herself into him.

"You," he says, dropping a kiss onto the tip of her nose. Everly rolls her eyes, but her cheeks pink beneath her makeup even though she tries to hide it by scrunching her nose to the side. "It looks great, love."

"You think so? There aren't too many poinsettias?" she asks, eyes scanning the room, then answers her own question with a snort. "Nah, that's not a thing."

Her smile is blinding when she turns it on him, and he wishes this party would hurry up so he could stop restraining himself. He wants to hike her dress up and devour her with his tongue, or rip it off completely and taste every inch of her skin. Giving himself a mental slap, he refocuses and takes a look around, ensuring there aren't any last minute details he can help with. Addison and Frankie are speaking casually with the party planners and decorator, so he assumes everything is taken care of, and he turns back to Everly.

"Ready?" Asim asks.

"Ready." She nods in emphasis, straightening her shoulders and looking him straight in the eye. His heart swells with affection for this incredible woman.

A short time later, the entire town turns up to support her. He greets many as they come in, welcoming them and wishing a happy holiday. Mr. Williams, from the senior apartments, shakes his hand with a proud smile on his wrinkled face. José Garcia, who works for the Parks and Recreation department, gives him a firm nod over the shoulder of his wife as he leads her into the ballroom with an arm around her waist. Fay, the owner of the sunset boat cruise, was here earlier but must have left for some reason as she comes striding back in with her shoulders thrown back and an air of surety about her that Asim can only admire. Chantel from the local handmade shop, Alex Gomez and Cindy Smalls, the baker and candy maker, respectively, come in like a storm trailed by a group of other locals, all laughing and joking together as they hang their coats and scope out the party.

Everly's parents' friends, local city council included, appear thrilled to be there, which is a relief. Everly had been worried they wouldn't like the change, but they don't seem to mind in the slightest; if anything, they seem to enjoy the opportunity to meet the locals and be a part of something bigger than any of them individually. He's even caught a few murmurs of how proud her parents would be, if only they were around to see the woman she's grown into, and he hopes someone who knew them tells her as much. Asim marvels at Everly's ability to pull together so many people from all different walks of life.

Asim keeps an eye on Everly as she flits around, ensuring everything is running smoothly and everyone is in their places. She organized every bit of this, but she doesn't want any of the credit. Instead, Addison will be the face of the event, acting as emcee and announcing each prize before the silent auction begins for the night. As drinks and hors d'oeuvres are floated around on trays carried by straight-backed servers, the music providing a soft backdrop to the elegant gathering, Asim checks his phone for any updates from his family.

Just as he's starting to worry, he sees his parents and sister, Farah, walk through the doors, eyes wide as they take in the grandeur. Asim slips along the wall to meet them, kissing his mother and sister on the cheek and thanking them for coming. They don't have time for much more before Addison is taking the stage.

Asim can't help but watch his future wife off to the side as she clasps her hands together, eyes bright and wide with cautious optimism as the main event of the night begins. Asim wants to be there next to her, holding her hand, but he also knows this is something she wants to prove to herself that she can do on her own, so he stays on the outskirts, ready to jump in if needed.

"This is very impressive, Asim," his father's low voice rumbles next to him.

"It is, I wouldn't have believed she did it all herself, but I know she's capable of anything she sets her mind to." His words are laced with reverence, and his mother reaches around to squeeze his arm.

"She's wonderful." She beams at him, full of pride for her future daughter-in-law.

Addison announces each donated auction item, and there are some good ones. Mrs. Langdon didn't show up in person, but Crooked Books donated a monthly special edition bestseller book for a full year, surprising everyone with her interest and contribution. Turns out, she's passionate about more than just cats and books, the support reflected in the donations of many other local business owners are too.

The sunset boat cruise is donating an entire boat to the auction, the owner of the candy shop is a retired ski instructor and they've committed to a full ski kit and private lessons for a weekend in the mountains, Roasted Coffee House donated a free daily coffee and pastry for a year, and the Sioria is auctioning the venue for any event in the next three years (there aren't many open dates in the next two, which he firmly believes is a good problem to have, even though Everly wanted the prize to be more immediate). Some of her parents' friends showed up with prizes to contribute as well, much to Everly's dismayed delight and last minute panic.

Addison finishes up and everyone wanders around the prize table to enter their bids, so Asim makes his way toward Everly.

He snags her around the waist, relishing the feel of her soft curves under his hands, and pulls her back into his chest. He leans forward, grazing her ear.

"Look what you've done," he says, angling her toward the prize table. "This is you."

She looks up at him, and he decides she needs to hear it one more time.

"You did this, Ever." He puts all the strength and conviction he has into the words, and she shudders against him. Asim swipes her hair off her neck and kisses her, trailing his lips down to her shoulder lightly before backing off. "I will never stop being impressed by you." He says, and he sees his words resonate through her.

After Addison announces the winners and the final tally comes through, they've raised thousands of dollars. Asim feels his chest puffing out and his muscles are practically bursting the seams of his suit as he holds himself back from Everly. There is nothing on this earth that could make him more proud of her than he is right now.

This is her moment, and although she didn't want to be in the spotlight, everyone still recognizes the work she put into it. He stands slightly behind her, one hand resting on her back tracing soothing circles, alternating with trailing up and down the back of her arm as everyone bustles about at the end of the evening. Everly reminds everyone to take a poinsettia as they leave, and many do so, their faces lit up with delight. People exchange hugs and handshakes, and nearly everyone thanks or congratulates her as they trickle out of the ballroom, wandering to the elevator and their respective rooms, or out the door to their homes.

"Thank you so much for coming," Everly says, greeting his parents and sister.

"We wouldn't miss it," his mom replies, pulling Everly in for a hug. "What an amazing night, so impressive."

"Oh, thank you," Everly stammers, turning to Asim for help, still not comfortable with compliments, though he's working hard on normalizing it for her.

Asim sweeps an arm around her, tugging her into his side.

"I couldn't be more proud." He drops a kiss to the top of her head and his sister takes pity on her, rescuing Everly so she doesn't suffocate from praise.

"Alright, alright." Farah links her arms through their parents, shooting him a wink. "We'll let you two celebrate in private, we're still on for brunch tomorrow, right?"

"Of course!" Everly's voice is about an octave higher than usual, and Asim has to hold in a laugh.

"Great! Have a good night!" Farah tugs their parents along with her as she turns and sweeps out of the ballroom. The three of them have a set of rooms reserved for the night, and they'll all spend some time together tomorrow.

"You're adorable." Asim drops his mouth to Everly's ear, grazing his nose along it and smiling at the shiver that courses down her back. "And very impressive." He kisses her neck, a light peck, but it's enough to have her melting into him.

Finally, the last of the guests leaves and the staff begins to clean up. Asim tightens his hold on his future wife and looks down at her.

"Ready to head home, darling?"

"Yeah," she sighs, shifting her weight from foot to foot. "Let's go."

They walk out to the car and Asim reinforces how proud he is of her going out on a limb and giving this a try. Every word is true, and he wishes he had more of them to fully express the depth of his feelings.

An unexpected chuckle slips from his lips as an image of her a year ago pops into his head. Everly looks at him quizzically as he starts up the car.

"Remember how flustered you were before last year's party?" he asks.

"You mean when you showed up at the crack of dawn and I was in my robe?" she deadpans, unimpressed. "Yes, how could I ever forget."

He does his best to hold in the grin, but his memories have taken hold and it's such a sweet picture, he doesn't want to let it go.

"Why do you look like that?" Everly's eyes narrow at him, and he tries to adopt an innocent expression. "What's your face doing? What are you thinking about?"

Asim doesn't want to keep anything from her, so he shrugs and decides to share.

"I was remembering how you kept reaching up to smooth your hair back." He looks at her out of the corner of his eye as he drives, easing around a corner. "I don't think you realized that every time you reached up, your already short robe inched up your legs a little bit more. It was tantalizing and torturous."

"What?!" She shrieks at him and he laughs. "You... you," she splutters for a moment, then shrieks again. "Tantalizing and *torturous?!*"

"Well, I was trying to be a gentleman but you were really doing your best at making it nearly impossible."

"And I suppose that's why you kept making me stay." She huffs out a breath and crosses her arms, not realizing all she's doing is accentuating her perfect breasts. This woman has no idea the hold she has over him. He catches her shooting a glare at him, but he can tell she's trying her best not to laugh.

"Why would I want you to leave or put more clothes on? You were intriguing and gorgeous. You *are* gorgeous. I wanted every single second I could get with you," he says, and it's the truth.

At first he just thought it was cute, the way she was embarrassed to be in her robe. Asim grew up with sisters; he didn't care that she wasn't all done up. He knew he should have let her get dressed, but he didn't want her to go. Once they started talking though, his world tilted on its axis and everything changed. He liked seeing the real her, he could tell the person she was used to hiding came out in those moments. Plus, well, he can admit to his baser urges too—each extra inch of enticing skin he saw made his blood hum. He wanted to cover her up and protect her and strip her naked all at the same time.

It was confounding.

"Why didn't you ask for my number?" she says, watching him turn onto Poinsettia Lane.

"I've asked myself that every day for a year," he replies, and she raises her eyebrows at him as they step out of the car and onto the driveway. "I truly don't know. I think you short circuited my brain. As soon as I drove away, I couldn't believe I left without any way of contacting you. I considered showing up at your house again many times, but I didn't think that move would get me very far." His voice is wry, and she giggles.

"I don't know, I was trying to figure out how to avoid stalking you too, so maybe it would have been okay." She pokes him in the side as he closes and locks the front door behind them.

"You little miscreant." He scoops her up in his arms, relishing her shrieking laughter as he carries her up the stairs to their bedroom before dropping both of them onto the bed.

Asim kicks off his shoes and slides down her body to remove hers, placing them carefully on the floor beside the bed. His eyes trail up her glittering golden dress, heating with every curve, when his gaze snags on her engagement ring. Asim lunges up the bed, almost feral in his need for her. He scoops her up again, putting her on her feet and removing her dress with shaking fingers, containing his need as best he can so he doesn't ruin a dress that holds such precious memories for her. His groan is animalistic when he sees she wasn't wearing a bra under it.

His own clothes he couldn't care less about. He rips his jacket and shirt off, buttons flying, and Everly's gasp has his already hard cock turning to steel in his pants.

"I need you," he says, and her rich brown eyes lock onto him, nearly as needy as his.

Shucking his pants to the floor as she drops her panties and reaches for him, he wraps his hand in her hair and backs her up to the wall. Her energy matches his perfectly, and she climbs up his body, her lips leaving a blaze of heat up his chest and neck, her legs wrapping around his waist as he grips one ass cheek, loving the feel of her in his arms. He pushes her back against the wall and takes a pointed nipple into his mouth, scraping his teeth along the soft flesh of her breast and sucking until she's writhing against him.

Asim squeezes the base of his cock, mentally telling himself to keep it together before angling it toward her center. He throws his head back, clenching his jaw as he slides home in one long, slow thrust, relishing the tight, wet heat of her surrounding him. His groan of satisfaction matches hers, and he drops his head forward again, looking down at her.

Everly's face is flushed, and the pink travels all the way down to the tops of her perfect breasts. He leans in and sucks on the spot she goes crazy for, where her neck angles into her shoulder, and she clenches around him.

He picks up the pace with her urging him on, both of them a frenzy of lust and need and want, until their desires are fulfilled and they come together, sweat slicked bodies slumping against each other and he slides them to the floor.

They breathe heavily, and Asim flips them around, sitting with his back against the wall and pulling her sideways into his chest so he can rest his head on top of hers. He kisses the top of her head before leaning his cheek against it, murmuring into her hair.

"You're mine forever, my darling, perfect, Ever."

Author Acknowledgments

Writing a book is hard, and self publishing is so much more than I expected. It feels absolutely wild to have an entire book I've written out in the world, and although terrifying, I'm so thrilled to be here. On that note...

Thank YOU, my dear reader! (Yes, I claim you now as one of mine). Thank you for reading, and if you have shared this book with anyone or told anyone about it or created content or recommended it on social media, thank you so very much. It means more than I can express with words on a page at the end of a book. I hope you enjoyed Poinsettia Lane, and I hope you are ready for the next one—you can probably guess who it will be about.

I'd also like to thank a few specific people who impacted this journey of bringing Asim and Everly into our lives.

Mercedes, who peer pressured me into writing with her. Without you, I don't think I ever would have started this journey! Thank you for encouraging me and always being ready to help me figure out how words work when I forget.

AnaCena, my unofficial editor and sounding

board, thank you for your knowledge, patience, and for reading this book so many times, and with such diligence.

Alexandra Samantha, Slexy Slex of the Kinklings. You have been such a joy to share this self-publishing journey with. Thank you for sticking with me, listening to my whining, and turning my pouts into smiles. You are truly a light in my life I wasn't expecting or looking for.

Yasmin and Karin, my authenticity/sensitivity readers, thank you so much for your time and the effort you put into making this book the best representation of Iraqi and queer culture it can be.

Andrew. Love of my life. Thank you for giving up evenings and weekends so I could spend time writing, then editing, then complaining about self-publishing. Thank you for cooking for me when I had no brain power left, and for taking Wixom out so I could have some peace from her grumbles. Thank you for haunting all the local libraries with me and always being down for a quick brainstorm session whenever I need one. I certainly couldn't have finished this project without your love and support, it means the world to me.

And... one more thanks for the readers!

A quick note from the author on mental health:

Millions of people at any given time feel anxious, and even if those symptoms aren't severe enough for a formal diagnosis, therapy can still help. Everly's experience of anxiety is just one of many ways it can look and feel; if you think you might have anxiety (or any other mental health concerns), **there is help out there for you**.

I'm a firm believer that no one is perfect, therefore we all have room for improvement and could benefit from counseling or therapy. If you think you may benefit from having someone to talk to, please give yourself the care and compassion you deserve by doing a quick google search for a therapist in your area. Many therapists offer online video sessions, so you don't even have to go in person.

If you don't know where to start and would like some help, please feel free to reach out. I would be happy to give you some tips to find a therapist that will be a good match for you.

Thanks again for reading,
Corina

Corina writes feel-good love stories with tension-building spice, funny and relatable characters, and Happily Ever After's that feel like a hug in book form.

After working at multiple greenhouses through high school and college, and now being a mental health therapist, Corina combines these passions to bring her debut novel to life.

When she's not reading or writing, you can find Corina forcing snuggles on her dog, rollerblading with her husband, playing the piano, or embroidering everything she can get her hands on, including book covers.

Check out her website www.AuthorCorinaBair.com for info on Corina's upcoming romance novels, sign up to her newsletter, and more.